MURDER IN THE MARSH

A Cozy Medical Mystery

MOLLY EVANS

KEEP UP WITH MOLLY EVANS

Sign up for Molly's e-newsletter at:
Mollyevansromance.com

Copyright information:

❧ 1 ❧

ONE FOR ALL AND ALL FOR ONE-ALEXANDER DUMAS

Being a travel nurse, taking short term assignments all over the country for three months at a time, could be totally awesome or a complete pain in my scrub pants. I never knew which it was going to be until my friend Jeannie Hatcher and I got to our new gig. I'm Piper Quinn. This one, a summer assignment on an island off the coast of North Carolina, seemed like a good idea when we booked it. We were tired of white snow and our white legs. We needed to rest and recreate at the beach, slathered up with sun-block for a few months to recover from our last assignment from hell.

We approached the nurses' station in the ICU and waited as a harried-looking medical secretary fielded sixteen phone calls and probably fourteen other tasks we couldn't see. She totally rocked.

"Hi. Sorry to interrupt," I said. "We're your new travelers and are supposed to meet the charge nurse here." After our day-long classroom orientation getting to know all the gory details about this hospital, we were ready to book out of there as soon as possible. I'd rather work a twelve-hour shift than sit in a classroom for eight. Shudder.

"Oh, yeah. That would be Audrey. Hold on, and I'll notify her," she said, answered the phone and typed something into the computer at the same time. She totally had multi-tasking down.

As we waited, the familiar sights and sounds of a critical care unit buzzed and tweeted around us. There was no place like home. Unless you were, like, really at home, but critical care was our second home. And yes, we were weird.

"Hello there." A normal-looking woman, mid-forties, wearing dark blue scrubs with a white lab coat tied around her waist, three pens sticking out of her hair and glasses perched on top of her head, greeted us. I sighed in relief.

I've found my people.

"Sorry if we're late. The Director Of Nursing kept us a little longer than we expected," Jeannie said.

"Yes, she likes to hear herself talk. Or likes others to hear her talk," she said with a smile and a quick roll of her eyes. I was going to like her. Or I was just like her. Either way, I thought we were going to get along just fine.

"I'm Audrey. Come with me, and I'll show you all the essential stuff you need to know about this place." She led the way down the hall to the break room that looked just like any other hospital break room I'd been in.

This one had a TV on with local weather station covering a storm out in the Atlantic. July was the start of the hurricane season in the Atlantic Ocean. That much I knew, as I'd thought about planning a Caribbean vacation in October once, but then reconsidered when I saw the radar with lots of little circles of storms heading to the islands.

"You're both experienced travelers, right?" Audrey asked, redirecting my attention to the present and away from vacations I hadn't taken.

I nodded.

"Yes," Jeannie said.

"Good, then I won't have to worry much about either of you." I could almost see the wheels spinning in Audrey's mind as she tried to figure out whether she was going to have issues with us or not. Not all travelers were created equal. Some needed more oversight than others.

"We've been travelers for four years each," I said, clarifying how experienced at this unconventional lifestyle we were. Jeannie and I had met on our third assignment and had been travel-buddies ever since.

"Great. I don't have to tell you that new travelers usually require more work on our part than experienced ones." Whether she realized it or not, Audrey sighed in relief, making me wonder what had happened with travelers to make her so tense. As a nurse, you quickly developed an ability to read people. Right now, I was reading Audrey was tense.

"Correct." Jeannie frowned. "I was wondering though, about something the DON said, that travelers aren't working out well here. Can you tell us what that means? She was kinda vague about it." We had to prepare ourselves if travelers weren't well liked. It had happened before, so I felt better prepared if we knew the atmosphere we were walking into.

"Yes, she would say that. She actually went to bat to get travelers accepted here, then a number of them have just bailed in the middle of their assignments lately." Audrey said. "Or so I've heard. I'm mostly concerned about my own staff, so I don't know what's going on with the other units in the hospital." She lifted one shoulder in a shrug. With the duties of a charge nurse in a fast-paced ICU, she didn't have time to think about the needs of other units when she had her own shifts to cover.

"Audrey, can you come here a second?" She was called away by another staff nurse, spoke briefly, then returned to us.

"Another one bites the dust." She pulled a pen from her hair and wrote a note on her clipboard. The frown on her face indicated she was none too happy about it, either. After she finished her note, she returned the pen to her hair with its mis-matched companions.

"What do you mean? You have a patient going down the tubes?" I asked, as I hadn't heard the usual flurry of activity or escalation in alarms when a patient was crashing.

"No. A traveler didn't show up for her shift. She came for orientation, worked one week, and has apparently bailed like the others. No one can get ahold of her, and now we're stuck to fill the shift." She shook her head and pressed her lips together. "Darn it. I'd hoped she was going to work out."

"Is she a first-time traveler?" I was so on it.

"You guessed it."

Jeannie pushed her lips out a second. She always did that when she was thinking about a problem. "I wonder if we could go talk to her, give her some support and see if we can get her to come back to finish her contract. First assignments can be tricky, and you don't feel like you've got anyone watching your back." That had been the case for both of us before we met. Now, we were our own off-beat support group.

"That would be awesome." Audrey's brows shot up at

the idea. "If you can find her, then she needs to get back to work ASAP." Audrey moved to a computer at the nurses station, plugged in a password, pulled up a few documents, fumbled for a pen in her hair, then scribbled something down on a scrap of paper. "Kelly McCall. This is her phone number. Out of state area code, of course, and her local address." She handed me the paper. I don't know why she did. This was Jeannie's idea. Audrey looked at me like I was the leader of this two-pack of tacos, but I wasn't all the time. Most of the time, but Jeannie took the lead sometimes. Either way, one of us got the other into trouble. But I took the paper, looked at it, handed it to Jeannie. She did that thing with her lips again, pulled out her phone and took a picture of the paper. *Smarty pants.*

"Just in case I lose it or something," Jeannie said.

Snap. Good idea. I took a picture, too.

"We're almost outta here," I said and nodded at the clock on the wall. "Why don't we swing by her place now and see what we find? She could have simply gotten cold feet, packed up her stuff and headed to parts unknown. She might not even be there."

"Do you know where she's from? Her home state?" Jeannie asked.

Audrey thought a second and pushed her glasses back up onto her head. "I'm not sure. I interviewed so many travelers for the positions, but I think it's Iowa or Idaho. One or the other sticks in my mind. She didn't have any sort of accent I could identify, so it could be either, I guess."

Iowa or Idaho? A vast difference between the two, and about a million corn fields, but I let it slide. Audrey obviously wasn't up on her US geography.

"Cool. Let's go." I was ready to get out of there, check

on the new chick, and get some chow. Orientation days were long and made me hungry.

"Let's look at the schedule before you go, so you know what your shifts are next week." After a few minutes of studying the schedule, she made a few changes, then printed us each a copy.

Once in my SUV, I plugged the address into the GPS, and Jeannie slid into the shotgun seat. "Wow. She must be paying through the nose for that place. It's on one of the streets to the beach." The hospital sat town center. Though it wasn't a huge town, it was a few miles to the beach, where Jeannie and I both wanted to be lying on a blanket, covered in oil and soaking up the sun every day we weren't working. That was our deal about coming to Oak Island for the summer. Work as little as possible. Lounge on the beach as much as possible. The last two assignments had been tough, and we deserved the break.

"Maybe not. She could have gotten a deal for the summer through Air B&B or something. Or Craig's List, though that wouldn't be my first choice," Jeannie said and gave a shiver of disgust. I didn't think it would be anyone's first choice for safe housing, but you never knew. She could have simply lucked out with a little old lady who wanted a roommate for the summer.

"Even a room in someone's house for the summer is going to be pricey if it's as close to the beach as I think this one is," I said and pulled out of the parking lot.

It wasn't. It was on the marsh side of the little island. The choicest beaches were on the southern tip of the island and on the northern end, the marsh was a completely different atmosphere. Homes had been built along those streets, too, and homeowners listened to bullfrogs and night insects rather than the smooth drift of the waves along the beach. Both were wonderful, but the beach was more costly.

Kelly either lucked out or had some money set aside for summer housing at the beach. Since it was her first assignment, I was betting she got lucky.

We pulled into the moderate sized home. A small sedan sat in the driveway with the windows down an inch to let the car breathe, and a dash protector was tucked into place with the visors. Iowa plates. Great. She was still here. Maybe she'd simply overslept, and we were now her wake-up committee.

"This is good. Nice. Conservative. Maybe she forgot to set her alarm or something. Or her phone died. That happens sometimes if you aren't used to the routine of things," Jeannie said. She tried to see the best in everyone and give them the benefit of the doubt, unlike my jaded and suspicious self. Sometimes her way worked, sometimes it didn't, like her last boyfriend who'd gotten one too many passes, as far as I was concerned. Rat bastard.

"Sometimes." We got out of the car and approached the door to the little pink house on stilts. We walked up the wooden stairs, holding onto the banister, careful not to get splinters from the weather-worn wood.

"Should we call her first, or just knock?" Jeannie was conscientious. I just wanted to pound on the door loud enough to wake the dead. If she were asleep, that oughta do the trick.

"Let's just knock," I said. I raised my hand to do just that as there wasn't a doorbell in sight, when I noticed the door wasn't latched and only rested against the frame. "Ugh-oh."

"What?" Jeannie had turned around to check out the

view, but spun back quickly. "What's wrong? That's your *something's-wrong* voice."

"I'm not sure yet." Hesitation in my movements, the sun burning down on us, making my antiperspirant work harder than it had to, I used my cell phone to push open the weathered white door. "Door's unlocked and open. Not latched," I said, biting my lower lip in hesitation. Should we go in? Should we not? Should we call the cops for a welfare check first? We were here now, so might as well just barge on in.

"I'm sure a lot of people don't lock their doors during the day," Jeannie said. Again, my friend the dreamer.

"Yeah, but in a high-traffic area like this, it's not a good idea," I said. Even in low traffic areas, it wasn't a good idea. Bad things happened in the sun and the shade.

"Maybe she just doesn't know enough yet, and where she comes from is a much safer place," Jeannie said, her voice tentative as she was coming to the realization we might not find what we'd hoped for. As a rule, Oak Island was a safe place. I'd checked it out online before we took the assignment. Few college students vacationed here because it just wasn't a party town. More older adults and retired people lived here. You've never lived until you've been to a swinging bash at the old-folks home. They could really rock it sometimes, but Oak Island just wasn't that kind of place.

Intrigued, curious, and a with sinking feeling of dread circling my ankles like a bad-tempered Chihuahua, I pushed the door wider. That would either give us a better visual of what was going on in there, or give a potential killer a better shot at us.

"Nope. I don't think she got lucky. I think she got darned unlucky." The Chihuahua took a big bite out of my ankle, and my guts churned unhappily. "Pretty sure Kelly didn't blow off work."

Jeannie moved closer and looked at the pristine white-tiled foyer. It looked like someone had spilled a bucket of red paint on it. Except we knew that that particular amount and color of dried paint was really pints of dried blood.

"Oh, dear. That's not good," Jeannie said and held onto my lower arm with a tight grip.

Not good at all.

2

DOESN'T EXPECTING THE UNEXPECTED
MAKE THE UNEXPECTED EXPECTED?-
UNKNOWN

"We've got to do something," Jeannie said, stating the obvious. Not like we're gonna walk away from the situation now. If we hadn't seen what we'd just seen, we might have been able to walk away in good conscience. But now? No way. My conscience would have me turning the car around and coming back for more if we even attempted to leave. Some people could walk away from scenes like this, but people like me and Jeannie actually run toward them. Must be in the DNA.

"Something awful happened here. We're definitely calling the police, but we should go in and see if she's hurt, if she's even here," I said. "Or if it's even her blood."

"Oh, right. I hadn't thought of that," Jeannie said.

Under normal circumstances, I wasn't normally a First Responder, but I was right now. So was Jeannie. We liked the structure of the ICU where there was some stability to the patients coming through the door, not like the unknown crisis every time the ER doors opened.

This situation in front of us was totally something else.

Kelly's life could depend on our actions at this very moment. Stewing about it, delaying while calling the cops, waiting for them to come, wasn't going to save her life.

We were.

"I'm calling 911 right now," Jeannie said and pulled out her phone.

"I guess that leaves me going in," I said and girded my loins, bracing for whatever was going to happen on the other side of that door. I wasn't afraid to go in. I'd been in my share of disasters, including the home of one crazy, hoarding, home-care patient, but I was cautious as I entered. My blood was humming along my veins, much faster than the normal three to four miles per hour it usually ran. Unless I was attending a code. Which felt about the same way now. I took a deep breath, hoping it wasn't going to be my last.

Adrenaline revved my nerves up to full capacity. Even the hair on my arms and the nubs on my legs stood straight out. If that didn't get your attention when you're walking into a strange house where someone may have been murdered, nothing would. Might as well call in dead yourself.

"Hello? Is anyone here? Kelly? Kelly McCall, are you in there?" I called out, hoping she would answer, or at least groan. Hoping the bad guy would know someone was coming in and high-tail it out the back door, or maybe a convenient side window.

No answer. Nothing. Not even the room breathed. Houses have their own atmosphere, an energy about them, but this one felt like I was walking into a vacuum, like the life had been sucked out of it already, and was waiting for someone else to animate it. Each cautious step I took through the foyer, around the blood pool, over a well-worn pink backpack, and down the hallway, brought me closer to the main part of the house.

It was trashed. Someone had been looking for something. Or a fight had happened here. A quick glance in the small kitchen revealed nothing more than one knife missing from the butcher block holder. That didn't mean anything by itself. A lot of people had incomplete knife sets.

Get a set of steak knives as a wedding present? Bet you someone uses one outside at a barbecue and it never makes it back to the block. Stuff like that. Or when your husband uses it to cut up galvanized metal in the garage for a project he already has ten tools for, but finds your steak knives a better deal. He'll be lucky not to end up with one in his eye. Knives go missing all sorts of ways.

So the missing knife could mean nothing.

Or it could be the one lying on the disheveled bedding in a bedroom dead ahead. Or straight ahead. Yes, something awful had happened in this house. Ears echoing with the wild pulse of my heart, I wasn't sure what I was going to find when I entered that bedroom. Not sure I want to find anything at this point.

"Piper?" Jeannie hissed in my ear.

A very undignified yelp escaped me, and I spun to find Jeannie right behind me. "Geez. Why didn't you call me sooner?" Hand over my chest, I was certain my heart was going to pound out of my chest cavity. Fortunately, I had two sets of ribs, two lungs and a breastplate to keep that from happening.

"I called you three times," she said in a harsh whisper.

"I didn't hear you. And why are you whispering?" I whispered back, because it seemed the right thing to do. Like speaking louder would be irreverent. Like talking during a college lecture. Or talking on your cell phone in a waiting room when the sign clearly stated not to.

"I know you didn't hear me, that's why I came closer. Someone might still be here," she whispered again, her frightened brown eyes darting around, looking for someone to come in and yell *boo* at us.

"Did you talk to the police? Are they coming?" I spoke in my normal tone, but after the whisper, it sounded like I'd shouted a profanity in church.

"Yes, someone will be here, but it may take thirty minutes or more," she said.

"What?" I gasped, giving up the whisper for louder communication. "How can it take that long? This island is five miles long. How long does it take to drive five miles in a screaming cop car?"

"Apparently, they don't have their own police force on the island, so the next town over is providing service, and it'll take them that long to get here," she said, looking as unhappy about it as I was.

"Seriously?" I bobbed my head in disbelief at that one. I thought we were taking an assignment on an island in North Carolina, not another planet.

"Seriously." Jeannie wasn't the type to pull a prank like that one on me under those circumstances. Not when someone was missing, and with the size of the blood pool, we could assume was dead.

"Did you find anything?" She dropped the whisper now, too, but cringed as her voice echoed off the pink plaster-painted walls. Must have been a sale on pink when this house was built.

I pointed to the bed. "A knife. A bloody one. Empty space in the kitchen block where it belongs," I said in a condensed version of events.

"Oh, that's bad." Jeannie's eyes widened.

"Yeah," I said. Unable to come up with anything else. She was right. It was bad. I was afraid it was gonna get badder before we were done.

"A body?" Jeannie made a cringing face like she didn't want to hear the answer to that question. I didn't either. But we needed to. If Kelly had any chance to survive, it was up to us, right now, to help her.

We turned toward the bed and the bedding that looked like it had been dragged toward the other side, between it and the window that faced the marsh. The old metal blinds designed to keep out the heat were all twisted up and wonky. Would take an act of God to get them back in order.

"I don't know. Yet," I said. I knew I was gonna know in a few seconds, because there was no way we were leaving this room without finding out if Kelly lay on the other side of that bed. Dead or alive.

Feeling much like Scooby Doo and the Gang, we tiptoed in. We clutched onto each other, and with breathless anticipation looked on the other side of the bed.

We sighed together.

"Nothing. That's good, right?" Jeannie asked. With that kind of unfounded hope, Jeannie really should have been a politician.

"What about *under* the bed?" I asked. Clever assailants had been known to shove bodies under beds in hotel rooms leaving them for housekeeping to find, which was why I always checked under hotel beds before climbing into one. Call me paranoid, but I wasn't gonna sleep on top of a corpse, no matter how cheap Motel 6 said its rates were. They could leave the light on for someone else.

"I'm not looking under the bed," Jeannie said, her eyes

wide, her face a pasty white, like she was certain her child-hood monster was under there ready to jump out and scare her again.

"What if Kelly's under there bleeding to death, and we can save her? We have to do it," I said, firm in my determination to do the right thing, no matter how scary it was. There was little chance of her being alive at this point, but we had to be certain. Not knowing an answer was never an answer. Not for nurses. That mantra had been drilled into our heads in nursing school, and the rules hadn't changed since.

"Okay. Okay." Jeannie nodded and huffed in a few breaths of fortitude.

"We're nurses. We can handle this. We've handed worse," I said, trying to bolster her courage and give mine a kick in the ass.

"We have? When?" Jeannie asked with a frown, her eyes narrowed in suspicion.

"We haven't, but I thought it sounded good right now." We all needed reassurance now and then. It was my turn to reassure Jeannie that the Bogey Man wasn't under the bed about to yank her back to her six-year-old self cowering under the covers with a flashlight.

Together, we knelt on the laminate floor. Good choice for a beach house. Sand could be swept up quickly, and you wouldn't spend years trying to get it out of the carpet. One of the downsides of living at the beach. Sand found its way into everything, and I mean everything. There wasn't a crack, of any sort, it wouldn't get into.

Nothing under the bed except a few dust motes someone missed on their last cleaning. I was so demanding a refund on my cleaning fee the next time I booked through Air B&B.

We backed out of the house carefully, not touching anything except the floor and only 'cause we had to. I had not yet perfected my levitation technique.

"Now what?" Jeanie asked when we were outside on the little porch. She breathed a sigh of relief, and I hauled in a few deep breaths to get some oxygen back to my brain.

"Now, we wait for the cops," I said. That seemed the most logical thing to do, but I wasn't always about logic. I was action oriented, and sitting on the sidelines had never worked for me. Would likely never work for me. I was either playing on the team, or I was going home.

"We should call Audrey. Let her know we didn't find Kelly," Jeannie said and bit her lip in hesitation. It wasn't a call she wanted to make and neither did I, but it had to be done.

"Yeah. She's going to have to replace Kelly on shift tonight," I said. I looked back at the hall and the ginor- mous blood pool that had dried, probably some time yesterday, maybe the day before. "Probably for the rest of her assignment. I don't think she's coming back."

"No, me either," Jeannie said and her shoulders dropped.

"We need to do something, though," I said, anxiety curdling the contents of my stomach. We were women of action. We didn't just stand around waiting for the cops to come in and save the day. We were the day-savers most of the time, and this was no different. Well, it was a whole lot different, but we still had to do something.

"What can we do?" Jeannie asked. She always asked that question, and it was always up to me to answer it. I didn't always come up with a *good* answer, but I couldn't let this one hang in the air that way. We were nurses. We were doers. We got the job done when no one else could. We ran toward disasters instead of away from them. It may not be the brightest thing to do, but it's who we were, how we we're wired. "Who knows when the blood was actually left there? It's dry, so at least a few hours, possibly a day," I said, speculating aloud. I looked at the unrelenting sun as it headed toward the horizon, felt the humidity in the breeze wafting from the marsh. If we hadn't been standing beside a crime scene, it would have been a lovely end to the day.

"We've already contaminated the scene by walking in here," Jeannie said. "The police won't like that." She was a people-pleaser. Me? Not so much. I liked to live dangerously.

"We had good reason to. If we found her injured, we could have done something, but if we didn't, and she died because we didn't act, I couldn't live with myself," I said. The grim reality was that Kelly had probably been dead for some time, and there was nothing anyone could have done to save her. At least we knew she hadn't bailed on her assignment. Now, I wished she had.

"Me, either," Jeannie said. Sadness crept into her voice, but I was still full of piss and vinegar, and righteous indignation. Someone had killed a fellow traveler, and I wasn't going to stand there doing nothing while they got away with it.

"There's something we can do. Right now," I said. Ideas just popped into my mind like that. I often questioned their validity, but not today.

"What? We have to wait for the police to come investigate, don't we?" Jeannie asked, hesitation in her voice. She was so by-the-rules, sometimes I wondered why she hung out with me. Maybe it just balanced our friendship. I was out there, she wasn't ,and together we made a good team. One got us into trouble. Usually me. The other got us out of trouble. Usually her.

"No, we don't. We can start the investigation ourselves. Actually, we already have. But we can do more," I said. Excited now, I faced Jeannie and grabbed her arms. "I have some basic supplies in the car from our last home healthcare assignment. I've got blood tubes, sterile containers, everything. We can take samples, label them so they aren't mixed up, destroyed or damaged, by the weather. Heat and humidity can taint samples, we both know that, so we've got to do something to protect them. There's probably ice in the freezer. That'll help preserve everything." My mind was on fire, thinking of the right thing to do and the right way to do it, as soon as possible.

"Are you sure we should do that?" she asked, hesitating. I got it. I really did. I'd watched all the cop shows where people inadvertently screwed up a crime scene by walking all over it. Time was essential now, and we weren't going to screw anything up. Unless it was a killer.

"No. I'm not sure. But Kelly didn't bail on her first assignment. Something bad happened to her. Something horrible. And it's up to us to help her. Even if all we can do is help solve her murder," I said. As awful as that sounded, it was true. "We'll write it up like a code. Every minute, every movement we make, so it's documented. Will that ease your mind?"

"Yes. And you're right. We may have been too late to be the welcome committee for her, but at least we can help figure out what happened to her. That may be of some comfort to her family," Jeannie said. With a resigned sigh, she nodded. "Okay. Let's do it."

"I'll go grab the box from the car," I said and reached for the keys in my pocket.

"Give me the keys, I'll get it," she said. I handed her the keys, and she raced off to the SUV just a few feet away in the sandy driveway. In a minute she was back with my kit, gloves, and all the stuff we needed to tackle this endeavor. Maybe the cops would be pissed at us. Maybe they'd be thankful for our efforts. Who knew? I just knew Jeannie and I needed to do something purposeful, not sit around like helpless females waiting for someone else to do the dirty work.

We were nurses.

We did our own dirty work.

Nurses were trained for dirty work. With sterile gloves on, a sterile field set up, I took samples from the edge of the blood pool, from the bed, bagged the knife in a haz-mat bag for transporting blood tubes to the lab, and labeled it.

Jeannie noted the time and the place the samples were taken from. She took pictures of everything to document the scene, and our process, as we moved through the home, trying to keep our focus on the essentials, trying to ignore the fact that this was the blood of another nurse we were scooping into vials.

"Look at this,"I said. I held up a molar hiding just under the edge of door to the bathroom. "Someone had their tooth knocked out."

A mean look came into those pretty brown eyes of Jeannie's. "I hope it was the bad guy. I hope she clocked him a good one for doing this to her." She growled in her throat. "Maybe we didn't know Kelly, but once upon a time we were just like her. New to travel nursing. Not sure if we were going to like it or not. Not sure if we could do the job. Not sure if we were going to make friends on the assignment or not," she said, finding her fire.

We could totally relate to Kelly's fears, for they'd been ours at one time.

"Okay, I think that's it," I said. I rose from the cramped position on my knees and placed the bag with the molar in it on the table with the rest of the evidence. When the crime lab arrived, we'd have to complete a chain of custody form for each piece, labeled with date, time, my name and location where it was taken from.

Jeannie looked toward the door. "I think they're coming now. I hear sirens."

I looked toward the sound of the sirens, then back at the scene behind me. "That's all we can do for now."

❧ 3 ❧

TAKE A PICTURE, IT'LL LAST LONGER-HIGH SCHOOL

So, the cops arrived amid the fanfare of sirens, red and blue lights, followed by an ambulance and a rescue fire engine. And a lot of hot, hunky men in uniform.

They knew how to make an entrance. After watching them approach under the weight of various equipment, a sheen of sweat on their faces and arms, muscles working hard, I decided they needed their own calendar. It would sell like hotcakes and probably pay for their own police force on-island.

Sigh. There were some perks being keenly-trained observers.

"Officer? I'm Piper Quinn, and this is my friend Jeannie Hatcher. We're travel nurses from Oak Island hospital. We came to find Kelly McCall after she didn't show up for her shift. We discovered the scene, and Kelly is missing."

The diligent, and slightly sweaty, officer wrote down our names, asked for our numbers, but was unlikely to ask us out for drinks later. "What's a travel nurse?" he asked with a seriously stupid look on his face. My respect for an office of the law just dropped a few notches.

"We take short-term contracts to help with staffing shortages at hospitals across the United States," I said, trying not to be irritated that he didn't know what travel nurses were. Most people didn't. That was the long and short of it. But it was my life. Life had been amazingly dull and boring until I took my first travel assignment. That's when I truly began to live, and I wasn't about to stop now.

"Huh. Never heard of it," he said, dismissing it as unimportant. I felt an eye roll coming on, but controlled myself.

The team of First Responders waited for the scene to be cleared before entering the little pink house. That was the job of Officer Shipper in front of us and his backup band of boys in blue. Secure the scene before anyone else went in. We could have told them we'd checked the house, but I didn't want to admit to compromising the scene too quickly. They'd be figuring that out in a few minutes.

"House is clear," one of them said as they left the small house. Not one of them was under six-feet-tall, two-hundred pounds of lean, honed muscle. All wore Matrix-type shades, but no hats.

I wondered if they knew about the incidence of melanoma for people who worked outside and didn't wear protection? I just hoped they wore good sun-block.

Another officer with amazing chocolate-brown skin, sporting a sharp, fade haircut approached, holding one of my lab bags containing the knife in his gloved hand. "Shipper? There's a whole slew of stuff like this in the fridge and on the table. Like someone processed the scene already. Was the crime lab here before us?" he asked, then turned those reflective sunglasses on us. "Ladies? Know anything about this knife and the rest in there?" He indicated the house with a nod in its direction. "Looks like you did more than discover a crime scene." There was a rich, deep timbre to his voice that made me wish he had his own radio show, late at night, playing smooth jazz, so I could stay up past my bedtime listening to him talk into my ears. A girl from the sticks in rural Pennsylvania could dream, couldn't she?

Officer Shipper turned to us, and I sensed the disapproval behind those mirrored shades of his. Oh well, it could have gone either way. It was a fifty-fifty shot whether processing the scene was going to be favorably received or not. Check the *no* box for Shipper's vote.

"Did you touch anything in there?" Shipper spoke sharply to both of us, but looked at me. Like I was the culprit. I was, but he didn't know that. Unless he was psychic, and that would be really interesting, but doubtful. On TV shows the cops always consulted psychics, because they weren't psychic themselves.

"Yes, we processed the scene due to the urgency of the day getting late and frailty of the samples. We know she's been dead at least an hour, probably much longer, because that's how long it takes for a blood pool that size to dry. We grew concerned that the weather, heat, and humidity were going to negatively effect the integrity of samples, so we bagged and tagged everything," I said and turned to Jeannie who was looking a little green. She so hated confrontation. I, however, was just getting warmed up. "Jeannie video documented the whole thing as well as recorded on paper each specimen, time and location it was collected, then we put everything in the fridge." Had to move entirely too many bottles of prune juice to fit it all on the top shelf.

"You shouldn't have touched anything, you know that, right?" Shipper asked and took a wide-legged stance, then shoved his shades up on his head, giving me an icy, blue-eyed stare, which I didn't care for. In return, I gave him my best I-can't-believe-you-just-said-that-to-me face. Patients said unbelievable stuff all the time, so I had this face down-pat.

I took a step closer to Shipper. He didn't back away, but his brows twitched up as he watched me. I'd impressed him with that swanky little move. I hadn't intended to, but it was a nice bonus.

"We had to make sure Kelly wasn't in there bleeding to death while we were standing out here like scared little girls waiting for daddy to come home and check under the bed," I snapped, making it very clear why we were there. Seriously? Who did he think we were? *Amateurs*?

Jeannie leaned closer to me. "I was, actually. I'd have waited," she whispered.

"We're professionals, with a serious concern for the safety of the nurse involved, so don't give me any shit about compromising a scene. We. Didn't." I felt like crossing my arms over my chest and huffing out a breath like an indignant five-year-old told to take her bath, but I resisted the urge. It was close, though.

"It's okay, ladies. You did the right thing," my new favorite cop said.

I squinted at his name tag, nearly blinding me as the late afternoon sun glinted off of it. "Thank you, Officer King."

"No problem." Then, Officer King took off his shades to reveal stunning hazel eyes that would have been completely overlooked if he'd had his own radio show. That would have been a sad waste of eye candy. At least for me. I adored men in all shapes, sizes and colors. With so many options, who could choose just one? "Cut 'em a break, Shipper. They're civilians," King said and even had half a smile for us.

"Not completely. We're all public servants, just with different jobs," I said, reminding them we were all equal in that capacity. We'd all chosen to help others in need, and here we were all doing it together.

"They compromised the scene," Shipper said with a slight whine to his voice, clearly not sharing King's philosophy, but cast me a sideways glance to see if I was going to get any closer to him.

"By trying to save a life. That's what nurses do, or hadn't you noticed?" King said and raised one brow.

I so liked this guy. I decided to call him Officer-Dreamy-Voice-and-Luscious-Eyes, but only to myself. It was too long to call him that out loud in front of other people. It would be our secret. Or mine, anyway.

"Thanks, Officer King. I appreciate your support." I was so in love with him. I was sure we'd have beautiful children one day.

He nodded and gave a stellar smile. This guy was so wasted in police work. He could be a model, or an actor. But I was glad he was a cop. If I had to get pulled over for a speeding ticket, at least it would be worth the cost, just to look at him for a few minutes while he wrote up my ticket.

"No problem. Did you find any sign of her in the house?" King asked, compassion in his voice, knowing we hadn't been prepared for what we'd found.

"No, sadly. But that's her car over there with the Iowa plates. We didn't touch it," I said and nodded toward the little sedan.

"Oh, goody. Something *not* compromised," Shipper

said. I didn't like his sarcastic attitude. Sass and snark were *my* departments. Not his. Nobody out-sassed me. Except southern women. Nobody out-sassed them. *Ever.*

"If you'd like to get into it, you're going to have to find the keys yourself. Didn't see any," I said. There. That made me feel better. I wasn't going to do his job for him. At least not all of it.

"Great," he said.

Then something occurred to me, and I turned to Jeannie as I thought out loud, bounced the idea off of her. "Maybe Kelly was on her way to work when she was attacked at the door. Confronted by someone. Or someone followed her home from work last night and pushed their way into the house. That would explain the location of the blood pool, the backpack near the door, and why the door wasn't locked or shut tightly." I'd mistakenly assumed the backpack was by the door so it was conveniently out of the way, but she could just as easily have dropped it there during a scuffle.

"That's a good thought," Jeannie said and puzzled over that one, considering it from all angles, just like we did at work with patent problems.

"What about the knife? Got an explanation for that?" Shipper asked. He was patronizing me. I knew it, but didn't care. We could puzzle this out and at least come up with some kind of theory as to what had happened.

"She could have fought the guy off, run to the kitchen and grabbed it, then he used it on her." Jeannie added.

"That's one possible scenario," Officer King said, nodding, while considering Jeannie's hypothesis. "Not bad, ladies."

"What about the homeowner? Do you know who that is?" Shipper kept asking questions I didn't know the answers to, but that wasn't going to stop me. I was a nurse, and not knowing an answer was never the right answer. You theorized, you postulated, you used your nursing judgment until something made sense. You didn't give up on a patient or problem because the answers were hard to find. I wasn't going to give up on this situation, either.

"No, but in one of the bags on the table is a note I assume is from her, saying she'll be out of town for a few days at her sister's house and a phone number," I said. That was at least one useful piece of information to go on.

"Convenient. That could be your killer right there with a hand-written excuse of an alibi trying to throw us off track, and he's already murdered the homeowner," Shipper said. He was really lacking in team spirit. I'd bet he sat on the sidelines a lot in gym class waiting to get picked for a team.

"Possibly," I said. I gave him my did-you-seriously-say-something-that-stupid look again. "But let me just say, Shipper, he's not *my* killer, and that would be *your* job to find out. The footprints, in blood I might add, are larger than a standard female, which is a size eight-and-a-half-ish." I motioned for them to come into the house where I'd placed a sterile barrier over one pristine footprint to protect it. "It looks like a men's size ten, or so, running shoe."

"What makes you think that's the size?" Shipper asked. "Are you a foot expert, too?" He was so lacking in faith at my skills. Obviously, I was going to have to show him some proof before he'd see things my way.

"In our line of work, we see a lot of feet. But that's my best guess, if you want it or not, its up to you," I said and shrugged, getting more irritated the longer we talked to

Shipper. "Make your worker harder if you want to. I prefer to work smarter, not harder."

"Touché, Quinn," King said and held up one hand for a quick high-five. I so liked him.

As expected, the crime scene van arrived, and I signed a ton of documents handing over what we'd collected. I knew they'd do their own collection anyway, take fingerprints, lift the bloody footprint. Things I didn't have the ability to do with my meager supplies. Even if they duplicated my work, it made me feel good to have done it anyway. If it was worth doing once, it was worth doing twice.

Two police officers opened the pink backpack, presumed to be Kelly's, searching for keys. Apparently, they found some and headed toward Kelly's car. A wave of sadness and grief flooded me. I hadn't known Kelly. Never even heard of her. But knowing she'd likely died a horrible death just feet from where we stood hit me hard. The beautiful sunset lighting up the sky with pinks and orange slivers, looking much like melted sorbet, was lost on me.

I loved sunsets, but knowing that Kelly had seen her last one, and not even known it, was sad. Would she have done anything differently had she known? Could she have changed the trajectory of the events that had led to her death?

"Are you through with us for the moment, officers? You have our contact information if you need anything else. It's been a long day, and I'd like to put it to bed," I said. The piss and vinegar had run out of me, and my shoulders dropped as if I'd just tossed the weight of the world off of them.

Jeannie touched my arm, indicating she was ready to go, too.

"Yes, but we'll be talking to you soon," Shipper said and ran his cool eyes over us, trying to make us feel like we'd committed a crime when all we'd done was discover one.

"Ladies, take it easy tonight. Plan on coming to the station in Southport to make formal statements in the morning," King said and gave us each a card with his contact number and the precinct address on it.

"Thank you. We'll be there," I said. It would likely be the last thing we could do to help find Kelly's killer.

Slowly, Jeannie and I got into my SUV, buckled up and headed back to our summer apartment. It was close to town center, just a short drive to the hospital, and steps away from a charming little coffee shop called the Flying Pig.

I wished they served bourbon, 'cause I could have used a shot.

❧ 4 ❧

NURSES ARE ANGELS IN SENSIBLE SHOES-
UNKNOWN

The next morning after a fitful night of restless sleep, we managed to crawl out of bed and face the day. New place, new bed, new environment altogether, throw that in the blender, add a little unexpected murder, and you've got the makings for a Madness Margarita that would keep you up all night.

In any case, we showered, changed into normal people clothes, not scrubs, and decided to go out for breakfast. We hadn't been able to shop for groceries last night, so all the cupboards were bare. Mother Hubbard must have lived there before us.

"I remember somewhere from the orientation there's a restaurant beside the hospital that a lot of staff go to," Jeannie said. "Maybe we should try that."

"Convenient. Let's go. I'm buying," I said. We took turns buying and today was my turn.

"You got it. Let me grab a sweater in case it's chilly inside." Jeannie was born a Girl Scout. She was the most prepared person I'd ever met. We were on an island in the middle of summer, and she wanted a sweater. But knowing her, she'd need it, because she was almost always right about being prepared. Me? I'd just freeze and bitch about how cold it was in the restaurant.

We made it to the restaurant with a vibe somewhere between IHOP and Waffle House, with enough cracked red upholstery on the seats to keep me happy. Nothing like a real diner experience. Fat Pete's was clearing out. We got there just as the night shift crowd was leaving. They'd chowed down on a high calorie, high carb and fat meal so they could fall into a coma the second they hit the sheets. There was no better sleep than the carbohydrate-induced swoon after being up all night.

Jeannie and I found a booth. Neither of us was in much of a talking mood, but we did have to speak to the waiter. It was easier to give our orders that way.

"Buttermilk pancakes, short stack, side of bacon and hash browns," I said. That ought to keep me moving for a while.

"I'll have two eggs, over easy, whole wheat toast, and a coffee," Jeannie said. She ate lighter. Probably why was thinner than me, too.

"God. Add coffee. How could I have forgotten that?" I head-slapped myself. How could I have forgotten the nectar of life on a day like this? "Please," I said.

"Been a long night, ladies?" the waiter asked us, assuming we'd been up all night. We must have looked bad if that was his assessment of how we looked early in the morning. Or hung-over. We probably looked like that, too.

"No, long day yesterday," I said. "Bleeding over into today." It was the work hangover.

Jeannie brightened and faced the tall, thin man. "We're travel nurses. Most people don't know about them, but--"

"I know all about you travel nurses, missy." The expression on his face slammed shut from being open and receptive, in a move we hadn't inspired. Something else had, but we were paying for it. "You'll get your food in a minute," he said and glared at me. "And your coffee, too." Without another word, he turned and stalked away.

"Wow, what was that all about?" Jeannie asked and pulled her mouth to the side. "Somebody got up on the wrong side of the bed."

"Obviously, but not our concern today. We've got much bigger issues," I said. We came across grumpy people all the time. Didn't mean we had to diffuse every one of them. Especially before coffee.

"Yes, we do," Jeannie said and looked up as a coffee pot appeared beside the table, presented by a young lady who had not been our waiter.

"Coffee?" she asked in a sweet voice with slight southern drawl. She wore her brown hair in a high ponytail that bounced as she talked.

"Thanks," Jeannie said.

I simply nodded like a bobble-head, and held up my cup. Neurons were not yet firing.

"So, plan for the day?" I added milk and two packs of the pink sweetener. The blue stuff gave me headaches. It was a neuro-toxin, go figure.

"We have to go to the police station and give our report, then grocery store, and hit the beach in the afternoon?" Jeannie had it all lined up.

"Sounds like a plan. I hope they don't keep us too long at the station," I said. It was a nice drive to the station house in Southport, where I hoped to see

Dreamy-Eyes-And-Sexy-Voice again. Shipper could take a hike.

"Depends on what other kind of activity they've got going on," Jeannie said. She shrugged like it didn't matter.

"On a Saturday in a beach town? Hard to tell," I said. "They could be processing any number of cases, from shoplifting to car jacking."

Our meals arrived, delivered by the young waitress, Emily, who'd brought the coffee, not the waiter who had taken our order and then gave us the cold shoulder.

"Thanks. What gives with the waiter?" I asked and nodded in grumpy-butt's direction. He stood with one foot on a chair, leaning his elbow onto it, yucking it up with a bunch of men in scrubs. "He have something against women?"

"No, not that I know of," Emily said and gave a nervous glance in his direction. "Pete's not a waiter, though. He's actually the owner of the place." She shrugged.

"Seriously? And he behaves like that?" Jeannie's brows twitched. She tried very hard to be non-judgmental, but in this case I could see it all over her face. "That's not very good behavior for a business owner," she said.

"He's under a lot of stress lately, so he's not been himself. Poor thing." Emily clucked her tongue in sympathy for Pete, though it was obvious by the way her gaze kept darting to him, that she feared him.

"I beg to differ," I said, studying the man, trying to identify what his problem was.

"What do you mean? Do you know him?" Emily asked.

"No, but I know people. Stress and money only make you more of what you already are. I know you're young, but remember that. He's a prick, but he's hidden it well until the stress of his situation pushed him. He's just more of a prick now."

Emily hesitated as she rearranged our plates, having put them down in front of the wrong person. "I see," she said, her gaze downcast and not just because she was watching what she was doing. She was remembering an event or maybe more than one, that she'd mistakenly given him a pass on, but now was reconsidering.

"Don't take any crap from him," Jeannie said and patted Emily's hand. "You deserve respect, just like everyone else does. If he doesn't give it to you, go work somewhere else."

"Jobs here are hard to come by. I'm saving for school in the fall," she whispered. Fear filled her brown eyes. We shouldn't have suggested that. We didn't know her or her situation at all.

"In a beach town there have to be plenty of other jobs that won't require you to give up your dignity," I said, then narrowed my eyes. Emily was pretty, obviously naïve, and Pete was mid-forties, balding, slight paunch, and mean eyes. "Did he hurt you?"

Tears quickly filled Emily's eyes, but she dashed them away and shook her head. "No. Not in the way you mean, but he has hurt me," she said. She took a quick look to make sure he was still occupied and pushed up her left sleeve to reveal a variety of bruises ranging from bright purple, to yellow-green. "Same on the other arm. He pinches me when he thinks I'm not doing things the way he wants me to."

"Controller," Jeannie said. "That's what he is. We can spot 'em a mile away." Jeannie narrowed her eyes and glared at Pete.

"How do you do that?" Emily asked, eyes wide. "I don't

want to go from this situation to another one just as bad. Or worse."

"Real men don't punish that way, for starters," I said. As I took a deep breath to go on, she straightened abruptly.

"I gotta go. He's watching," Emily said, stepped back and pasted on her best fake smile. "I'll be back to check on you," she said in her best waitress voice, then moved to another table.

"What do you think that's all about?" Jeannie asked as she buttered her toast.

"I think the guy is a prick, just like I said, and doesn't know how to treat women." I knew I wasn't wrong in that regard.

"Maybe he's a misogynist," she said and slathered jelly on her toast.

"That's not an abbreviation for a massage therapist, right?" I got confused. Sometimes, there were just too many notes.

"No," she said and gave a snort. She was always trying to keep me calm. "A misogynist is a man who hates women. I guess they all have their reasons, but none of them are valid in my book." She motioned with her fork. "Let's hurry and get out of here. We can come back another time and help Emily if we have to."

"I don't like those bruises on her arms," I said. That wasn't right. Talk about a hostile work environment.

Jeannie dove into her eggs, obviously as ravenous as me. "Me either, but there's nothing we can do right now." Jeannie pulled out a small notebook, scribbled something onto it, tore it out, then tucked it under her plate.

"What was that?" I asked.

"I'm leaving her my number in case she needs anything," Jeannie said.

"That's nice of you," I said. It was. Just wasn't sure if Emily would reach out to her or not.

We tipped Emily well. We'd both been waitresses through nursing school, so we had an appreciation and understanding of her position, then scooted out of there.

The drive to the police station in Southport wasn't long in distance, but was made longer by throngs of people crossing the road in no hurry to get anywhere and lights that stayed red way too long. But we made it.

We pushed through the double doors and got no farther than the small lobby, encased in bullet-proof glass and one female office sitting in a booth, like she was collecting tolls on the Turnpike. Fortunately, we were the only ones in line.

After a short discussion of our purpose, she buzzed us through, and that's when it hit me. This was where all the action happened, all the activity, the energy and the buzz of a police station. Phones ringing off the hook. The clatter of computer keyboards. And the cacophony of voices, each with their own tone and vibration.

Sounded just like an ICU without the cardiac alarms.

"Ladies?" My favorite cop approached and led us to a quiet room where we could be undisturbed by anyone, especially Shipper, to give our statements. Officer King brought his own laptop and typed as we talked. Now, half a day away from the trauma of finding the crime scene, we could talk more clinically than we could last evening. I'd written down my findings on a notepad so I didn't forget any details, and we had Jeannie's notes from the evidence collection while we were there.

"That should just about do it," Officer King said. It took

two hours for all of us to be satisfied that we'd included everything.

"Where's Shipper? I'm surprised he missed this," I said.

"He's off today," King said. The sigh of relief told me he wasn't too fond of Shipper, either.

"But not you?" I asked.

"Nah. I like working the weekends. Less admin to deal with. Just get the job done, file the paperwork and go home," he said, nodded as he spoke.

"See?" I said. "You're more like us than you are Shipper," I said and was so glad. Maybe he could be my spirit animal.

"For sure." He raised his hand and gave me another high-five and one for Jeannie, too. "Thanks ladies for the statements. I'll give a call if any questions come up or if you think of anything, give me a call."

"I will." I leaned closer conspiratorially. "I think I'll call you just to listen to you talk. Has anyone ever told you you have a great voice for radio?" I asked.

"Yes, actually." He laughed, and I detected a slight reddening of the skin on his neck. He was secretly pleased by the compliment. "I worked in radio through college," he said.

"Oh, no way," I said and leaned back in my chair, then waggled my fingers for him to send some of it my way. "Come on, give us a sample."

He laughed and shook his head, thinking. "Okay. I'm a bit rusty, but here goes." He cleared his throat. "Welcome to WDVE radio, your home for all that cool jazz, made for late nights and long, slow weekends with your sweetheart." He sounded somewhere between Barry White and Howlin' Wolf.

"Yes!" I clapped. "I was right. You *do* have a voice made for radio."

"Awesome," Jeannie said, a big smile on her face. "That was great."

"Thanks, ladies. I appreciate that. Been a long time since I've thought about those days," he said with a nod, like they were good memories we'd stirred in him.

"So what are your plans for the weekend? Are you working?" he asked and escorted us from the conference room, back through the deluge of noise and mayhem of the bullpen, and to the front door.

"No, they actually gave us the weekend off, so we're going to get to know the lay of the land, then hit the beach," I said.

King took a look at my fair skin, my red hair and made a face of concern.

"Don't worry, I use a lot of sun-block," I said. Had too many burns as a teenager not to.

"Try an umbrella, sugar. I don't want to have to come visit you in the burn unit," King said.

I laughed, but nodded at the suggestion. "You are so right. We'll pick one up."

We waved goodbye and headed out to do just exactly as we'd planned. Grocery store. Health food store for Jeannie was a must. Scoped out the locations of a beauty shop, nail salon, Jiffy Lube and tire repair, as well as a plethora of seafood restaurants we'd likely try. We'd already discovered the coffee shop right across the street from a bunch of fun, touristy shops we'd get to later. First, we'd settle in to our new apartment, put things away, organized a little, then be ready for our next thirteen weeks.

Jeannie and I traveled together and shared housing

expenses. There was no reason we each had to have our own apartment on assignment when we'd be hanging together most of the time anyway. This way we had a roommie we could trust to halve the expenses with.

Our salaries varied assignment to assignment, and we had to pay for our own housing, just like everyone else in the world did. Most people thought travelers got paid an amazing amount of money, but we didn't. And we worked just as hard as anyone else for our paychecks. We just did it at various locations across the nation, uprooting our lives, thirteen weeks at a time. What better way to be employed full time and be on permanent vacation at the same time?

Score!

After staking out my territory on the beach blanket with my newly-purchased shade umbrella, a snazzy lime green, sporting a pink flamingo, planted securely, we settled in for a few hours of baking in the sun, probable napping, and sunset watching. Unless those scattered clouds on the horizon decided to organize and band together to form one righteous system to throw down some rain on our parade, it was going to be a nice few hours.

As I lay there sweating out the coffee I'd had for breakfast, I thought a good rain shower might just be the ticket to cool me off. No such luck, so I rose and made a dash for the breakers heading my way as the tide had turned and started to come in. Who needed a rain shower, when there was an ocean twenty feet away?

After another hour we packed up our gear, I realized we weren't that far away from the crime scene. The house Kelly had lived in briefly. There'd been no report of her death on the local news. Maybe a traveler or tourist death wasn't a good thing to report at the height of tourist season. But I wanted to satisfy my curiosity.

"Do you mind if we swing by Kelly's house again?" I asked Jeannie. I didn't want to totally refer to the area as a crime scene, because it was a house and still someone's home.

"Sure. We can probably walk across the marsh bridge, take a few pictures there. I think I saw some egrets and a few herons looking for dinner when we drove by," Jeannie said.

"Good idea," I said. I loved taking pictures, and had my big camera with a long lens for wildlife shots with me. Made my bag heavy as hell, but when I wanted a shot, I wanted a shot. Never knew when we were going to come across something worth stopping for.

We'd just stepped onto the wooden platform that led to the footbridge across the marsh. The tide continued to rise and wading birds tiptoed through the shallow water, their keen yellow eyes and sharp bills ready to snatch the next unwary little fish for its dinner. The brilliant white of the egret feathers against the bright green of the marsh grass was a stunning contrast. I watched one of the great blue herons that had joined the crowd, as he stalked through the shallows. Then I swallowed a sudden lump in my throat and my mouth went dry as I realized the white object I was seeing wasn't that of another egret lying in the grass. First of all, they don't lie down unless they're nesting, that much I knew. And secondly, they didn't have brown hair pulled back in a braid.

"Dammit. Jeannie. Look there," I said and pointed toward the heron, feeling the happy buzz of the day fading away and feeling bad that I was going to destroy Jeannie's.

"Nice. Did you get a picture?" She smiled and reached for he phone to take a picture.

"Past the bird. Focus on the grass behind it."

"Why? What's there?" She took in a sharp breath. "Oh. I see now. Somehow, I'd hoped . . . Well, I'd just hoped." She pulled her phone from the outside pocket of her beach bag. "We're gonna have to call Officer King," she said.

"We are. But how's it going to look that we discovered the crime scene, and now we've discovered the body?" I didn't usually give a rip about what people thought of me, but finding bodies was a whole new twist.

"I don't know, but we've got to follow through," Jeannie said. She looked overhead for the sun, now waning on the horizon. "They won't have much time before sundown to get over here," she said. She pulled Officer King's card from her wallet and dialed the number.

"Officer King, this is Jeannie Hatcher. Yes, hello again. I'm sorry to report we've got more bad news. I believe we've just discovered Kelly McCall's body in the marsh." She gave him the location of where we were and ended the call with a sigh. "Now, we wait again. Same deal as yesterday," she said and set her bag of beach essentials on the wooden planking of the bridge, and adjusted her hat so it shaded her face more fully against the waning sun. She too was born of pale skin that burned easily.

"How have people walked across this foot bridge all day long and not seen a body in the grass over there?" I asked. Incensed, I shook my head. "Are people that self-absorbed?"

"You know as well as I do that people are largely unob-servant, don't look for anything out of the ordinary, and are usually focused on their phones instead of the glorious nature around them," she said and lifted one hand to eloquently encompass the beautiful marshland around us. "We're trained observers. We miss very little."

"Yeah, I know. Sometimes I just wish we could skip being so damned observant," I said as I watched the great heron continue on its way, nonplussed by the body of a woman floating not three feet away.

5

A BOY'S BEST FRIEND IS HIS MOTHER--PSYCHO

"Mother, it's time for breakfast." He knocked twice on the door frame to her room where the elder woman slept twenty hours of the day. Watching her chest, he looked closely to ensure she still breathed. With relief, he watched her thin chest rise and then fall again. At least it was something. She lived. For how much longer, he didn't know. He knocked on the bedroom door again, not wishing to startle her from sleep, but his schedule demanded that she wake now. She had to be fed, bathed, set in her chair by the window until he could return later to change her, try to entice her into having a few bites of food for lunch, then put her back to bed for the remainder of the day. There would be no food in the evenings. She never ate past sundown. Had claimed that was how she'd kept her figure slim for so many years. Even with the life draining out of her, she wouldn't eat after sundown.

One more loud knock, and he entered the room. An odd, sickly fragrance clung to the air. She was ill. He knew that. He just couldn't live without her. Couldn't face the thought of her leaving him. He'd have no purpose if she died. He lived to care for her. What would he do with himself if she left him?

She stirred, first a twitch of her brows, then the slack mouth closed, her eyes fluttered, and she drew in a deep breath. "What time is it?" The rich, contralto voice she'd once had was gone, replaced with squeaky vocalization.

"Time to get moving, Mother." He pasted on a sweet smile, the one she'd always loved, but never looked past. He'd practiced that smile since he could remember, using it to get what he wanted out of her, but after many years, he'd stopped using it and just took what he wanted. Her car, her money, her signature on documents turning assets over to him.

"Yes, dear." She rose with his assistance and sat on the edge of the bed, oblivious to all he'd done.

"Take a minute so you don't fall. I can't have you falling any more. I don't want to take you back to the hospital and have you end up like Father." That would be the worst thing he could think of. Having her hospitalized, taken out of their home. Taken away from him.

"Where is your father, dear?" There was that annoying, raspy voice he hated, screeching in his ears. She couldn't help it, he knew that, but it didn't make it any less annoying. How his father had stood it, he didn't know.

"He's in the living room." He answered her question, but didn't give her any more information. She was like a child, accepting things at face value. She believed anything he told her.

"Oh. Been up with the sun, I'll bet," she said with a slight laugh.

He didn't answer. He didn't tell her Father was in the living room and had been there since his death two months ago. Father now resided in a plain brown box filled with his ashes. Father hadn't prepared for his demise, and his mind had been too far gone to do anything about it by the time he took sick.

Now, *he* had to deal with his step-mother alone. She was the only mother he'd known, but she wasn't his birth mother. She'd died of a fever shortly after his birth. His father hadn't waited long to find a new wife and a mother for his son, so Father didn't have to be both parents to an unwanted child. If he'd been just one parent, that would have been enough, but Father had had a business to run and shunned the son that had killed his wife.

"Help me get to my chair." She held out a gnarled hand, fingers twisted with arthritis, too weak to support herself to get from the bed to her wheelchair. Even a few feet, she couldn't go without assistance. Couldn't make it to the toilet by herself, couldn't tell when she had to go any more. Pissed herself more often than not. It sickened him to take care of those needs, to clean up what she soiled, what she ruined. To buy more clothes from the thrift store because she ruined everything. She'd always ruined every-thing, but she wasn't going to ruin him any longer. He'd see to that.

Roughly, he grabbed her arm and hauled her to her feet, the flesh squishing beneath his hand.

"Ow, you're hurting me," she cried out as he tore off her saturated pajamas and threw them into the nearby bin. He hated this part of caring for her, so he did it as quickly as possible, not wanting to touch her any longer than necessary.

"Be quiet. You're fine. I'm not hurting you." He didn't care if he hurt her or not. He needed her and if some small amount of pain kept her living, then so be it.

"Yes, you are. You're always rough." She batted at him with one hand, but he slapped it away. There wasn't enough strength in her limbs to hurt him.

"It's nothing more than you deserve for pissing in the bed," he said. He'd have to buy a new mattress again soon if she didn't stop.

"I didn't do that. Someone else did." She took one more whack at him. "Stop blaming things on me."

"Someone else was in the bed with you?" He scoffed at the absurdity of that notion.

"You should be ashamed of yourself, thinking that. I've never been unfaithful to your father. I'm not going to start now," she said.

"Just shut up, will you?" Some days he had no patience for her, and today was one of them. Once he put her in her chair for the day, he could go to work and forget about her for a few hours. Forget about the futility of his situation and find distraction in his work.

Finishing up with her in the bedroom, throwing a load into the washer, he fed her as quickly as he could and put her in her chair by the window so the neighbors could see her. A bright bird feeder attracted some entertainment for her through the day. During peak season he had to fill the damned thing every day. One of these days, when she died, or he killed her, he was going to stop filling it. The birds would have to fend for themselves, the way he'd had to.

OFFICER KING APPROACHED US WITH HIS SHADES ON TOP OF his head, eyes now guarded, not open and casual like they'd been before. He suspected something. He suspected us.

"Ladies." Wearily, he approached, taking the wooden stairs to the platform two at a time with his long, long legs. Bet he had thighs I could bounce a quarter off of.

"Officer King," I said. I held out my hand, determined to be my usual bubbly self, even though we'd found another major downer on our second day in town. The feel of his hand was warm and strong, and he didn't try to crush my hand the way some men did to prove their superiority. Thankfully, he didn't give me one of those limp-assed handshakes, either.

"So your afternoon at the beach didn't end all that well, did it?" he asked.

"Afraid not," I said. So not a good ending.

"Why don't you show me where she is, so I can radio the crime lab with what they're going to need," he said. Didn't sound like Officer King had had a good day, either.

"This way," Jeannie said, her mouth turned down at the corners.

The three of us walked a few more feet and stopped. "There, just past the blue heron." It had returned, heading back the direct it'd come from, then stopped, holding statue-still as we disturbed its fishing venture. The only sign of life was the uber-slow movement of one foot that it raised and eased forward.

King focused past the bird and saw what we'd seen. The white of her scrubs had caught my eye first, as I'd been seeing white egrets. My mind had tried to make another one, but couldn't make the shift and her scrubs merged together until I saw what was really there.

47

"I see her," Officer King said with a sigh. "I'm glad you found her," he nodded toward the body, "but now it leaves us with two problems."

"What are those?" I had a sinking feeling I wasn't going to like what he had to say. One problem of this magnitude was enough. Two? I couldn't imagine.

"First of all, that's not Kelly McCall, and since it's not, we've got us a second murder," Officer King said.

I knew people said their jaws dropped when they got bad news, but I actually felt my jaw drop all the way to the bottoms of my sparkly pink flip-flops. That's how far my jaw dropped.

"Wow. I was not expecting you to say that, Office King," I said. Not at all.

"I wasn't expecting to say it, Piper. At this point, I think you need to call me Charlie, though." His lips turned down, and he shook his head, taking in the enormity of the situation. "Mmm-mmm-mmm. Sure wasn't expecting those words to come out of my mouth," he said.

"You're kidding. That's not her?" Jeannie asked. Her jaw was apparently matching the position of mine. We'd had no idea what Kelly looked like, we'd only been given her number and name.

"Unfortunately, no." Charlie reached into his pocket and extracted his cell phone, pulled up an image of a woman who looked like a pixie with short, spiky blonde hair and sparkling blue eyes. Full of life. Full of mischief. I'm certain we'd have been friends and gotten into trouble together. "Got this from her MDV photo. Doesn't match what we're seeing over there with that long, brown braid." He sighed again. "I was hoping this was going to be a one-time deal, but obviously, it's not."

48

"What did you hope was going to be a one-time deal? Kelly's death?" Jeannie asked and adjusted her hat again.

"We had a nurse go missing from the hospital just last week. We never found any trace of her, not even her car. Just nothing until now," Charlie said. "Ever'body thought she'd just quit and left."

"Seriously? Kelly wasn't the first one?" I didn't know whether to sit down, hyperventilate or faint. But I never fainted, so we could cross that one off the list. I might hyperventilate and say nasty words now and then in stressful situations, but faint? Pfft, never.

"That's really bad," Jeannie said and stepped closer to me. We stared at the female body floating in the marsh, bobbing a little with the incoming tide. "So we have a body and no name, and a name and no body."

"Could be the killer was rushed on this one, but had more time to dispose of Miss McCall," King said, thinking out loud.

Neither of us had anything to add and just stood there staring as the sun waned further in the sky, as night creatures came out of hiding and began tuning their songs. Frogs, cicadas, locust and crickets I recognized. But other, dark creatures that slithered in the night, made no noise at all. Those were the ones I feared.

Those were the ones nightmares were made of. With darkness teetering on the edge of the marsh, mosquitoes rose to feast on our juicy, blood-filled flesh.

"I'm going to need your statements again, but this time let's do it in the squad car and get away from all these bugs," Officer King said.

We turned to go, but he paused. "Hang on. I have to call this in and get people out here before they can't see a damned thing." He turned away and pressed the mic on his shoulder radio, called in the details to get recovery personnel out there. There would be no rescue. Whoever lay in the marsh was already dead. They only needed to recover the body. Different sense of urgency.

Lightning bugs began flaring, their little bodies glowing briefly in the twilight. They created an enchanting, yet creepy atmosphere, lighting the way to darker shades of night. Deeper in the shallowy marsh unknown creatures lurked, just waiting to unleash their mayhem on the unwary.

An unseen owl hooted in the trees bordering the marshland.

"That's a bad omen," Jeannie said and jumped at the sound, her eyes darting around to try to locate the source of the sound.

"You don't believe in omens, now, do you?" Charlie asked, his eyes darting around, looking for the location of the owl. There was no smile in his eyes or on his face. He was serious, his expression unreadable, waiting to see what our reactions were. He offered no indication as to what his beliefs were. With that guarded face he could play poker with the big boys and totally clean up in Vegas.

"I don't know what I believe sometimes," Jeannie said and rubbed one arm, then walked again toward the squad car, but her gaze drifted back to where the owl had given away its position.

"How about you, Piper? What do you think?" Officer McDreamy asked me. Now wasn't really the time to get lost in his eyes, but if I didn't have some kind of distraction, the situation was going to seriously spook me, and it took a lot to do that.

"I grew up in the heart of the Appalachian mountains, spoon fed on mystery and lore. Of course I believe in omens, but over the years I've discovered most things we attribute to omens have very human motivations and hands behind them," I said.

I got a nod of respect on that one. "Well said, sugar. Well said," Charlie said.

I wasn't insulted by the endearment. I'd been around enough southerners to know that *sugar, sweetie* and *honey* were words everyone used all the time. No wonder I couldn't lose weight. Even the atmosphere was loaded with carbohydrates.

We grabbed our belongings and followed Charlie to his squad car parked on the edge of the marsh and got in. We sat there out of biting range of the mosquitoes that had risen like a black tide of death from the marsh, and told him our stories. Spent the afternoon on the beach, the umbrella with the flamingo, everything. Even how I'd fallen asleep for an hour and not ended up scorched. Thank you, SPF-50.

"And that's it. We were just going to take a walk past Kelly's house, the crime scene, before we left and then discovered the woman floating in the marsh." Though we'd found a body and that was distressing enough, imagine if we hadn't decided to take that walk. The woman could have lain there for who knew how long before being discovered.

"Nasty business this is," Charlie shook his head and clucked his tongue, sounding much like an old woman who's just discovered her chicken coop had been dese-crated by a fox.

"We've never come across a situation like this before," Jeannie said, and it was the truth. Most of our assignments were pretty ordinary. Work, work, work, go to bed, finish the assignment and go on to the next one. Throw in a bit of hiking, sight seeing, and the occasional night out clubbing with the girls and waking up the next morning with my back out of joint. Ibuprofen and ice packs anyone? Other than that, pretty much run-of-the-mill.

"We've never had a run of murders like this, either. Two in two days? Bad stuff there," Charlie said and pulled out his laptop, did some typing.

"But we don't know if the marsh body has been there for a few days or not. Yet. Or exactly when Kelly was murdered. Right? You can't have gotten much help from the lab between last night to this afternoon," I said. Despite TV shows magically coming up with lab results in minutes, reality was they took days to weeks to be processed. No smoke. No mirrors. No instant mass spec.

We finished up and Charlie drove us over to where my SUV was parked, so we didn't have to walk alone to the parking lot in the dark after just having discovered a body, or become feasted on by the nasty little bastards just waiting for us to get out of the car. I appreciated that he looked in the windows of my SUV with his super-duper-high-intensity flashlight that would blind a blind man. He didn't just drive up and let us hop out into an unknown situation like some guy drooping off a date in the middle of the night past curfew. There were still gentlemen in the world willing to make a little effort for others around him. Charlie was one of them.

"I'd like to say I hope to not talk to you again any time soon," I said as he stood beside the vehicle, waiting for us to drive away. "At least not about stuff like this. Maybe you can call us for lunch sometime." That would be so much better than a friendship entirely defined by death.

"I know what you mean. I hope to not see you two any

time soon, too." He gave a crisp nod and returned to his cruiser.

"Such a nice guy," Jeannie said and adjusted the AC vent to her liking.

"Sure is. I hope he doesn't find any more bodies, though. It's just too much paperwork."

℀ 6 ℀

NEVER UNDERESTIMATE A SMART WOMAN
WITH A NURSING DEGREE—T SHIRT

Normally, night shifts started at either six or seven pm. Ours was six, meaning we'd get off work at around six-thirty am. We could give report in the mornings, head down to the beach for a quick walk before full sunrise, then head home to sleep for a few fitful hours. By the third night-shift in a row, I was in a walking coma, and so was Jeannie. We were lucky we could safely negotiate home, brush our teeth and strip off the cruddy scrubs before collapsing on our beds.

When my eyes started to twitch, that's when I knew it was time to head to bed. Or learn to sleep standing up. Still haven't perfected that one, yet. Nursing schools should teach that skill and how to levitate patients. It would cut down on a lot of back injuries sustained from turning patients that couldn't move themselves. If I ever got elected to the national board of nursing, I was going to work on that. But since I was probably never going to run for that office, I was unlikely to be elected. Go figure.

All bright and shiny for the next few hours, Jeannie got our assignments and settled in with our orientation nurse.

The first three shifts of an assignment travelers were usually buddied up with a staff nurse who showed us all the essentials for working on a particular unit. Then, we were on our own for the next three months. That's why assignments were thirteen weeks. The first one didn't really count, as it was all orientation. Hospitals didn't figure they would get their money's worth out of the travelers the first week.

"This is Sherm," Audrey introduced me to a bear of a man, mid-forties, who barely fit into his black scrubs. Usually women wore black scrubs to hide an over abundance of body fat, but Sherm, Sherman I presumed, looked bad-ass in them with not an ounce of excess to hide. I wondered if his last name was *Tank*, cause he sure looked like he could plow through anything. Like a human combat vehicle. With a high and tight haircut, eyes that looked for suspicious people, I was guessing he was former military. Probably a medic, then got his nursing degree when the military spat him out.

"Hi, Sherm. I'm Piper." I held out my hand for the man-hand-crusher-test. He took my hand in his tough-skinned one and gave it one tight shake. Yeah. The bones in my hand were still where they belonged. Awesome. Wouldn't have to file for workman's comp in the morning.

He nodded once, still assessing whether I was going to cut it here or not. "Pleasure," he said. Probably wasn't, judging by the irritated lines around his mouth, but he'd deal. So would I. Neither of us had to like each other. We just had to work together for a few nights a week. Didn't need to swear a blood oath for that.

"Okay. Jeannie, come with me. I'll introduce you to your preceptor," Audrey said. Jeannie waved quick and turned away to face her own fate.

"Let's get on it," I said to Sherm. "What's our patient load, history and all the fun facts." I took a quick look at the room behind Sherm's massive shoulders and saw our patient was on the ventilator, a respirator, had a variety of IV fluids and drips hanging from poles, run through calculating pumps that ensured each drip infused at the proper rate.

"The first patient--" Sherm gave me report as if we were going off shift, so I had as much information as possible. I knew how to take care of this patient. I'd taken care of countless post-op surgical patients who weren't able to be successfully extubated, or removed from the respirator, in the recovery room. They needed a slower process, and more observation, to ensure they were stable. Hence, the ICU.

We ran through the machines, the monitor, all the stuff necessary for me to care for the patient's tonight.

"Great. Thanks. I'm trained on EPIC charting, but I still need to test drive my user name and passwords to make sure they work," I said.

He nodded to a bedside computer. "Try there. It's the closest one, and you don't have to fight for one at the desk." After I signed in, we sat to watch the monitor. "I hear you and your buddy found the dead nurse," Sherm said. It wasn't a question. He wasn't asking. He was stating a fact that he believed.

What could I say? Audrey probably had told some people who had told some people and then those people shared bits and pieces of the truth. It was like playing that kids' game of *telephone*. The first person in line was given the statement and told the next kid in line. By the time it got to the end of the line, the statement in no way resembled the original one. I played that a lot as a kid. But I was going to have to straighten this out right now. If I could.

"Yeah. I guess we did," I said. There. Straightened out. Next question.

"You guess? Did you or didn't you find a body?" Sherm's uni-brow wrinkled as he looked down at me. I was willing to bet his DNA was straight Neanderthal. Maybe Homo erectus. I always got those two mixed up.

"We found a crime scene, but no body," I said and hesitated, but it was going to come out sooner or later, so I might as well spill it. "Then yesterday we found a body, but no crime scene."

"No shit?" He watched me, trying to figure out if I was feeding him a bunch of crap. I'd surprised him. People loved being the first one to have a bit of juicy gossip to share with others. It elevated their status among their peers. Most of us really haven't evolved much from middle school.

"Unfortunately, no shit. Charlie, Officer King, said they'd had a report about a missing nurse last week, and is now trying to figure out if the one we found in the marsh last night is her. Kelly's body still hasn't been found." I hated saying that out loud. The more I said it the truer it became.

Surprisingly, a flare of compassion surfaced in Sherm. He put his beefy hand on my shoulder and gave a quick squeeze. "I'm sure that was difficult for you and your buddy. Jeannie's her name, right?" he asked.

"Yeah. And it was. Pretty much a shock to both of us. We'd decided to see if we could give Kelly some extra support since this was her first assignment. We turned from welcoming-committee to body-discoverers," I said. I really didn't like that job title.

"Well, we'll keep you busy tonight and maybe you can forget some of those visions bouncing around in your head," Sherm said, having some sympathy for me, knowing distraction was a good way to cope for a while.

"Thanks, but how did you know that was going on with me?" I had my suspicions, but I'd learned it's best if people tell you their stories, rather than guessing what they were. Being former-military, I'm sure he had a few images floating around in his memory he'd rather forget, too.

"Two tours in Iraq. Two in other places," he said. Other places he couldn't talk about. Memories surfaced in his dark eyes, and he let me see the effect they had on him for just a moment, then he cleared his throat and glanced at the cardiac monitor again. "Normal sinus rhythm, but a little tachy. Not unexpected for post op."

Got it. A little glimpse into the real Sherm, then back to business. "Why don't you print me off a strip from the EKG, and I'll do the measurements?" I asked. Back to the business we were both there for, taking care of patients.

Sherm cast a sideways glance at me. We had an understanding. Those who've gone through traumas recognized each other at some level, and his respect for me rose half a notch. "You got it. If you don't have calipers, they're some on the desk," he said.

"Nope, got my own." What self-respecting ICU nurse wouldn't have her own set of calipers to measure the QRS waves on a cardiac strip? Although the machines could calculate it, it was good reinforcement to do it manually, ensuring the nurse knew that the patient's heart was operating on full steam, or not. Sherm handed me a few inches of the cardiac monitor paper, and I got to work measuring things and recording them on our flow-chart.

At the end of our shift, we gave report to the day crew coming on to care for our patients through the next twelve hours.

There were a lot of things I liked doing, such as reading, hiking, napping or watching a movie, but few of those activities did I enjoy twelve hours in a row. It was no wonder people were grumpy at the end of their shifts. Twelve hours of staring at monitors, listening to the alarms and phones, turning and basting patient's all night. It was exhausting.

Three days of our week started and ended like that. We'd finished our week of orientation. Basically a crash course in all things Oak Island hospital. Where the supplies and linens were kept, policy and procedure books, OSHA policies and how to report any incidents from a finger stick with a used needle to a wet spill on aisle seven.

The morning of the third day, historically people have risen, but on this third morning we were headed to bed.

"Hey, Curly? How about you and Jeannie joining us for some chow?" Sherm had affectionately decided to call me curly, 'cause he couldn't remember Piper. Duh. How hard was that? I think he just wanted to give me a nickname.

"Sounds good, but let me check in with her." I dashed around the corner and caught Jeannie mid-yawn. After a quick discussion, we decided to go for it. Not just to make nice with the local nurses and try to amend their beliefs on travel nurses, but we were hungry.

My favorite food was anything I didn't have to make myself.

With a sudden energy surge in anticipation of low-grade carbs, I dashed back to Sherm and a few other night nurses that had gathered.

"Let's go. I could eat a horse," Sherm said.

"Please don't," Jeannie said and made a face of disgust.

"I won't, I promise," Sherm said with a twinkle in his eye. "But if a small pony wanders by, I'm not making any promises."

Jeannie laughed and gave him a playful pat on the arm. "Okay. I'll buy that," she said and adjusted her backpack over one shoulder. "Where are we going?"

"Place close by. We can all walk together. It's our ritual after third night on, and you're welcome to join us since you'll be on our rotation," Sherm said and led the charge to the ICU exit.

Jeannie and I looked at each other. We must have done something right, to be accepted and invited to the core group after just a week. Score.

We'd totally found our people.

℈ 7 ℈

IF THERE ARE NO UPS AND DOWNS IN YOUR
LIFE, YOU'RE DEAD - INTERNET

W e followed Sherm and the crew through the
hospital and its secret hallways, down access
stairs that led to the outside and across the
lawn where a path had been worn through the nice green
grass. Although a sign prominently stated walking on the
grass was discouraged, people obviously didn't agree with
the sign and continued on their way to wherever they
were going.

Primarily, to the restaurant nearby. It boasted breakfast
and coffee twenty-four hours a day. What sane night shift,
or for that matter, day shift worker, could pass up that
advertising?

Unfortunately, it was the place where we'd been so
rudely treated the first day. Oh well, maybe grumpy-ass
Pete wouldn't be working today.

As we entered, a little bell over the door chimed our
arrival. *Ting-a-ling.* We're here. Feed us, it seemed to say.

We found a table to accommodate all of us, our back-
packs or survival bags, or whatever we needed to get
through our shifts. Every nurse had one. It was only the

contents that varied person-to-person. Some people brought books in case of a slow night, or an actual real bonafide break, some brought pictures of their kids to set up on the desk so they gave themselves the feeling they weren't missing anything while their kids slumbered in their beds. We all had our own adult version of a security blanket we brought to work.

Emily, our waitress from the other day, approached with a handful of menus under one arm and a hot pot of coffee in the other. The smile pasted on her face made her look as if she were actually happy to be up at that time of the morning on her summer vacation. She was good.

"Hi, y'all. Welcome to Fat Pete's. I think y'all have been here before right?" she asked and relaxed a bit. With a crowd of regulars she didn't have to keep up the facade..

"Yeah, we're all frequent fliers here," Sherm said, taking the lead, refusing the menu. He knew what he wanted as did most of the others. They'd been doing this together for some time.

Jeannie and I, however, took the menus and drooled over the selection of high-fat, high-carb breakfast of dreams and made our selections.

"So where's Pete?" Sherm asked. "He's usually around when we come in."

Emily took a quick, panicked look around, then leaned between me and Sherm. "I'm sorry. He saw y'all come in and headed to his office." A quick flush crept up her neck. She wasn't going to get away with lying to her mother with that reaction.

"Really? He never misses jawing it up with us," Sherm said. "He's always got some new conspiracy theory for us about why roaches can't be killed, or why insects are going to take over the planet one day."

"I think I know the reason he isn't coming over," I said, ready to make my confession to my new comrades. "We came in the other day, and he made it pretty clear he wasn't fond of travel nurses." I shrugged. "Don't know why, though."

"Hmm. Interesting." Sherm gave that some consideration and added a generous amount of cream and sugar to the giant mug Emily sat in front of him. Usually restaurants gave you those small mugs and advertise *endless* refills, when the first mug was only half the size of a regular one, anyway. They tried to make you think you were getting something for nothing, but I knew better. Half the coffee for twice the price. Talk about conspiracy theories!

We talked to the others about staffing issues at the hospital, our previous assignments, and why we traveled. Each of these fine nurses, men and women, permanently lived on or near Oak Island. They had homes, and families, and were firmly entrenched in their community. Sometimes they could imagine taking off and leaving all their cares behind, but others looked at us as if we'd lost our minds when we told them we actually enjoyed moving to a new location every three month, packing all of our worldly possessions in the backs of our cars, and heading to parts unknown.

Maybe we were on the fast track to Nutsville, but it was an awesome ride.

Except for the dead people part. That was a new stop on the crazy train.

"I filled everyone in on how you'd found the crime scene and no body, and a body with no crime scene," Sherm said. He was taking the lead position of dispersing juicy information this morning.

If I were a naturally suspicious person, which I was, I might be supposing that we'd been so quickly accepted into the group because we had a juicy story to share. Which we did. But I'd like to set that aside and believe we'd been accepted because of our excellent nursing skills, and they liked us. They *really* liked us.

Who cared, as long as I had pancakes. And coffee. That I didn't have to make.

"Yes, we've certainly had more adventure the first week here than anywhere else," I said and raised the mug with life-sustaining nectar to my lips and breathed in its delightful scent.

"That's for sure," Jeannie said and dipped her tea bag in a pot of hot water. She was not as fond of coffee as I was, but I'd forgiven her for that long ago. She had tea first, then coffee.

Pete appeared at the doorway of the back room, where I assumed his office was hidden. He was pretty scrawny for owning a place with *fat* in the name. I wondered if he'd lost a bunch of weight, 'cause he looked kinda sickly, as if he hadn't seen the sun much lately. Or had recently suffered a severe gastrointestinal virus that I really didn't want to know about.

I nodded to Sherm. "There he is if you wanna have a chat with him," I said and kept my gaze on my mug.

Sherm was good. First he lifted the fork loaded with a Denver omelet sprinkled with hot sauce into his mouth and chewed, then he lifted his head as if thoroughly enjoying the bite, but it gave him the posture to observe Pete without letting him know that he'd been spotted out of his hidey-hole. Sherm nodded. "Excellent." Anyone else might have mistaken the complement for the food, but I knew he was talking about the intel on Pete.

Then Sherm eased his gaze to me and spoke quietly. "Wanna see what that was all about?" he asked.

I gave a stealthy upward twitch of my brows. This was gonna be good. Jeannie and I discriminated against no one, so when someone gave us that kind of rude treatment, it surprised me. Shouldn't, but it did. "Bring it."

Sherm raised one arm in the air and emitted such an ear-piercing whistle through his teeth that I jumped. I think my heart may have stopped for at least two beats. Maybe three. *Wow.* I was so never sitting beside him at a sporting event. "Yo. Pete. Come on over here," Sherm demanded in that deep, booming voice of his. I imagined no one had defied that voice when he'd been in the military.

For a second, Pete looked like he'd had a former life as a deer caught in a headlight, and had hesitated for just a second too long. Then the expression of surprise disappeared from his face, and he plastered on a fake smile that was way worse than the one Emily had initially used. Pete approached, and I could tell by the rigid lines in his body language that he was none-too-pleased to be summoned by someone, even though that someone had brought lots of other someones that paid his bills.

"Sherm, how are you?" He took Sherm's hand in his, and I saw the grimace the little weasel hid quickly. Sherm had given him the strong-man-handshake-test, and Pete failed. I so liked Sherm more and more. I was going to bake him some cookies.

"Hey, I wanted to introduce you to some new nurses at the hospital, and I want you to treat them extra special for me." Sherm put a hand on my shoulder and gave a quick pat. "This here's Curly, cause I can't remember her real name's Piper, even though she has a name tag on." He indicated Jeannie across the table. "And over there's Miss Jeannie."

Pete's face was gonna crack. I just knew it. And he was going to ruin the beautiful breakfast I had not yet had the pleasure of.

"Yes, I believe we met the other day," Pete said. He didn't hold out his hand, and I didn't want to shake it, or I'd have to use my hand sanitizer again. "I understood them to be something other than staff nurses." He was trying to slam us and appear like he wasn't slamming us, but we were onto him.

"Oh yeah, did I forget to tell you that?" Sherm shook his head and gave his best Gomer Pyle impression. "Surprise, surprise, surprise. They're actually the best of the best, Pete. They're travel nurse on assignment, and we're lucky enough to have them here for the entire summer, so you'd better treat 'em right." There was no sparkle of amusement in Sherm's eyes now. He meant what he said, and Pete damned well better do it.

"What do you mean, *the best of the best?*" Pete had bitten on the tempting bait Sherm had dangled in front of him. Sherm had deliberately, and sneakily I might add, hooked Pete into taking the bait and now, Sherm was going to reel him in. Without knowing it, Pete was giving up what was going on *without actually asking him* what was going on. I'd have to remember that technique next time I was in a similar situation. Or in a bar. Or in jail. Whatever. Pete finally gave up the pretense. "They're travel nurses. How can they be the best of the best if they can't keep a job for more than a few months?"

"Actually, that's a mistake for you to think that," Jeannie said, trying to correct his erroneous believe about travelers. She was so sweet, but I was afraid it was wasted here.

"Oh, really? A mistake?" Pete asked, the sarcasm dripping from his teeth. He was gonna need a bib, but we weren't at Red Lobster.

"Yes, really." Sherm took command again. "These two are very hard-working nurses that having come to help us out for the summer, our busiest time, and have *chosen* to patronize your establishment because they heard it was the best of the best, too."

Pete's mouth slammed shut with a splat. For a second, he considered Sherm's words carefully and his own more carefully-er. "Yes. Well. I see." Back again was the fake smile, but the watery blue eyes remained cold, devoid of any warmth. I was reminded suddenly of the feeling I'd gotten at the marsh last night when it had turned dark and slithery things had left their sleeping dens to hunt. I think Pete must have been one of those in a former life, too. Maybe he still was, and we just didn't know it.

I AWOKE HOURS LATER TO THE FRAGRANCE OF FRESHLY CUT grass wafting in through the window I'd left open a few inches. Although we'd recently discovered two crime scenes, I wasn't worried about someone breaking into our apartment. The window was designed to snap into place every two inches and lock. I liked the circulation of fresh air mixing with air from the air conditioner as I slept. I also turned on the ceiling fan and a small fan on my bedside table stirring white noise that kept me from being a complete insomniac. It drowned out a lot of excess noise and allowed me to sleep deeply for a few hours.

Jeannie was up already. I smelled coffee. We brought our own coffee pot and custom blend. We weren't spoiled or anything, we just liked what we liked, and since neither of us kept a permanent residence, it was essential we had the basics of feeling like we were living in our own home instead of a rented apartment all the time.

I brought some artwork for the walls and a few pieces of regional pottery and stuff from other assignments. It helped me to feel like home was wherever we were at any given time. Meant I carried my life in my car, but without it, I'd be homesick for a place that didn't exist.

My home had been in western Pennsylvania, in the heart of the Appalachian Mountains. Halfway between Pitt and Penn State universities, where college sports ruled, and women were treated like they were in the nineteen-fifties. Drove me nuts. But it was my home of origin.

I hadn't found the home of my heart yet, and neither had Jeannie. She had a great relationship with her parents who lived in Missouri. When we traveled near there, we'd swing by and spend a few days with them at their farm of pygmy goats and alpacas. For those few days I had a home and a loving family. Guilt by association, I guessed.

Her mother always sent us off with boxes full of home-baked goods and sometimes freshly-picked fruit from their small orchard. Cherries, apples, peaches and pears all grew there in abundance with little effort. It was an ideal setting in the lower range of the Appalachian mountains ruled by its own mystery and lore.

A quick rap on my door was followed by Jeannie's voice. "You alive in there? We have to go to HR soon."

"Ugh," I said and slapped a hand over my eyes. I'd forgotten about that one last orientation task we had to take care of. "Yeah," I croaked, sounding like the frogs in the marsh. "I'm alive. Or at least I think so. I'm not quite in my body yet." My spirit was still floating around in the ether, not yet assimilated in my physical form.

"Well, get moving, sister. We have an hour to get there." She opened the door, and a draft of heavily conditioned air sneaked into my room.

"What time is it?" I asked and reached for the bottle of water I kept beside my bed. It enabled me to sleep better if I didn't have to physically leave the arms of Morpheus to retrieve water. I could just open the bottle, take a sip, put it back on the table, hardly waking up. Much. Unless I drank too much, then I had to get up to pee sixteen times. There was a fine line between hydration and exceeding bladder capacity.

"Noon. A bit after. I couldn't sleep," Jeannie said. She sighed and entered my room, perched on the end of the bed, as graceful and ethereal as one of the blue heron's we'd seen in the marsh.

"Too many pancakes this morning?" I sat and leaned back against the headboard.

"No. Too many images in my mind. Of the girls we found," she said.

She could call them girls, since they were. We weren't much older, but in that moment we both seemed older than our thirty years of age. Age wasn't always a number, sometimes it was the wear and tear that aged a person.

"Yeah, I get it." I sighed and began to unbraid my hair. If I left it loose while I slept, I'd end up with one large mat of hair knotted at the back of my head that took too long to comb out and was painful. So I braided it, which helped. I'd heard Oprah say she slept on a satin pillowcase, but so far I hadn't been willing to cough up the money for one.

"Our appointment is at one, so you have time to

shower and dress, grab some coffee, then we can go." I stretched and my Winnie the Pooh night shirt stretched with me. Most days when I woke, I felt like Pooh. Oh, bother.

"OK. OK. I'm up. I think." Swinging my legs over the edge of the bed and standing helped me get all of my neurons firing in the right direction. "Shower." I staggered to my private bathroom as Jeannie left and closed the door behind her.

We headed to the hospital. This time Jeannie drove her hot little Mazda six-speed convertible sports car. Why not have a sports car in an electric blue that got awesome gas mileage if you could?

The humidity on the island was entirely too high for my curly hair. I looked like I'd just gotten a perm, though I'd never needed one. Mother Nature provided enough curl for my entire life. Thanks, bitch.

We found our way to the HR department, that wasn't all that far from the nursing director's office we'd frozen to death in the other day. We entered HR and found one man who looked like Humpty Dumpty's cousin that had totally not been put back together again. Looked a few pieces shy of a full egg.

"Hi," he said in a distracted voice from behind a giant pile of files and stacks of papers surrounding him. He sat up straighter, and we could see at least his eyes over the stack. "How can I help you?" He stood, having given up trying to see us around the piles.

"Yes, we're new travelers and have a one o'clock appointment to finish up our on-boarding process," Jeannie said. She was so nice.

"Oh. Really?" He harrumphed and sat down again,

pulled his keyboard forward and signed into something. "Hmm. I don't see you on the schedule."

"Really? Maybe we got the day mixed up or something." She pulled up her phone calendar.

"It's Wednesday, perhaps you put it on the wrong date or something," he said, suggesting we were there in error.

"Actually, it's Thursday. Could you look at your Wednesday schedule?" I said. I wasn't getting out of bed for nothing. We were here. We were going to do this. Whether Humpty liked it or not.

"Seriously? It's Thursday?" He looked startled and squinted a paper calendar on the wall. "Well, rats. I lost a day somewhere." He gave a little chuckle, but it wasn't very amused sounding. "I was on vacation last week, and I'm still trying to get back in the swing of things." He moved to another desk and rifled through another pile of file folders. "What units are you in?"

"We're both in the ICU," Jeannie said and moved forward as he tried to balance way too many of those file folders. They looked like they were gonna go over. "Can I help you?"

"Nope. I got it." He shuffled some more, nearly lost the whole load and secured it, clasped against his chest. "Sorry. Give me just a minute." With one foot, he pulled a desk chair out, then dumped the entire contents of his hands onto the chair. "There." He looked at us. "Now, where were we?" he asked.

"ICU? On-boarding process?" Jeannie reminded him.

"Right." He sat on his chair and scooted to yet another desk.

"Don't you have any help?" she asked. "You're buried in files."

"Nope. I'm it. The entire HR department right here." He

gave a brittle smile, obviously trying to bite back a comment.

"How do you keep all of this organized?" I asked. That was a trick question, as he obviously wasn't keeping it organized at all.

"It ain't easy. This is an improvement after the last HR person left." There was that brittle smile again. Bet he had a comment about that one he was biting back, too.

"Seriously?" Jeannie's eyes widened. "You need some help."

"They won't hire anyone full time, and this is a nightmare. Would you want to walk into this mess?" he asked us.

"Uh, no. No, I wouldn't," Jeannie said, always honest.

"But, in any case, we just need to finish up with you and then you don't have to look at it any more the way I have to," he said. Martyr much?

"Since you were on vacation last week, maybe you didn't hear about the travel nurse that disappeared," I said, spreading the cheery news. We didn't know if the body we'd found in the marsh was a traveler, so I couldn't count her.

"Really? Which one?" His brows shot up.

"What do you mean, *which one?*" I asked and almost reached past the piles of papers to grab him by the neck, but my arms weren't that long. "There's been more than one gone missing?" I thought about the second nurse Charlie had mentioned at the marsh, but surely there couldn't be more than that, could there?

"Yes, there has been more than one." He hoisted himself from the chair again with maximum effort. "Give me a minute." He opened a file cabinet, then closed it quickly, moved from one desk to another searching for something when he pulled a thick file from beneath a box that a dead flower in a pot sat on. "Aha. There it is." He opened it, thumbed through a few pages, then returned to his chair and collapsed back into it like he'd just run a marathon. "They're all here."

Jeannie and I looked at each other. "All? How many are there?" I asked and swallowed hard, pretty sure I didn't want to know the answer to that question.

"Three. I think. With the new one, that makes four."

I though my jaw dropped before. Now, it was in the sub-basement of the hospital. I couldn't fathom that many nurses missing, or just walking away from assignments and no one noticing.

I held my hand out. "Can I see that file?" I had to see what was going on here.

He snapped it shut. "I'm not sure. HIPPA and all that rot."

"HIPPA only applies to protected *health* information. The files don't contain their medical records do they?"

"Besides, if the nurses are presumed dead, HIPPA no longer applies. It's considered public access information, like arrest records or autopsies," Jeannie said. That was total bunk. I was so proud of her for coming up with that on the fly. I hadn't thought of it, but it worked. And although autopsies *were* public information, you had to pay for the records that sometimes took months to have completed. You just couldn't look up your neighbor's autopsy report online to be nosy and see what they died from.

"Really?" He gave a confused frown. "I'm going to have to look that up."

"Don't worry. We're not going to blab anything about anything to anyone. We're just trying to figure out how many travelers are missing, and why no one's put this together yet," I said. How could that many employees be missing from one employer and no one noticed?

"Because I've been on vacation, or didn't you hear me say that? I'm entitled to a two week vacation every year, and I just got back, or hadn't you heard that either?" he snapped. Maybe HR wasn't the place for him to work. Maybe food service would be easier for him to handle. The color of his face reddened and not in a good way. The jugular vein trotted away in his neck, and the vein in his forehead looked like it was gonna pop. What a mess that would make.

"You know, you don't look very well," I said. I approached on one side and Jeannie the other. She put her much gentler hand on one of his shoulders. I'm certain mine would have been closer to his neck.

"Why don't you take a breath? You're sweating now and getting upset," Jeannie said and put one hand on his wrist, checked his pulse and looked at her watch. "Are you having chest pain?"

"Chest pain? No. I'm fine." He looked back and forth between us as if he were being assaulted on all sides. He was, so I couldn't fault him for that.

"You know, the first sign of a heart attack is *denial that you're having a heart attack*," I said. I really didn't think he was having one, more like anxiety because he'd come back to his job, and we were messing it up for him. Some people with OCD couldn't handle changes in routine, even if the routine was a mess.

"I'm not having a heart attack, I'm thirty-seven years old." He sputtered as the sweat poured off of his head, and he wiped it away with one hand.

"Seriously, when was the last time you had your blood

pressure checked or your cholesterol?" Jeannie asked. "Your age doesn't protect you from a heart attack. You're more likely to die from it."

"My doctor's been after me to lose some weight," he admitted and looked down. I'd be willing to bet the doctor wanted him to lose more than just *some* weight.

"It's okay. We all have our health issues, but you seriously don't look good right now," I said.

"Why don't I go with you to employee health?" Jeannie asked, offering to go with him.

"We don't have employee health any more. Staffing cuts. Have to go to the ER now," he said, his breathing was getting faster.

"Okay, then why don't I walk with you to the ER?" Jeannie gave him her best calming nurse-voice I'd heard her use countless times with stressed patients and families. Always worked to get them settled down quickly.

"Your pulse is really erratic, and that's an indication of something going on," I said, trying to overcome her nurse voice. We needed him out of there, not settling down.

"What? What's going on?" His eyes widened, and he looked like he was really going to have a full blown panic attack.

"We don't know. The only way to find out is to go to the ER and have your symptoms checked out by a doctor," Jeannie said.

"But I don't have any symptoms," he said, obviously sticking to his story.

"Denial will get you nowhere, Jerry." I said and stepped back. "Unless you're ready to let go and die an unnatural death at an early age, then that's a whole different story." I gave him the options.

"No! No, I'm not ready to die." Yep. Panic attack on the way. With a side of anxiety covered in hot sauce.

Jeannie took him by the arm and urged him to a standing position. "Then let's go now, so you make it to your next birthday."

A downtrodden look covered his face and his shoulders slumped. "That's tomorrow," Jerry said.

"Well, good. If we go now, you'll probably live to see another day," she added with a bright smile.

"Probably? he asked, now looking to her as the authority figure.

"Probably," she whispered. "But we have to go. Time is essential when it comes to surviving cardiac death."

"Cardiac death?" He looked to me to confirm her statement, as if I knew more than she did. I didn't, but it was important to present a united front.

"It's important. Just go. We can come back another time to finish the paperwork," I was so self-sacrificing. I glanced around, but there was no sword nearby for me to fall on.

"Okay. Okay," he said and walked with Jeannie out the door and down the hall to where the signs pointed to the ER. That would probably take at least an hour.

Awesome. I rubbed my hands together and faced the piles of files, looking at the one he'd just set on top. Alone at last. I hurried around the desk and sat in the chair that was still warm from Jerry's body heat. Ew. I took a breath. At least it wasn't sweaty.

୫ 8 ୭

My fingers trembled a little as I reached for the file. I'd never committed an act of espionage, so I didn't know if this qualified or not. It wasn't state secrets, or anything to do with Homeland Security, but still. It was private contents I wasn't supposed to be looking at, or have access to.

I'd consult Wikipedia later about the definition of treason.

The contents of the file could be a whole lot of nothing, or it could be the key to what had been going on around the hospital regarding the travel nurses. Jerry had indicated there were more than a few people who'd just up an left their assignments, but that didn't usually happen. Nurses didn't just walk away like that. Not even the rare, whimsical travel nurse.

I opened the file. The first page indicated a name and demographics of a nurse due within a week. I picked up the phone and dialed her number. No time like the present to get information or cause random acts of chaos.

The phone rang four times and dread stirred in my

stomach. If it went to voicemail it could mean she was a smart night nurse and turned her phone off during the day so she could sleep. Or it could mean she was in a dead zone. Or it could mean she was dead.

It could also mean she didn't answers calls from numbers she didn't recognize. I didn't. Do you know how many wrong numbers and sales calls I got on a daily basis? Entirely too many.

But at the last second, as I held my breath, the phone clicked.

"Hello?" The voice did sound sleepy. But at least she wasn't dead.

"Hello, is this Miranda Archer? I'm calling from HR at the Oak Island Hospital, just wanting to welcome you to your new assignment." What else was I going to say? I was sitting in the chair at HR, calling on the HR phone. I never said I was an HR employee.

"Oh, hello. That's really nice."

Rats. Now I'd started a precedent I hadn't intended to. "Yes, we have a lot of travel nurses and wanted to make sure everyone has what they need to have a great start to their assignment." Winging it here, but it seemed to be working.

"Oh, great. This will only be my second assignment, so I'm glad to hear a friendly voice on the other end of the line," Miranda said.

"That's me." God, I sounded overly enthusiastic, even to myself. I should be in sales. "Can you tell me when you'll arrive?" I looked at her file, but couldn't see her exact start date. Looked like the document was unfinished.

"Yes. I'll get there on Tuesday next week. Should I come right to HR then? I have an email directing me to a general orientation," Miranda said.

"No, go there first, then they'll give you the appointment time to come here," I said. That's what they'd done with us, so it figured they'd continue the same way with everyone. "Let me give you a contact number for another travel nurse who will show you the ropes and make sure you have everything you need for a successful assignment," I said. I gave her my name and number and told her to call when she arrived.

"Oh, that would be great. I still have so many questions about being a travel nurse." The relief in her voice was palpable. This wasn't a game I was playing here. This was a real life and death scenario.

"We'll see you next Tuesday. Be safe driving. Pace yourself, take a break every two hours whether you think you need it or not. Eat, hydrate and all that good stuff." Well-used tips of the experienced travel nurse. I should write a book. Or at least a pamphlet.

"I will. Thanks again for the tips. I really appreciate it."

We ended the call, and I sat for a second with my hand on the phone. Jeannie and I had intended to be the welcome committee for Kelly the night we'd found the crime scene. Now, I'd just inadvertently made myself the welcome committee for Miranda. Maybe Jeannie and I needed to make something official. I'd have to have a chat with her about it and maybe we could get something going for real to help out, and connect with, other travelers coming in. Everyone needed support. Even people as independent as travel nurses.

Back to work. Back to *snooping* just didn't have the same ring to it.

I flipped the page with Miranda's information over, then looked at the next page. I read more this time and saw that Josh Vine was scheduled to be arriving in two weeks. He could wait. Next one, and the next one. I finally got to the batch of nurses who were a few weeks into their assignments.

They were from everywhere. They were assigned to different units. They were from a variety of agencies, other than my own.

If I called my agency and asked what other travelers were coming here, they might not have any, and that's where the issue lay. It was why no one put it together, and why it had been overlooked. There were multiple agencies involved and none of them connected to each other. Jerry was the only one who had all the information, as scattered as it was, and he'd been physically absent for two weeks. Mentally, probably a bit longer.

There was no continuity to the influx of travelers. No single entity, except for the chaotic HR department of one. Each unit cared only about their own staffing needs, that was pretty typical. So when one traveler didn't show up, the hospital assumed the worst. They assumed the nurse had simply walked away from their assignment and the hospital got someone to fill the gap as soon as possible, never checking into what had actually happened to the nurse. That wasn't their job. Their job was to take care of patients and fill staffing shortages.

But assuming nurses just bailed had serious conse-quences the hospital units probably weren't individually aware of. That had been a grave error for Kelly and at least one other nurse. We still didn't know her name.

If nurses didn't finish their assignments, they didn't get paid everything they were due. They lost out on hundreds of dollars of mileage reimbursement and travel expenses. And most nurses, travelers or full time staff, had high levels of integrity. They simply never walked off a job and left their patients behind. Ever.

I checked my watch. Time was passing, so I scooped up the entire file and moved to the photo copier. Making a copy of the entire file would be simpler and easier. Certainly more efficient. Maybe after four years, Jeannie was finally rubbing off on me.

So I'd just put the whole file on the copier and was about to push the button when the HR door opened.

Dammit. I'd been lucky so far that no one had entered. My heart headed into overdrive, and then I relaxed a second. Maybe it was just Jeannie coming back.

"Hey," I said and turned to face a complete stranger and pasted on a smile. Double damn.

"Hi, I'm new here and was wondering if you could help me out." A small woman, mid-twenties, pink spiky hair and a long sleeved shirt that I was betting covered up a bunch of tattoos, stood hesitantly holding her backpack just inside the door.

"Hi, there." Gulp. I hit the start button and set the copier to doing its job. That made me look more like I worked here, didn't it? "How can I help you?" That sounded very official. Even though I'd never worked in HR, I had a hospital badge identifying myself as belonging in the hospital, if not that particular department, and I was a public servant helping a lot of people. I could so wing this. I took a seat behind the desk but couldn't see her, so I came back around. "Pardon the mess. Someone's been on vacation."

"Oh, right." She bobbed her head and looked like a pink chicken. "So, like I said, I'm new here, and I can't figure out where I'm supposed to go next." She held out a piece of paper listing events that looked familiar to me. It was the same print out Jeannie and I'd received in our first orientation day.

"Let me have a look at that." I read it and verified that was correct. I checked my watch. "Looks like you're set to meet the DON, then go to your unit for your schedule." Surely I could recall events from just one week ago, right?

"Yeah, but where is the DON's office? I thought it was in this hallway, but I can't find it," the woman named Mitzi said.

"Come on, I'll show you. It's a pretty cold place in there, so I hope you have a hoodie in your pack." It was a chip off the old iceberg.

"Yeah. I do." Her eyes brightened as we approached the door just a few down from HR. "There it is. I completely overlooked it, thanks."

"Hey, wait a minute. Let me give you my number," I said, needing to confess. "I'm a traveler here, too. I don't work in HR, I just happened to be here. If you need anything, give me a call." I couldn't in good conscience mislead her any longer. Her life might depend on her reaching out to me instead of HR.

"Great. Thanks."

We exchanged numbers, and I felt a bit better that I'd made contact with a new traveler. Maybe Jeannie and I could do something to prevent her from disappearing, or leaving the assignment a little too early.

Back in the HR department I scooped up the copies that were crappy, with black streaks running across some of the. They were readable, but someone needed to change their toner cartridge. *Jerry.*

I found a manila folder and stuffed my copies into it, then grabbed a Sharpie from the desk and scribbled my name in big letters. To a casual glance, it would look like I had a file of information that belonged to me, not some info I'd hijacked without permission.

I moved toward the door and tucked the file under my left arm, placed the original file on top of the stack I'd gotten it from just as the door opened again.

Was there such a thing as a triple-decker-dammit? If so, I was saying it now.

"Piper?"

"Jeannie!" I peeked around the stack of files three feet high. "Good, you're alone. How's Jerry?"

"Panic attack. They gave him some Vitamin A, our friend Ativan, to calm him down. I think losing the day right after vacation was not good for him," she said.

"No kidding. He does need to drop some weight, or the next time it really could be a cardiac issue for real," I said. Events like that came out of the blue for people like him. For people like me and Jeannie, we saw it coming a mile away.

"Always better to err on the side of caution." She opened the door and we left, headed back to her car. "What did you find?" She asked that so casually, as if we did this all the time. Her espionage skills rivaled mine.

"I don't know yet, but I did talk to two travelers, one on the phone due in on Tuesday, and one that just got here. I gave them my number as a contact," I said.

"Busy little bee, weren't you?" She put the car in gear and shoved on her sunglasses. "Let's go to the Flying Pig and see if we can make some sense out of that information."

"Good plan," I said. Any plan that involved coffee got my immediate cooperation.

We settled at the large main table that resembled a giant wooden spool of thread. Just no thread. Probably had had cable wrapped around it at one point. The decor was eclectic, pig-style. Looked like an antique shop, but most things had some sort of pig theme, even bumper stickers with their logo on it.

Jeannie opened her hand toward me, asking for the file. "Let's see what you got, Sherlock."

She pulled out the pages and divided them into two piles, one for her, and one for me. "I don't know what we're going to find here, but I think this is the key to it," I said.

Our drinks arrived, cold coffee milkshakes first thing in the morning made the day worth getting out of bed for. Although it was afternoon now, we'd just gotten up, so that still qualified as morning for us. Add a nice whopping shot of whipped cream on top, and we almost had ourselves a food group. Some day I'd make an application on its behalf to the Department of Health for top billing on the food pyramid, but not now. I had too many things to do today.

I sorted information my way. Jeannie sorted her way. Of course, being the more analytical-minded of the two, she sorted by alphabet. I sorted by time.

She pulled out her computer and opened a new spread sheet. She knew what spread sheets did to me. I broke out in hives. I thought I was allergic to them, but she was calm and didn't appear to be scratching. Maybe she had an immunity that protected her.

She plugged data into the program, then reached for my pages and plugged that information in, too. In between, she guzzled her black tea latte and nibbled an orange poppy seed scone, drizzled with white icing.

"What are you seeing? Any pattern yet?" Patience was

not my strong suit. I wasn't sure I had a strong suit. Maybe a few good runs, but not enough for a full house.

"No, not a pattern, yet." She frowned and squinted at the screen. "Well, maybe."

"Do tell. I'm not getting near that spread sheet," I said and resisted the urge to scratch my arm.

"It appears that only one of the travelers has actually left before their assignment ended," Jeannie said and squinted at the screen, but I didn't think it was going to help.

"What? That can't be right, can it?" I asked. Despite my misgivings and lack of access to antihistamines, I scooted my chair closer to Jeannie so I could see her screen.

"From four units." Though Oak Island wasn't a major hospital, it was sizable enough to require outside staffing to fill their shortages, especially during the height of their busy season.

"Show me." I hunched closer to her laptop and squinted, hoping that would help.

"I set it up by date of arrival, date of departure, date gone missing, then unit, and then agency," she said. Her hand shook when she reached for her drink.

"I see," I said. I did see. Though it was sporadic over the last two months, four female nurses had gone missing from all except for two units. Pediatrics and obstetrics. "Huh. That's weird. We know travelers are great, no matter what unit they work in, but Peds and OB seem to have not been affected by the weird factor." I didn't know what else to call it, as they were the exception, the anomaly.

"Look at this," she pointed to the graph with red dots to the far right.

"You made a graph?" I asked. Seriously? She needed to get out more.

"No, the program makes it for me," Jeannie said. "But yes, it's a graph. In any case, it's skewing the stats."

"Don't you have to remove those that do that? What happens if you remove those from the scenario?" The only thing I remembered from my statistics class was something about throwing out the top and bottom numbers, which were the outliers, and using the other information from which to deduce your theory. And that's about all we had. A theory.

She punched a few keys on the keyboard and hit enter again, then turned the screen toward me. "Then it appears that thirty percent of travel nurses have disappeared from this hospital over the last two months, and no one has noticed," Jeannie said.

"Thirty percent? That's outrageous." I was shocked. I knew my voice rose because a few patrons looked up from their game of checkers. Seriously, they were playing checkers. They didn't move, just looked up to see what the ruckus was about. I was the ruckus, so I waved and pasted on a smile that said I wasn't going ballistic on anyone. I leaned closer to the computer and nearly pressed my face to the screen. That probably wasn't going to help me any more than it had helped Jeannie. "What do you mean, thirty percent?" I whispered. "How could that happen without anyone noticing?"

"Simple. HR guy, Jerry, was on vacation. Each unit is de-centralized. When they have staffing issues, they find their own solutions. They don't have a single nursing supervisor in charge of staffing, they do it themselves. Seems like all of the travelers have come from different agencies. Including us. But we just got here, and I'm really hoping that neither of us is going down the way the others have." We didn't even know what that was, but we didn't want to take that fork in the road, no matter where it led.

"Hell. Me, too." I had plans to live to a ripe, old age, sitting on my porch in my rocking chair, swatting mosquitoes with a fly swatter.

"We need to make better friends with Jerry when he comes out of his Ativan-induced-high," Jeannie said. "Let him know we're available to support him."

"Why would we do that?" I could usually see her logic in most things, but not this one. I needed more explanation.

"You started it, so don't blame me." She picked up her latte and sipped again.

"What did I start? I didn't start anything. Did I?" What had I started? A riot? A fashion statement? A cliché?

"Yes, you did," she said and gave me a look. So, she was right, and she knew it. I had to catch up. "The welcome committee. By giving two travelers your number and telling them to call when they got here, you involved us. Or one who's coming, and one who's here already," she said, clarifying the details. "Remember?"

"Oh, right," I said and sat back in my chair. "I did do that. But you're okay with it, right? Since we were going to do that for Kelly, anyway."

"Oh sure. Just so long as no one has my number," she said, but I caught the sparkle in her eyes.

"Brat. Drink your latte, and let's go for a drive." That was something normal for us. Long drives for sight-seeing and being tourists on our days off. Since the sky was overcast, there was no sunning on the beach today. Might as well take a drive.

"Okay. Where to? There's a nice park, Fort Fisher, a bit north of here. Have to take the ferry over, then we can walk around, take some pictures there." She shut down her laptop, gathered all the notes and stowed everything in her bag.

"No, I wasn't thinking of that, but we have to put it on the list of places to go. That sounds cool. I was thinking maybe we should go to Southport and show this information to Charlie. It might help, right?" I said. I didn't know if it would or not, but it seemed like the right thing to do. It was at least another piece of the puzzle we'd inadvertently fallen into. I just wanted out of it before all the corners were put in.

"Oh, I see," she said and some of the pizzazz drained from her eyes. "I was hoping we could put some of this aside for a little while."

"I'd hoped so too, but with this new information we've just compiled, okay you've just compiled, could be really important to the investigation," I said. I couldn't in good conscience take credit for her work. At least not this time. Maybe another time when people's lives weren't on the line and nobody was looking.

"True," she said and pushed out her lips again. I gave her some time, because there was no telling how long the pushed-out-lips were going to stay that way while she considered the issue. The less I interrupted, the faster she processed the question.

"Okay, but first, I think I need to add some more information to the database. More than what I put in. Like their phone numbers, home addresses, and if we can find it, their local addresses," Jeannie said. Travelers generally found their own housing. There wasn't a database of nurses addresses, since everyone worked for different companies.

"That might be stretching the boundaries of privacy

and-or stalking laws," I said. I'd consult Wikipedia for that one, too. Maybe I needed to download it and have it on my phone to be available for such circumstances.

"Oh, yeah. Hadn't thought of that. Maybe Charlie can help us with that part of it," she said. There went the lips again.

"Hopefully." I picked up my drink and sucked down about half the frozen and blended coffee drink. "Oh, ow." I pressed the cold cup against my forehead and scrunched my eyes closed as pain mushroomed in my head like a bomb going off. The only thing keeping it intact was that it was firmly attached to my body. *Oh, the pain.*

"What's wrong?" Jeannie asked.

"Sphenopalatine Ganglioneuralgia," I gasped as the pain in my head shot past the top of the one-to-ten pain scale. *To infinity, and beyond!*

"Brain freeze?" she asked after a second of thinking. Score one for her. "But what you doing?" Jeannie asked.

I didn't open my eyes. I couldn't. The freeze was still on, but my mouth wasn't impaired. "I saw somewhere that if you have brain freeze you should hold the cold glass against your forehead," I said.

"That's stupid," she said.

"I know, but when you have brain freeze you'll do anything to stop the pain, right?" I asked. Maybe Wiki-*how* would be more helpful.

"The brain freeze occurs because the soft palate in your mouth has become extremely cold extremely fast and sends the message to your brain that you need to do some-thing about it quickly," she said, little miss logical.

"I was doing something about it," I said.

"Something helpful," she said. Smart ass. "Like pushing

your tongue against the roof of your mouth to warm it up. Or drink something warm."

"I think the point of drinking something really cold is to cool you off. Having a warm drink defeats the purpose of the cold drink, you know?" I said. I could be a smart ass, too.

"Fine. Give it a second," she said, speaking to me like I was a toddler having a tantrum.

"Okay, I'm good again," I said and opened my eyes. In an instant the pain evaporated. There were still miracles in the world. *Hallelujah!*

"Don't drink it so fast next time," Jeannie said.

"Yes, mother." I shot her a playful look.

"*Stop acting like a child, and I'll stop treating you like one,*" she said with a sassy shake of her head and a bland look tossed my direction. "OMG." She gave herself a headslap.

"Yeah. You sound just like my mother. Or your mother. Or both," I said. I shivered with the memory, having dreaded hearing those words from my mother. But now that she was gone, it was kind of comforting to hear them again, even if they came out of Jeannie's mouth. I might have nightmares, though.

"Come on. Lets go for a drive. See Charlie. Then we can swing by the fort on the way back. We don't have to be anywhere for four days, so what the heck? Let's live it up," Jeannie said. She stood, and we cleared our table. We couldn't leave a mess for someone else to clean up after us. It as so un-nursey.

"Right on, sister," I said. We left, and I realized I didn't have my camera with me. If we were going to take that kind of a trek to the fort, I needed shoes other than my gorgeous, pink, sparkly flip-flops, and also my camera. No camera, no sightseeing. "Let's stop by the apartment. I need a few things first."

"Okay. Me, too. We can pack some water and grab a few essentials," she said. Knowing her, there would be a sweater on her list.

In the end, we decided to take my SUV as everything was already in it, except for us.

We drove straight to the Southport police substation. We'd get water, and probably more coffee-laden frozen drinks again, later.

❧ 9 ❧

WEATHER FORECAST FOR TONIGHT: DARK -
GEORGE CARLIN

"Suppose we should call Charlie and see if it's at the station?" Jeannie asked. "He could be out doing something."

"Hmm. That's a good idea. He'd only been there on Saturday because we told him we'd come in. Can you look up his number and punch it in?" I asked. I had a navi and phone system in the over-priced, but really cool, SUV. I could look at the screen and punch in a few numbers, or even call up a directory from the steering wheel if I wanted to, but I had yet to actually to talk to the inanimate object I rode in. The GPS voice telling me what to do was enough already. Sometimes it was very bossy, telling me where to go. Bitch.

"Sure." Jeannie said and opened her contacts. I pulled up the phone screen on the navi system, and she dialed it in, because I was, like, driving. After two rings it was answered.

"Officer King, how may I help you *on my day off*?" He emphasized the last few words to make the caller feel guilty. I knew that trick. Had done it myself to people, but we weren't just people. We were...*us*. He should know that by now. We didn't follow anyone's standard rules. We just made them up as we went along.

"Oh, no. Charlie? This is Piper and Jeannie." She cringed. I didn't. He told us to call him any time, and I tended to take people at their word. If they didn't want me to do something, like call them *any time*, they shouldn't tell me to call any time. Because I will.

"Hey, ladies. When it comes to you, two, I never take a day off," he said. Genuine pleasure pulsed in his voice, not the fake public servant crap people said for good PR when they were talking to someone they had to.

That made us laugh. "Obviously, you haven't seen us at the end of a stretch of night shifts," I said. "It's not pretty."

That made him laugh. "I'm sure after a few hours of sleep, you'll be as gorgeous as ever," he said.

"Well, you're about to find out. If you're available, that is," Jeannie said. "It's your day off, so we don't want to disturb you. If you want us to talk to, uh, Shipper or someone else, we'd be glad to," she said. She might, but I wouldn't.

"Actually, we wouldn't. Jeanie is too nice to say it, but I'm not," I said. I really had to say it out loud. Otherwise, to me it was like lying. An omission of the truth was still a lie, wasn't it? "I'm not terribly fond of Shipper, so if you're available, I'd rather talk to you, know what I mean?"

That made him laugh hard, and I wanted him to reconsider the radio show gig. What a laugh that was. Just listening to it made me feel better, forget the fatigue in my bones, and that I'd recently almost frozen my brain to death.

"Now, that's the best bit of truth I've heard in a long time, sugar," he said when he could breathe again There was that syrupy sweetness again. After three months in the south, I was seriously going to have to reconsider my diet, and go to a convent or some place where they took vows of silence, and skipped words like *honey* and *sugar*.

"Glad I could help you out and bring a little levity to your day," I said. It was in my job description under, *other duties as assigned.*

"You certainly did that. Where are you ladies anyway? I'm heading to Oak Island myself right now," he said.

"We're headed to Southport right now," Jeannie said.

"I hope we don't have a head-on collision. That would just ruin my day," I said and looked for a cruiser coming our way, buy didn't see any.

"Mine, too. Let's meet somewhere other than the substation. I'd rather stay outa there, or they're likely to really put me to work," he said. I could empathize with that.

"How about the Flying Pig? You know it?" Jeanie asked. Even though we'd just been there, we could deal with another trip for sugar, fat and caffeine.

"Sure do. See you there in five." He ended the call. Probably because he shouldn't be talking on his cell phone while driving. He probably didn't text while driving, either. Good man.

"Awesome. U-turn time," I said and made a squealing sound in my throat, but continue to drive safely to the next light, made a left hand turn into a parking lot, and then pulled out when the lane was clear.

"That's your idea of a U-turn?" Jeannie asked, a baffled expression on her face. "What about the squealing tires sound you just made?"

"Well, it's safer to make two left turns, rather than do a U into oncoming traffic. I don't want to end up as a patient in my own ICU, do you?" I gave her a glance and returned to watching the traffic.

"Uh, no. Very good point," she said and looked at the traffic. "It's pretty slow now, so we probably wouldn't end up with any serious injuries." At the beach people always assumed a vehicle was going to stop for them no matter where they crossed the road. Wrong. But as a good citizen and a nurse, I couldn't in good conscience plow down anyone in front of me, no matter where they crossed the road. I would swear at them like a sailor, but I drew the line at outright mowing them over.

"Not willing to risk it," I said. I might be all balls and brass with my mouth, but when it came to safety, I was by the book. "Flying Pig, here we come. Again."

"Try not to freeze your brain into the next ice age this time," smart-mouth Jeannie said.

"I was thinking of doing just that since the first one today felt so good," I said. Yeah, sarcasm was sweeter than revenge, which you could really only do one time. Sarcasm went on and on.

Jeannie gave me that *I'm-a-telling-you-now-that-if-you-do-it-again-I'm-a-giving-you-that-I-told-you-so* look. It was complicated, but I got it.

We re-entered the colorful establishment, got in line behind one person and gave our orders by the time Charlie pulled up in a big, black SUV with the Southport Police logo emblazoned on the side of it. No mistaking whose vehicle that was. He wore casual, civilian clothing today, but wore the reflective sunglasses to protect his eyes. Smart. Denim shorts that showed off those nice legs of his, and a Bob Marley tee shirt with the singer's hair flying back. The epitome of all things Bob.

"I thought you were off?" I asked when he sat with us.

"I am." He looked outside where I indicated with a delicate twitch of my finely-arched brows. They came in handy now and then for non-verbal communication. Like now. "Oh, you mean the big, bad SUV I'm driving?" he asked.

"Yes. I thought you turned them in every day or something," Jeannie said.

"In some cities they do that. Here, we like to show our presence wherever we go. Makes the public think we're out on patrol even when we're not, and it discourages casual criminals from being completely stupid when a cop is around," Charlie said. Our drinks arrived, and we each took a sip of our own frozen bliss in a plastic cup with a red straw.

"So, what's the thing you wanted to talk to me about?" he asked. The cop eyes were back. He was assessing us, even if he didn't know he was assessing us. My nursing evaluation skills came in handy at times like that. It was good to know that someone was looking at us the way we were looking at them.

"We came across some information that might be useful. The ever-helpful Jeannie has put together a spread sheet of the information to more easily compare it," I said. That said a lot without actually saying a lot.

"You *came across* some information?" Charlie repeated my words slowly, digesting them, as if he were trying to decide how to handle them. Pepto, or go for the burn? He turned with those gorgeous eyes of his narrowed slightly. *At me.* Seriously? I knew he was a cop, but what had I said to make him believe I'd come across the information by nefarious means? I needed to figure that out quickly so I didn't do it again the next time I came across information I'd obtained by nefarious means.

"Yes. That's correct. That's what I said," I said. I stared him down, but I couldn't prevent the blush from rising up my neck. Damned Irish blood and skin. Gave everything away, and it was too hot to wear a turtleneck.

He pressed his lips together a second, then shook his head. "Never mind. I don't want to know how you got the information, just lay it on me. Whatcha got?" he asked and looked at Jeannie.

She was the one with the power point in her head. "We discovered that not only have two nurses gone missing, presumed just to have abandoned their assignments, but a total of four nurses have, too. All from different units in the hospital," she said. There it was in a nutshell. With sprinkles on top.

"What?" Bemusement crossed his face. He removed the shades from the top of his head and placed them on the table. It was a delay tactic, whether he knew it or not, to give him a second or two to digest that information.

"Let me show you the dates and times first," Jeannie said and pulled up her spreadsheet, then the graph of the travelers coming and going over the last two months. Charlie whistled, impressed.

"How did no one catch this?" he asked the same question we had. Puzzled, he looked to us for answers we didn't have. We weren't the travel-nurse-police.

"There are a lot of issues. A lot of pieces to this pie," I said. We explained how the HR guy had been on vacation, had no help, the hospital units only dealing with their own staffing issues, and how de-centralized nursing worked. That each unit was responsible for obtaining their own staffing when they were short on nurses.

"That's crazy. Just crazy," he said and shook his head again. In the artificial light of the coffee shop I could see the lines of fatigue beneath his eyes, and the lines on either side of his mouth had deepened since we'd seen him just a few days ago. The case, or something else, was taking a toll on him, and it showed. He didn't look like he was sleeping well, or he was worried about something. The usual reasons people looked like hell.

"Yeah. That's what we thought, too," Jeannie said and slumped a little in her chair. She hated not having the answers to any question. Even one as bizarre as this.

I took a sip of my frozen drink that had way too many calories in it, but I didn't care. Lives were at stake and people were missing. And I'd been up all night. My ass could handle a few more calories. I'd run them off later.

"We, well I, gave two travelers my contact information. One is here, and one is coming next week. She's supposed to call me when she gets here." I paused a second, not sure I wanted to say this out loud. Once something had air time, it usually became real. "I sort of started a welcome committee for the travelers, so we can keep track of people coming in." I pointed to the screen. "With the information we have here, we can contact other travelers already here and invite them to our little circle of support, and warn them about stuff that's been going on. I'm sure their agencies haven't warned them, because they simply don't know." I shrugged. "No one does. Except us."

Charlie nodded. "Those are really good ideas, ladies," he said.

"I didn't think of it, Piper did," Jeannie said, giving me the credit for accidentally creating a welcome committee that I was now going to be responsible for. "I just put it all together here," she said and pointed to the computer screen.

"Damned fine ideas and cooperation. I wish we had

that between agencies. Hell. Even between departments in one agency would be a help," he said and sipped his concoction, pondering the situation. "Could you email me a copy of that document? I'd like to take it and your explanation up the food chain a notch. Might even go to the Feds, too. This could be big, ladies. We, rather you, may have stumbled on a situation. It could even be something as bizarre as human trafficking. Vulnerable people who have no one in the immediate area to report them missing? To know they're even missing in the first place?" He clucked his tongue in disgust. "It's certainly worth thinking about," he said.

"Yes, the agencies are all over the country, the nurses are from all over the country, too," Jeannie said.

"Wow. That's crazy. I never knew anything about travel nurses until this situation came up," he said. "Shipper thinks he knows everything, and I overheard him telling someone he'd never heard of travel nurses before now, either." He didn't have to say that made him feel good, too. To know more than the know-it-all was da bomb.

"At least he admitted it, right?" I asked with a cocky toss of my head.

"Yeah, and there's no one person or entity watching out for any of it. No overseer, so to speak," Jeannie said typed the email address from his business card into her program and hit send.

"And that's good. That's free enterprise, capitalism, and all that, but this is a very unique situation, isn't it?" I asked. I'd never run across something like this, and I was certain he hadn't either.

"Very unique." Charlie pushed back from the table and stood. "I'm going to have to think about this for a while. Figure out which way to go with it and let you know. In

99

the meantime, be careful out there. Be suspicious of every-one, and I mean everyone. Don't take anyone for granted just because they're another nurse. It could be a nurse behind all of this," he said.

"I don't know if I can do that, Charlie," Jeannie said. "Be suspicious of everyone? Really?"

"Even the people waxing the floors. This person knows how nursing schedules work. Don't underestimate him." A hard glint eased into those amber eyes. "Trust no one. Except each other," he said.

"Thanks." She nodded. "We'll heed the warning," she said, but I knew it was going to be hard for her to do that. She was such a trusting soul. I was the more suspicious-natured of the two of us.

Leaning all of his weight on one hip casually, he picked up his drink and gave a look around the shop. I knew he was sizing up everyone from the lady behind the counter to the gentleman in the corner who'd hobbled in using a walker. Everyone was suspect, right? "In the meantime, what are you two going to do on your day off?" he asked, trying to lighten the dark mood that had fallen around the three of us.

We filled him in on the trek to the fort and the ferry ride across the inlet we wanted to do. Maybe being away from the hospital for a while would protect us. Lighten our hearts, too.

"That sounds like great fun. Just remember, the last ferry comes back at seven or eight, I forget which. If you miss it you'll be swimming back or spending the night alone on the island, which I'm sure you don't want to do," he said, sounding like a tour guide, but one we should listen to.

"No, we don't," Jeannie's eyes widened. "After what we

found in the marsh the other day, I'm pretty sure I don't want to be outside anywhere at night here." She gulped. "Thanks for the advice."

"Good to see you ladies, but I have some personal errands to run today." He towered over the two of us and everyone else in the shop, his head narrowly missing a piece of pig folk art suspended by clear fishing line from the ceiling. Pigs really did fly. "Be safe out there, and I'll be talking to you again about your findings," he said and gave me a raised eyebrow. "No matter how you found them."

"What?" I squeaked. "I'm sure it's public information." I cleared my throat. "Somewhere."

"I'm sure you think that, but right now I don't want to know." He grinned then and the Charlie we'd been getting to know emerged. He gave us a two-fingered salute. Maybe he'd been a Boy Scout earlier in his life, 'cause it wasn't a cop salute, or a military one. Maybe he'd made it up just for us.

"Okay. So off to the fort now? Or how are you feeling?" Jeannie asked me.

I leaned back in the chair and sipped from my drink, more slowly this time, and performed a self-analysis. Sometimes in the afternoons I got headaches behind my eyes from the three nights of being up. Sleep deprivation reared its ugly head, telling me I couldn't sleep at night, but I couldn't sleep during the day either. Bitch.

No headache now that couldn't be dealt with. A little muscle fatigue, but more of a heaviness in my chest that wasn't a physical ailment, but from the emotional distress of discovering how many nurses were really missing.

"Not feeling real great, but I think a nice boat ride over to the fort, then maybe some awesome seafood for dinner might just do the trick to shake it. How about you?" Food always made me feel better. Especially if I didn't have to prepare it.

"Same. I could either binge a tub of ice cream while wrapped in my fuzzy robe and slippers while watching Netflix, or take a long drive and a short hike." She peered through the big window of the coffee shop to get a look at the sun. It was waning. We were a bit late in the day for driving to the fort an hour away and ensuring we'd get back before the last ferry of the day. "I'm not sure I want to brave the chance of not catching the ferry back, so how about we do the fort tomorrow and just go eat something wicked tonight instead?" she asked.

"Good plan. I hit Sherm up last night for some restaurant recommendations, and I have a list on my phone." I patted her on the shoulder. "Let's go."

Dinner was a lovely meal eaten on the deck of restaurant that wasn't far away, but was hidden down a surprisingly long dirt drive that opened up onto a road that was a resort on one side and a boat dock on the other. Condos fanned out along the shore, far enough back that they didn't take the financial hit of being right on the beach. A row of luxury beach homes took that formidable position. But at the dock, where sailboats, fishing vessels, and a variety of other sea-going boats resided, was an upstairs restaurant with a bright blue awning and a fancy cartoon shark painted on the side of the building. Looked like Charlie The Tuna, but with more teeth.

"That has to be it," I said. The lot was packed. A few trucks with empty trailers hitched behind, probably fishermen or boaters out for the day, took up two parking places each. But I found a spot at the end of the row.

I grabbed my camera from the floor in the back seat

and locked up the car. Maybe I'd be able to score some nice pictures from the upper deck of the restaurant and get some shots of the boats coming back to the dock, against the varying colors and mood of the sunset. Those kinds of pictures always brightened my day and would be a great addition to my photo journal.

First things first, we secured a table outside on the deck under a shaded area that also sported a nifty misting system spritzing water intermittently.

"Just lovely," Jeannie said and turned her face up into the mist. The blissful expression on her face said it all. We were off for a few days, could sit here after the sun went down and drink Margaritas as long as one of us was safe to drive us home.

We ordered, talked about our separate experiences with our preceptors at the ICU, their different styles, and whether we thought we were ready to go solo on our next scheduled shifts.

"Danielle is a great preceptor. She, of course, said I could hit her up for anything new that came up after orientation, and if she ran across anything interesting, she'd let me know." In a general ICU, you never knew if you were going to have multiple trauma from car crashes, or take care of someone who'd had multiple medical problems from a cardiac arrest and recovery, to a patient who was in multi-system-organ-failure from the little cocktail of drugs they'd ingested, having trusted their cousin's best friend when they'd said it was *okay to take.*

"Good. Sherm's the same way, too," I said. Solid. Reliable. Looking out for me, whom he now considered his little sister. Or at least an extended cousin come to visit for the summer.

My plate of sizzling scallops wrapped in bacon entered

the picture. Nothing compared to the melt-in-my-mouth succulence of perfectly-prepared scallops. The rasher of bacon wrapped around them didn't hurt, either. Everything was better with bacon on it. Even bacon.

Jeannie sashayed closer to her delicate-looking white fish with a colorful cilantro-mango-lime salsa on top.

We'd already shared some oysters on the half shell, and perfect margaritas, so-called because that's what the menu said they were. Perfect Margaritas, so we were well on our way to a magnificent end to the day.

The sun continued westward, nearing the horizon and spread brilliant orange wings to signal the end of its participation in the day. We sat outside on the upper deck of the restaurant that overlooked the sea. A small peninsula reached out into the bay and trees had grown up on it over the years. A wide channel cut through the grass and marshland big enough to accommodate various sizes of boats headed from the marina out to the open ocean. People could also fish around in the brackish water for creatures seeking refuge in the tall marsh grass, or protection from turbulent tides of the deeper sea. Either way, the view was just stunning.

"What a nice day," Jeannie said and emitting a long sigh of relief, her cheeks puffing out a little. "I'm starting to feel better about things." The tension in her jaw eased, too. Things were finally settling down. We both felt it. Or the tequila was doing laps around our brains making us believe we were relaxing. Either way, I was good with it.

"I know what you mean," I said and I did. There was a certain amount of responsibility one acquired when discovering bad news and dead bodies the way we had. Though we'd had no input into how they'd gotten that way, we had a kinship with them that couldn't be denied.

A certain responsibility to find out what had happened to them. "I'm starting to feel human again."

"That's because of the tequila you just ingested," she said and slurped down the last vestiges of watered-down margarita among the melting ice cubes.

"Don't forget the fine meal, too." I sighed as the sun melded into pinks against the blue of the night sky. "I just feel a bit better with a nice meal, nice scenery and good friendship," I said. I raised my water glass and held it out to her, "You know what I mean?"

"I certainly do," she said and clinked her water glass with mine. We limited ourselves to one adult beverage, then stuck to water or iced tea afterward. Getting snockered and arrested for a DUI would totally ruin an assignment.

Half an hour later we were back at our apartment and the smile slid from my face like a melting ice cream cone in the heat. I froze in front of the door, suddenly reconsidering my state of bliss.

"Did you forget your keys?" Jeannie asked and stuck her hand in her purse, looking for hers. "How could you lose them between the parking lot and the door? It's three feet away." Slight exaggeration, but I got her point. That wasn't the issue. Not at all.

"No. We don't need keys," I said and took a step back, grabbed her hand as I continued to walk backwards while keeping my eyes on the door.

"Why not?" she asked.

"The door is already open."

❧ 10 ❧

I LIKE TO DISSECT GIRLS. DID YOU KNOW I'M
UTTERLY INSANE? - AMERICAN PSYCHO

"Mother, I'm working the late shift tonight," he said as she drifted off to sleep. He didn't think she heard him. Though she wasn't completely deaf, she'd been half asleep in her chair by the time he'd taken care of her physical needs, removed the teeth from her mouth, scrubbed them and put them into a cup on the sink. That sickened him. Holding another person's teeth in his hands, having to scrub the slime and bits of food from them. He'd gagged tonight. The task never failed to get to him, but tonight, it had overwhelmed him.

Tonight, he must work. Tonight, he must get the visions of her teeth out of his mind and fill it with something else. With his work, his mission, his need. His revenge.

Closing the door most of the way, he made sure it was cracked a few inches so the night light in the hallway shone in on her. If she awakened in the middle of the night, she could see where she was and not freak out the way she had when the house was completely dark. She'd

MURDER IN THE MARSH

fallen in the hallway a few times trying to find the bathroom when it was right there in front of her. After that,
he'd purchased a six-pack of night lights and put them
through the entire house. At least her part of it.

He could see in the dark. Cats eyes, Mother had always
said. He'd had cats eyes from the time he'd been small. He
could negotiate through the house without disturbing a
single piece of furniture because he could see the shadows
in the dark and knew where everything was. Where
everyone was.

Now, that life-long skill came in handy for other
reasons as he silently and quickly moved through the
house. The hall clock chimed eleven. His father hadn't
been able to afford a real grandfather clock, so he'd bought
a cheap one that hung on the wall. It was the same sound.
Had the same timing mechanism. The same setting to
chime on the hour. But every hour he was reminded that it
was a fake. Just as he was a fake.

When the chime echoed into silence, he slipped on the
gloves he needed and left the house. Though it was still
high summer, he needed the gloves for work, so he might
as well put them on now. Why wait until he got there?
That just wasted essential time. If you weren't ready to go
to work when you got there, you were a slacker, trying to
get something for nothing. That's what Father had always
said. *Be prepared when you go to work. You're there to work,
not dawdle around and talk, but to work.*

Work called for him now, and he left the house through
the side door in the garage. He'd recently oiled the
squeaking hinges and sticky brass knob. Now, it opened
and closed with ease, silently, the way it should.

Everything should work the way it was supposed to.
Everything had a design, and that's what it was supposed

to do. But things weren't working the way they were supposed to, now. People were changing things. People were deviating from the way things were meant to be. The way things were always supposed to be. The way he wanted them.

Stepping out into the night, he closed the door, but didn't lock it. No one bothered his house. It disappeared in the shadows past dark. If you didn't know the house was there, you wouldn't suspect its presence. Long ago it had been a quiet suburb, and he'd listened to the night sounds outside his window, the occasional stray cats picking fights. Over the years the town had grown up and built around the home that Father had placed there brick by brick. He'd built the home with his own hands, determined that he would die in the place one day. But one day had come too soon.

Taking the sidewalk onto the flagstones he'd painted black, he eased his way to his work, passing the restaurant by the hospital. Looking through the window as he walked, there were few patrons inside. At that time of night, most tourists were in their hotel beds or rental homes, tightly ensconced in their summer pajamas and summer-weight bedding. He knew those things because Mother had drilled them into his brain from childhood.

Summer weight bedding went on from Memorial Day through October first. Then the winter bedding had to be put on and kept there until the end of May. Didn't matter if Hell had opened up the vents in April and unleashed the hottest spring on record, the bedding wasn't going to be changed until it was *supposed* to be changed. That was how things worked. That was the order and nothing deviated from it. Nothing.

The light doilies under the lamps in the living room

and parlor had to be changed at the same time. Things had to be *just right* for company. What would people say if they came to visit, and you still had your winter doilies out when it was past Memorial Day? People would talk about you, that's what would happen, Mother had said, and had dragged him around by the ear until each and every doily had been changed properly.

Then she smiled sweetly and told him what a good boy he was while his ear throbbed with pain for hours.

Fists bunched up in his pocket, he clenched the blade he carried there. It was black, very sharp and encased in a worn leather sheath he'd made from an old shoe washed up on the beach a long time ago. He'd known as he'd made it then, that some day he would need the blade to protect what was his, and he'd been right.

In his other pocket, he thumbed the coil of jute cut from the spool in the garage. Father had always been tying things up with it. Tomatoes, vines, squash and cucumbers in pots that had lined the porch every summer for as long as he could remember. At the end of the summer when the plants died and no longer bore fruit, Father untied the jute and placed it in an old coffee can, then put the lid on it, stored it on a shelf for use the following season. Depression era survivors, his father and step-mother were. They'd been young at the time, but had learned early on not to throw anything away that could be reused.

After Father's funeral, he'd gone to the garage and pulled the old can from the shelf, taken it out to the dumpster and unceremoniously dispatched it inside. He wasn't going to re-use jute ever again. For his work, he needed fresh, strong fiber that wouldn't break against the stress he put it through.

The scent of cigarette smoke came on the breeze

toward him. Vile habit he couldn't abide. How did they do it? How did people inhale that acrid smoke into their lungs without coughing and gagging? Pausing beside a stand of Norfolk Pines, he waited until he saw it. The light, the glow of the cigarette as a nurse pulled the ghastly chemicals into her body, then tilted her head back and expelled the smoke from pursed lips.

She leaned against the old red brick building, one foot on the ground, one foot bent at the knee and pressed against the building, looking much like a stork with her pink spiky hair and long sleeved pink shirt beneath white scrubs. The little creature was his, just for the taking. She'd propped open the back door. Staff weren't supposed to do that, but they did, ignoring security policies to go outside to smoke at the back of the building.

He breathed hard, felt the racing of his heart through his veins. The buzz in his head built as he pulled the jute out and edged closer to her. She was tiny. She was nothing. She was going to be his. It was her fault and the fault of others like her.

It was all their fault Father had died. They could have saved him, but they didn't. They were too busy. Were too involved in other things to help a man strangling to death in his own sheets. They'd found him dead, hours later, when it had been too late to save him. The worst were those temporary travel nurses who said they came and went. They weren't stable. Had no home. How had they been trusted with the life of his father?

Then she pushed away from the building, crushed her smoke under her foot and reached for the door.

Anger pulsed in him as she escaped into the building, but then his dashed hopes reemerged as she laughed and held the door open for another. He couldn't hear what was said, but he guessed it was cigarette talk between them.

Lifting his nose, he sniffed the air again, and watched the other nurse begin the ritual all over again. They all did it. They all engaged in the same ritual, in the same way every time.

He had his own rituals. They would see just how.

Head bent over the blue-white light from her phone, she lost herself between the cigarette and the mindlessness of the screen, unaware the instrument of her death lay hidden just feet away.

Seizing his opportunity, he stole through the damp grass at his feet, past the stand of trees. Breath short, he lunged forward and used his superior strength to spin her about. Caught her off guard, and in the half second it took her brain to catch up to what was wrong, he whipped the strand of jute around her neck.

And pulled.

She made no sound. He felt her attempts to draw breath against his hands, felt her claws scratch at his hands and wrists, then dropped to her sides. Fumbling, she tried to escape as the life force dimmed, tried to--

The lightning flash of pain in his left thigh caused him to lose his grip on the jute just long enough for the stinking female to escape. With a hand to her throat, she took in a gasping breath and dashed in through the door. Just as he reached for it, she slammed it in his face. He pulled back to the shadows. Limping, reeling from the pain in his leg, he felt the hot drip of blood rushing down his leg. Crying out, he tried to hold it in, but couldn't. Couldn't stop the whimper from escaping his lips as he staggered to the side door in the garage. Not caring that someone might see, he flipped on the light over the workbench and looked down.

A pen. A black pen stuck out of his leg. The bitch had beaten him with a pen. Oh, she would die for this. He would put the pen through her eye and kill her that way. Shove it into her brain, force her to watch with one eye until she could see no more.

Smacking off the light, he made his way through the dark into the house and to the bathroom in the bottom floor. He'd never make it up the stairs with the pain he was in right now. He rummaged in the bathroom closet through the guest towels, to the every-day towels, down to the old towels that resembled rags and pulled three of them out. Mother would never tolerate it if he soiled one of the guest towels or even the every-day towels with his hands, let alone the stain of blood that could never be cleaned properly.

Stripping his upper clothing off, he tossed them onto the floor. Somehow managed to remove his shoes and socks, loosened the jogging pants and slipped one leg out of them, groaning as the position pressed on the painful protrusion in his leg. Taking one of the old towels, he rolled it up and clenched it between his teeth. He turned the water on, then stepped into the shower. Reaching for the pen, knowing it was going to kill him, he pulled it out with a scream he couldn't muffle, even with the towel.

Agony threw stars in front of his eyes, and he clutched the shower nozzle to keep from fainting. The bitch. She was going to pay for what she did to him, and what they'd done to Father. All of them. They'd killed Father, but they weren't going to kill him.

Looking down, he watched the burgundy life force exit his body and whirl down the drain. People thought blood was just red, but it was rich, dark, burgundy. He removed the towel from between his teeth with a hand that trembled, and pressed it against the hole in his thigh. Throwing his head back, he pushed his face into the stream of water and screamed out the pain in his body, his heart and his soul. They would pay. By all he held sacred, he would make them pay.

来来

WE RACED BACK TOWARD MY SUV. I HIT THE REMOTE fourteen hundred times to unlock both doors, and we dove in, not caring that we looked like idiots running across the parking lot for a Chinese fire drill, as long as we were inside and safe.

We slammed the doors shut and locked them manually, then I gasped in panic and hit the overhead light like a kid who thought the monster in the closet had returned. I'd forgotten to look in the back seat the way Charlie had done the other night, making sure there was no one there waiting to strangle us, or at least me. A perpetrator could only strangle one person at a time, right? So it was a fifty-fifty shot for either of us to survive.

"Call 911," Jeannie said and hit the panic button on the navi panel. She pushed several times. "Why isn't it working? This is an emergency, and it's supposed to work no matter what."

"Only if the car is on," I said. Slight oversight in design. I was going to write them a nasty letter. If I lived through the night.

"Well, turn it on," she screeched, the pitch of her voice rising higher than a dog howling at bad music. I hit the start button on the panel with hands that trembled, and the V-6 engine roared to life.

"I'll call 911. You call Charlie," I said and hit the red

emergency button on the panel, told the operator what the emergency was, that we were safe in my vehicle and weren't going into the apartment until the police arrived. I took a breath and took an assessment. I think I might have wet my pants. I think I might have wet Jeannie's pants, too.

"Charlie, this is Jeannie and Piper. I'm sorry to bother you again on your day off, but we got home and the door to our apartment was hanging open, just like Kelly's was," she said and panted in a breath. "We're okay. In Piper's car outside the apartment, but we're scared shitless," she said. That was something. For Jeannie to curse, even a little, she had to be wigged out pretty bad. "Call us back and tell us what to do. We've already called 911, but we'd feel better if we could talk to you." She ended the call and held the phone in her lap.

"Oh, my God. He didn't pick up?" It never occurred to me that he wouldn't pick up when we were in our hour of need. Couldn't he sense our panic and know we needed his assistance? Apparently, not. In an emergency situation, everyone was the center of the universe, and we weren't immune from the notion either.

"No. I suppose he's entitled to have a day off without people like us bothering him," she said and shrugged, then reached out to hold my hand in her icy one. I turned down the AC. "He could be in the shower, or out with friends, or even in bed already." She looked at the clock on the dash. "It's almost midnight. If he has to be at work at six or something, he could already be asleep and simply not heard the phone."

This time I chewed my lip. Charlie wasn't our savior. He wasn't even on duty, so he owed us nothing. At least the thought of that voice of his gave me some comfort.

Jeannie's phone rang, and she picked it up. "Hello?" she said, then leaned toward to me. "Charlie, I'm so glad it's you. Actually, both of us are glad it's you. Let me put you on speaker," she said.

"You said you called 911, right, and you're safe?" he asked.

"Yes, we're all right. Freaked out as hell, but we're okay," Jeannie said. Score two cuss words for her tonight.

"I checked in the back seat like you did the other day, but it's just my junk in here," I said. Big relief. Except my pants still felt wet.

"Did you check under the cover in the far back?" he asked and I froze. The cover I pulled across anything back there so people weren't tempted to break in if they saw packages or something they wanted.

"I didn't." I looked at Jeannie's wide eyes. "I don't want to get out of the car to check. If someone's out there, we'll be targets as soon as we get out of the car."

"And if he's inside you'll be targets inside the car," Charlie said, providing a diabolical double dilemma.

"Charlie? What do we do?" Anxiety now began to settle in my bones. The margarita having completely worn off, I was getting ready to sprint into full panic mode.

"How long ago did you call 911?" he asked, and I could hear rustling in the background of wherever he was.

"About ten minutes," I said. It felt like two hours, though. Maybe we'd gotten sucked into a time warp and not known it. General Relativity could take a hike as far as I was concerned.

"Okay. They'll be there before I can get there," Charlie said, relief evident in his voice.

"Are you in Southport still?" If he was, that meant a thirty minute wait, even if he came sirens flashing.

"Yes, dammit. I'm in the ER," he said and huffed out an irritated breath.

"Oh, no. Are you okay?" We looked at each other. Our hero had been injured and was still willing to come help us. He was a double-duty hero to us now.

"Yeah, I'm okay. Just had a mishap tonight. Hurt myself. Damned stupid, but I had to come get a tetanus shot, a few stitches, and an antibiotic shot in the ass," he said. The grumble in his voice was totally understandable. We'd taken care of patients who'd injured themselves in a variety of ways, and the thing they all had in common was irritation at the stupidity of the situation that ended with a trip to the ER and a shot in the ass. Or two.

"Really, you don't have to come. You need to take care of yourself." Jeannie was letting him off the hook. "I feel better just talking to you," she said and nodded at me with a glare, trying to get me to let him off the hook, too.

"Yeah, Charlie," I said without enthusiasm, sounding like Eeyore. Glum, with no hope for the future. "Take care of yourself. The police ought to be here soon, right?" I looked out the back windows, but didn't see any rescue lights yet.

"It's change of shift, so they could be a little later than usual." He paused, and I could almost hear him thinking. "No. I'll come. I can't leave the two of you alone in this situation. Not after all you've gone through to help us with the investigation, and some very creative acquisition of intel," he said. Now, I heard the affection he had for us returning to his voice. Everything was going to be okay. I just knew it. "You ladies sit tight, and I'll come get you. I'll call the duty cops and let them know what's going on, then I'll be there as soon as they get my leg bandaged up."

"You don't know what a relief it is to hear you say that,

though I really don't want you to come, I really want you to come," Jeannie blurted out exactly what I was feeling. We were nurses and could pretty much take care of ourselves, but not when there was an apparent serial killer on the loose targeting nurses. We weren't going to be able to take on that one. Not without some major help. Or a rocket launcher.

✣ II ✣

Time never slowed as much as when you were waiting on someone else. At midnight. When a killer was on the loose.

Or, if you were waiting for the answer to the Jeopardy question. At least they had music. That stuck in your head. Eternally.

Right then, we had nothing.

I tried to practice my meditation breathing, but nothing helped. I kept an eye on the door to see if anyone came out or went in, or lurked around it. Even the most innocent of people could have walked by then, but at that time of the night and as freaked out as we were, it would have looked like lurking.

The phone rang, and we both jumped. "Geez!" I said out loud, then said some rather nasty things under my breath while Jeannie cleared her throat and answered the call.

"Hello?" she said. "Oh, Charlie. Let me put you on speaker again."

"Ladies, at least one officer will be there shortly. Apparently, something went down at the hospital. Everyone is already over there trying to figure it out, but they're pulling one or two patrol units to come check your apartment. Then I'll be there as soon as I can," Charlie said.

"What happened at the hospital?" I asked, a sick feeling of dread tightening up places that ought not tighten. At least not in public. I wasn't sure I wanted to know the answer to that question. Maybe a grief-stricken family member had come in and caused trouble. Maybe the ex-boyfriend of a nurse had come in to cause trouble. Maybe I just didn't want to know what kind of trouble it was. But I had a bad feeling I already knew what kind of trouble it was.

"I'm not sure. A female nurse was attacked while on a smoke break," Charlie said and there was a hardness to his voice that hadn't been their earlier.

"Yet another reason not to smoke," I said.

"Amen, sister," Charlie said. "But with that incident and the possible security breech at your apartment around the same time, it's just not a safe night for female nurses to be out alone."

"I have a revolver," I said, "but it's in the apartment."

"Don't even think about it," Charlie's voice was sharp, like I'd never heard it before. Jeannie and I looked at each other, feeling uncertain now. "Statistics are off the charts about women having their weapons taken by an assailant and used against them." He took a breath. "I'm glad you have one, but at this point, I'm glad you don't have access to it. Just hang tight, and someone will be there shortly."

"Thanks again. I'm going to put you in for a commendation," I said, certain once again that he was our savior.

"You can't do that," he said with a muffled laugh that

ended in an exclamation of *ouch*. "But I appreciate the sentiment.

"I know the governor," I said, totally confident in that false statement.

"You do not," he said, utter disbelief in his voice.

"Well, one day I might and what better way to meet him--"

"It's a her."

"--her, than to make a commendation for one of the boys in blue?" Made sense to me.

"Piper. You just can't do that," Charlie said.

"I don't care if I can't do it. The world is full of people who were told they couldn't do something, and they went off and did it anyway." I crossed my hands over my chest, though he couldn't see me. "I'm putting in a commendation anyway," I said.

"Piper, you are something else." More rustling in the background. "Hold on. Getting my walking papers now."

The sudden flash of red and blue lights reflecting off of the cars around us alerted us that at least one patrol car was near. "I see cop lights," Jeannie said. "Thanks for staying on the line with us."

"Should be Sullivan or Wayne coming. Make sure you ask for their ID when they pull up. Otherwise, you stay in the car 'til I get there," he said, reminding us of a safety tip we wouldn't have thought of. Wasn't everyone who drove up in a cop car at midnight flashing lights a real cop? Apparently not.

The police cruiser parked in the middle of the lot. They didn't know what my vehicle looked like, so it was up to us to get out and flag him down. And expose ourselves to an attacker, but hopefully, the blue light special had scared him off.

The officer who'd arrived was tall, young, another high and tight haircut, white male, wearing the summer uniform of the local police, so he looked the part. He carried a large, super-duper flashlight, the kind that Charlie had, and shone it around with one hand, while keeping his other hand on the butt of his weapon. I described him to Charlie. "That sounds like Sullivan, but make sure when you get out," Charlie said.

Carefully, I pulled on the door handle, which immediately turned on the inside dome light and blinded me for a second. Blinking several times, I eased from the car and shut the door. "Hello?" I called out.

The officer immediately turned toward the sound of my voice, but remained in the same alert stance with his hand on his weapon. "Are you the lady that called about the apartment break in?" He had a nice voice, too, but not nearly as warm and rich as Charlie's. Unfortunately, no radio show for him.

"I'm supposed to ask or your ID," I said and stayed back a few feet from him. If he lunged or something, I could at least sprint a few feet before he caught me. I'd never outrun him.

"King told you to ask, didn't he?" The cop chuckled a little and lowered the flashlight beam to his chest, illuminating his name badge and his shield prominently displayed. It matched the one Charlie and Shipper had worn the other day, not that I was an expert or anything, but I was becoming one pretty quickly. The tension in my chest eased some.

"Okay, Jeannie. He's good," I said and called to her through the open window, and she stepped out. Charlie was still on the phone on speaker.

"Sully? That you?" Charlie asked.

"Yeah, it's me. What do you want me to do? Wayne is one the way, but he's ten minutes out," Sullivan said, speaking to Charlie on Jeannie's phone.

Since we'd called Charlie first, I guessed that meant he led the investigation, but as Sully was the first one at the scene, he was supposed to lead the investigation. At least they were trying to work together. Cooperation. I loved it.

"Wait for him. This guy's dangerous. No telling what he'll do with the opportunity to kill a cop. Just hang tight. I'll be there in twenty," Charlie said and the line went dead.

"I guess we're in your hands now," Jeannie said. Her eyes were wide. Vulnerability showed in her face. The kind of emotion I had a hard time conveying, but Jeannie was more open than I was. She'd be the vulnerable one, and I'd come in and kick some ass. Just hoped I wouldn't break my foot.

"What do you think could be going on?" I asked Officer Sullivan. I meant with the whole thing. What the hell was really going on with, just, everything?

"Hard to say. Could be the suspect who attacked a nurse at the hospital. Timing is about right. He could have tried you two first, then got frustrated when you weren't here, and looked for another target. Once a suspect is in a frenzy, they have to act. They can't not act. It becomes a compulsion." He shrugged. "Or it could be that you forgot to pull the door tight. Simple as that. Humidity swells wooden doors, especially in the summer, and they don't always latch tight. If you're not from here, you might not know to give it a good tug." He looked around the area with his flashlight again. Though he seemed calm and relaxed, his hand remained on the butt of his gun, and his eyes continued to check every shadow he could find.

MURDER IN THE MARSH

"Could just be some drunk college students looking for something."

"If it's them, I just hope they left my panty drawer alone," I said with a frown. I knew how male college students worked.

Sully gave a snort of a laugh and looked down at me. "I hope so too. I hope that's all it is. You can always replace some missing panties, but not your life."

"But we didn't leave the door unlocked or unlatched. That's for sure," Jeannie said. She was right. We'd both come from poor families, and we valued the possessions we had. We weren't going to leave a door unlocked for the casual thief to just walk in through. No matter how little we carried with us, they were our things, and we weren't likely to be so cavalier as to leave a door unlocked.

"Can we stand under the light more?" Jeannie asked. "I feel safer under the street light."

"Not advisable," Sully said. "If you're not comfortable, come closer to where I'm standing."

"Really? Why not?" She looked longingly back at the giant spot the street light had created, but stepped closer to Sully as advised.

"Just illuminates you as a target. If someone has a gun, you're just one big, bright bullseye for him to pick off beneath the light."

"Oh. I hadn't thought of that," Jeannie said and eased away from the circle of light we'd both once considered safe, and closer to Sully. Had to scratch street lights off the safe list.

"Just hang tight with me. Wayne will be here momentarily," Sully said.

He squeezed the radio mic on his shoulder. "Wayne? Sully. What's your twenty?" I loved cop lingo. Especially since it was being used around me. Made me feel like an episode of a cop show was being filmed in front of me. Except there were no actors. Nobody to keep us safe from harm except the couple of cops we'd grown to depend on very quickly. I think I needed to brush up on my martial arts training. I was rusty. I could make my own movie: *Karate Nurse*. Didn't have the same ring, though. Maybe Ninja Nurse. That would be better. And I looked good in black.

The radio crackled again. "Two minutes out."

"Good. He'll be here shortly. You'll be safe with me 'til he gets here." Sully was doing his best to remain vigilant and keep two nervous nurses calm.

"I think my prom date said something like that that when he tried to get into my dress," I said, trying to recall that foggy memory.

Sully laughed. "Charlie said you were a crack-up."

"I'm serious," I said. "I'm going to have to go through my yearbook again and see if that jogs a memory. I'm so gonna slap him at the next class reunion," I said. I'd learned a lot about male behavior since those early days.

More lights heralded Officer Wayne's arrival, and my heart rate dropped again. At least with two cops and one more on the way, this guy wasn't going to get away with frightening us for very long. I assumed it was a guy killing the nurses. I supposed it could be a female, trying to off her competition in some sick way, but it didn't feel like it.

Women were more typically poisoners, or the type to run you down with their car in the parking lot. And back up over you. Vicious that way. Not this. Not the brutality I'd seen at Kelly's place, or the woman in the swamp.

Just thinking of it again made me shiver. For a few hours today, Jeannie and I'd forgotten about the murders, but the memories of them came flooding back into my brain like a storm heading down a small creek to overflow the banks. There just wasn't enough room to keep it all in, and pretty soon it was going to be leaking out over the edges.

"You two get in my car and lock the doors," Sully said as Wayne arrived. Already their focus was off of us and onto our apartment.

Without another word, they drew their weapons Jeannie and I hurriedly got into Sully's cop car and locked the doors. We watched through the tinted windshield as they took positions on either side of our bottom floor apartment door and announced themselves. We couldn't hear anything over the hum of the running engine. I held my breath and gripped the steering wheel as they moved through the unlatched door, then rushed inside.

My pulse roared in my ears, and Jeannie reached out to squeeze my arm. Neither of us moved. Our focus was totally on the scene unfolding in front of us.

A sharp knock on the window beside my head disturbed my peace. Several things happened at once. I jumped. Then Jeannie jumped. Then I screamed like a little girl getting her first sight of a naked man.

It was not pretty.

I gaped and reached for my heart to put it back into place. Somehow it had escaped through the protection of my chest and landed on the floor.

"Cripe!" I yelled, holding back what I really wanted to say because Jeannie frowned on the use of foul language around her. "Jee-zuz." I had to have an outlet for the tension screaming through my veins.

Charlie stood there. He made a rolling motion with his hand. Being the superior mime-interpreter and charades player that I was, I immediately deduced that he wanted me to roll down the window.

Cop cars didn't have handles to roll down windows, but they did have fantastically quick buttons that did the same thing. I pushed the button.

"What are you doing in there?" he asked without preamble.

Jeannie leaned forward and waved. "Hi, Charlie."

"Hi back," he said. "Let me correct myself. What in holy hell are you doing in there?"

"Sully told us to get in his car, so we did," I said. I didn't see the big deal.

"Sully is it?" His brows twitched up.

"It's hard to go back once you know a person's nickname, so yes, Sully. He told us to get in, right Jeannie?"

"He did, Charlie. He and Officer Wayne went to check the apartment. They're there now," she said and pointed through the windshield to the grassy knoll in front of our apartment. I just hoped we weren't going to have the same situation as the grassy knoll of infamy.

"Have you ever been in a cop car?" Charlie asked, his mood not improved at our explanation.

"Not since college," I said with a sweet smile that revealed nothing. "It was just a one-time deal."

"Most people get in the *back* seat when they're told to get into a cop car." An exaggerated sense of patience hung in the air. Maybe he wasn't as interested in hearing my story as I was in telling it.

I looked around. I was in the driver's seat. Jeannie was in the front passenger seat. "Huh," I said and turned back to Charlie. "I guess we're not most people, are we?"

"No, you certainly are not," Charlie said with a shake of his head. He pointed a finger at us. "Put the window up and stay there until we come back." I started to put the window up, when he turned back to us. "And don't touch anything."

I couldn't really hear anything else he said, because I'd already zipped the window back up, so I just gave him a big, double thumbs-up.

"Think he's mad at us?" Jeannie asked.

"Why would he be? We were just doing what we were told, right?" I asked. With a little loose interpretation of the instructions. No harm done.

"We're in the front of a cop car," Jeannie said. For some reason she felt compelled to point that out to me. Like I didn't know. With all the gear around us, I'd figured that out pretty quick.

"But it's not *his* cop car," I said. I felt compelled to point that out to her.

"That's a good point." She pushed out her lips for a second. "Should we get in the back seat?"

"I'm not getting out of this car until they're back. And there's no way my hind quarters are fitting through that sliding window between the front and back seats." I gave her an assessing look. "Yours aren't either, but you're welcome to try. I just don't want to have to explain why you're stuck halfway between the front and back seats. Of a cop car."

"You're right," Jeannie said and folded her hands primly in her lap. "I'll stay right here, too."

"Good thinking." We didn't have long to wait.

Two of them, Charlie and Sully, returned together coming down the small hill of grass toward the lot. Wayne remained behind. Charlie still wore his Bob Marley shirt, but the shorts he'd had on earlier were now bore a dark stain on the left side and his left thigh was wrapped all the way around with gauze. Probably holding another dressing beneath it. I hadn't seen it when he'd been standing so close to the window.

"Here they come." Jeannie sat up straight and fluffed her hair, like she'd been waiting to be called for an interview.

I buzzed the window down.

"Anything?" I asked. I didn't have to explain what that meant.

"You'll have to come in and see if there's anything missing. Nothing appears to be out of order, and the apartment is clear. No one's in there. They may have left some time ago," Sully said, giving the quick synopsis of what was going on.

"Did you check under the beds?" I asked and narrowed my eyes, thinking once again of Motel Six.

"It's clear. No worries." Sully tried to hide a smile, but I saw it. He thought I was paranoid. But when there were bodies under beds, a person couldn't be too careful. Or too paranoid.

Charlie pulled on the door handle, but I'd secured the door as I'd been instructed. See? I could too follow directions. "Unlock the door, Piper," he said.

I complied, and Charlie opened the door. "Sully told us to lock ourselves inside, so we did." As gracefully as possible in my sparkly pink flip-flops, I followed the men to our door, caution and anxiety buzzing with angry wings around my head. Wayne stood guard until we arrived.

"All clear ladies, except one bedroom window was open a few inches," he said, the tone of his voice clearly disapproving.

"Oh, rats. I must have forgotten to close it. When I sleep I need a little more air, but usually always close it when

I'm up, and we go to work." Damn. If this whole thing was my fault for leaving the window open, I was going to be royally pissed at myself. "Did someone get in that way and just go out the front door?"

"No. Window doesn't look like it's been tampered with, but you definitely need to make sure you get it closed and locked from now on." Sully kept eye contact with me, letting me know his thoughts on the subject without actually telling me his thoughts on the subject.

"I sure will," I said. I was going to damned well make sure of it, even if I had to set an alarm on my phone to remind me. Was there an app for that?

"As you go through the apartment, look for missing items," Wayne said.

"Especially our panties," I whispered to Jeannie, but when the guys laughed, I realized I'd apparently spoken in more than a whisper.

We flipped on the lamps in the living room, the kitchen lights, the hall, bathroom and bedroom lights. Everything appeared to be normal. Appeared to be just as we'd left things. Even my rumpled bed, because I hadn't made it before we left. Sometimes I did, sometimes I didn't. Today had been a *not* day, because I was tired, and we'd had things to do.

I pulled out drawers, looking for clothing, jewelry, and yes, my panties. I moved to my bedside table and reached beneath it. My revolver was still there. I kept it beneath the bedside table rather than in it. If I had to grab it in a hurry, then it was one less step I had to make to have it in my hand and pointed at someone who didn't belong in my home. "All good here."

Jeannie returned to the living room from her bedroom. "Everything seems to be good in my room, too."

"Take pictures of everything when you can," Wayne said. "I had to make a homeowner claim a few weeks ago, and they wanted to have pictures of everything I had a claim on, or receipts that were non-existent." He huffed out an irritated breath. "Like I'm going to have twenty-year-old receipts. Take my advice. Take pictures of each other with the most important things around you. The TV, microwave, revolver and jewelry. Everything."

"Oh, my camera, too. I bought it a few years ago and there was no way I could find a receipt now if the need arose. Good point. We'll do that soon. Thanks for the tip." I held out my hand and shook Wayne's hand, then Sully's and then Charlie's. Felt like I was in a receiving line at a wedding.

"It's getting late. If we need any further information we know how to find you," Sully said and pulled out an electronic tablet and started punching information into it.

"So what happened at the hospital?" Jeannie asked. "Was there another travel nurse attacked?"

Sully stopped scribbling with the stylus. "What makes you think something happened at the hospital?" He had cops eyes for sure. He kept looking at Jeannie, the quick smile gone.

"Charlie told us," she said and looked to Charlie to support her claim.

"You weren't called in, so how did you know?" Sully asked him.

I trusted Charlie, but the situation made me nervous. How *had* he learned of the hospital incident? Anxiety started doing the cha-cha in my gut. That was so not a good feeling.

Charlie stood with most of his weight on his right leg. Whether he was aware of it or not, he gripped his upper thigh with his left hand. If what he said was true about his injury, the numbing medicine must have worn off. "I had the scanner on," he said. Maybe it was that simple and I really was being paranoid.

"I see," Sully said and relaxed his stance. He didn't want to believe Charlie was involved either.

"Not much to do when you're waiting in the ER other than stare at your phone," he said, looking uncomfortable. "Why don't we worry later about what happened at the hospital?" he asked, deflecting the conversation away from him. Sweat beaded on Charlie's forehead. I didn't think it was hot enough for him to be sweating that much. Something was wrong, but I didn't know what it was. Maybe he just wasn't wanting to share that information with his co-workers and we'd inadvertently spilled it.

"I think that's a good idea," Wayne said and looked at his watch. "We have to get back to finish interviews, and I'm sure y'all want to get to bed."

"Yes, it's been a long day." Started twenty hours ago. Or more. At this point I wasn't sure. Maybe I'd only slept for four hours and had been awake for twenty. Either way, my brain was mush.

We escorted the officers to the door and waved goodbye with hugs of thanks.

Then we re-entered the apartment, and as I turned to ensure the door locked, I heard it click shut and the dead-bolt slide into place.

Charlie stood just inside the door.

"What are you doing?" Jeannie asked before I could. I was frozen as I stared at Charlie.

"You ladies need to be given some lessons, and you're gonna get them right now."

🎋 12 🎋

IT'S ALIVE. IT'S ALIVE!-FRANKENSTEIN

"What are you talking about?" I demanded. I was so not okay with this. "You are way outta line, Charlie." What the hell was the matter with him?

"Am I? Or am I right on target?" There was a glassy look in his eyes I hadn't seen before. Pretty sure I didn't want to see it then, either.

"If you can explain things a little more clearly, maybe we can understand them better," Jeannie said, always willing to give people the benefit of the doubt. Right now, I wasn't sure that was the right option. We had to figure this out and fast.

"You two are the key to this entire investigation, and I don't want anything to happen to you," he said and stepped closer, his limp clearly evident, more pronounced than I remember it being, just minutes ago.

"Sit down, why don't you, before you fall down," I said and patted the rented couch cushion. This was an apartment we'd found that we could lease fully furnished for the summer, so the furnishings were pretty flimsy, but they did the job.

Charlie grabbed the back of the couch and put his weight on his hands, easing the pressure on his leg. "Yeah, I think I'll do that."

"Do you need a bottle of water?" Jeannie said. "You don't look too good right now."

"Yeah, maybe that'll help," he said, hobbled around to the front of the couch and eased into a position with his left leg straight out. "Maybe I'm just dehydrated.

Jeannie hurried to the fridge and grabbed a bottle of cold water. In warmer climates people always kept water in the fridge, cause no matter how long the taps ran, water would never get cold enough. And who drank unfiltered water any more, either? "Here you go," she said and handed him the bottle.

Hands trembling, Charlie took it and tried to remove the cap, but his hands fumbled. "I don't know what's wrong with me," he said and looked at us, confusion clearly written on his face. "I feel weak as a kitten, and that's just not like me." He shook his head. "Not at all."

"Tell us what happened to you today," I said. Maybe we could figure out if he was just dehydrated or something more serious was happening.

"I was gonna give you two some simple, but important, safety lessons to make sure you do every time you leave your place or get in your car, but I'm just not up to it now." He shook his head, still struggling with the bottle.

"Well, it is almost two am. You've got to be at work in the morning, don't you?" Jeanie asked.

"Nah. I took tomorrow off to get some work done around the place. You know, yard work, cleaning out the garage and the shed. Stuff you put off until you can't put it off any more." He nodded and tried to open the bottle again. I took it from his hands, unscrewed it and handed it back to him. Mostly because I wanted to see if his hands would shake again the way they had a few minutes ago, and they did. I wasn't being mean. I was assessing his fine motor skills. They sucked, buy why?

Something definitely was going on with Charlie, and it wasn't run of the mill fatigue. Maybe he'd come across some kind of rat poison or a pesticide or something in the shed.

Sweat appeared on his forehead earlier and dripped down onto his shirt, covered his face, and neck. I moved close to him and put my fingertips on his left wrist.

"Your pulse is going crazy," I said and placed my other hand on his forehead. "Burning up, too." Upon closer inspection I saw something I hadn't seen before.

"What?" Jeannie said and moved closer.

"Take off your shirt, Charlie," I said.

"What? No, that's ridiculous. I'm just a little warm, that's all." But as he raised the water bottle to take another drink he missed his mouth and water poured all over his chest and lap. "Dammit," he said and tried to stand up, but lacked the coordination to do so and collapsed abruptly on the couch again.

"What's wrong, Piper? What do you think is going on?" Jeannie sat on the other side of him and took his right wrist in her hand, checking the pulse for herself. Not that she didn't believe me, but every practitioner placed their hands on the patient and made their own assessments.

"I think he's having an allergic reaction to something he got in the hospital," I said. I spoke to her, but didn't take my eyes off of the man who was deteriorating right before our eyes. Without preamble, I raised his shirt and exposed his chest. Just what I expected. Raised red spots, welts, covered his torso.

"Oh, dear. Look at that," Jeannie said and was reaching for her phone just as I told her to call 911.

"Put the call in." I grabbed Charlie's keys that he'd set aside when he'd sat down, and ran for the door.

"Where are you going?" Jeannie cried.

"To get some help here fast," I yelled back as I dashed out the door and ran for Charlie's SUV. I hit the remote a thousand times in the few seconds it took me to reach the door. I hoisted myself up into the tall vehicle and slammed the door shut.

With trembling fingers, I reached for his police radio attached to the ceiling and pressed the mic. It was on channel nine, and I knew that was the emergency signal. "Officer down. Officer down," I repeated then took a breath. "We have an officer down and need rescue crew now, or he's going to die." There was no other way to put it.

Immediately a voice came back to get more information. "Who the hell is this? You're on a protected channel. Get the hell off," and angry male voice instructed.

"Sully? Is that you? This is Piper. Something's wrong with Charlie. I think he's having an allergic reaction, and if we don't get some medicine in him right now, he's going to die," I said. Statistically, if life-saving epinephrine didn't get into the body from the time anaphylactic symptoms appeared, a person only had minutes before their body tried to kill them. The body detected the foreign substance and went to work to eliminate it from the body. The bad part was that the immune system didn't know when to stop. Bee stings. Peanut allergies. Medications. Anything could trigger a severe reaction.

"Are you still at the apartment?" Sully got it. I heard the tension in his voice. He got that this was real and not some kids playing a hoax at two am.

"Yes. But I'm afraid he's going to die before we can get an ambulance here," I said, my hands shaking.

"There's emergency kits under front seat. See if there's anything you can use in it, and we'll be there. Just keep him alive, Piper. We'll be there." The urgency in Sully's voice made my nerves rattle more than before. He was depending on us to save Charlie's life.

"I got it!" As he talked I reached beneath the seat and found the black waterproof case with a bright red cross on it. I dropped the mic, clutched the kit to my chest and raced back to the apartment, praying like crazy that what we needed was in it.

I burst through the door, not caring that it didn't shut, and found Charlie on the floor, hands clutching his throat, eyes wide and swelling fast, his swollen tongue protruding through his teeth. Jeannie on her knees beside him, tears rolling down her face. "Piper! We have to do something!"

"We are. Right now." I was in nurse mode, and we were going to save this man's life. "Charlie, hang on. Talk to him, Jeannie," I said. "Just keep talking to him." I unzipped the kit and dumped it on the floor, I swished through the contents with one hand, spreading it out so I could see quickly what was in there, my eyes looking for the one thing we needed.

"Got it," I mumbled aloud. My heart raced nearly as fast as Charlie's. With one hand I tossed Jeannie the bite-block from the kit. It was a padded tongue blade designed for seizures, but it would help here, too. "Put this between his teeth so he doesn't chew up his tongue." I didn't even look at her as my eyes and hands focused on popping the glass syringe filled with Epinephrine out of the box, screwed the two ends of it together. It was professional grade. This was going to do the trick. At least I hoped it was going to do the trick. I looked at Charlie's face. His eyes were nearly swollen shut. Everything was going so bad, so fast.

He was dying right in front of us.

I pulled his left arm onto my lap and tied a rubber glove around his bicep. There was no tourniquet, but this would get the job done.

"What are you doing?" Jeannie asked "Just get it in him."

"He needs it in a vein. It'll take too long to absorb from the muscle now," I said. I waited two seconds for the vein to fill with blood, then pushed the sharp tip of the needle into the vein, released the glove and pressed the plunger of the syringe. I injected the life-saving medication directly into Charlie's blood stream. Not all of it, but enough to get the job done. My hands were strong and sure. I was trembling on the inside, but nothing and no one was going to save this man except us and this syringe of Epinephrine right now. I'd fall apart later.

Sounds of Charlie's ragged and distressed breathing broke into my concentration. His breathing was getting worse, and I looked at the syringe still in my hand. Should I give him the rest? If I did, it could lead to a cardiac arrest. If I didn't it would lead to respiratory arrest. Making the best decision I could at that moment, I pushed the remainder of Epinephrine into his vein. *Flo' help me now.* I prayed to Florence Nightingale. I prayed to Agatha of Sicily. She was truly the patron saint of nurses. I didn't care which one guided my hands, I just needed their help now.

"I can't get it in," Jeannie said, frustration showing in her voice as she tried to get the bite block between Charlie's teeth. If he bit down during a convulsion, he could sever his tongue and bleed to death.

"Take a breath," I said in a voice that sounded calmer than I felt. She did as I said, and the nanosecond that she took for herself made the difference for Charlie. She eased a finger inside his lip, to make room for the bite block, then slid it between his teeth on one side. "Is there another one?" she asked and held her hand out, not taking her gaze off of Charlie's face.

"No, but you can use this," I said and tore open a wad of gauze, folded it a few times to make a square and handed it to her. Her voice was soft and soothing as she told Charlie she was going to ease the gauze on the other side of his mouth, so he wouldn't chew up his tongue. He drooled out both sides of his mouth and it ran down his face and neck. His body was still trying to protect him with the hyper-salivation. Unfortunately, if we didn't get his airway protected, he could drown on his own secretions.

I couldn't hear any easing of his high-pitched, crowing respirations. His airway was swelling shut due to the tissues in his throat and tongue blocking off the essential route for air to get in and out of his body.

"He needs oxygen. He's dusky," she said, holding one of his hands up and looked at his fingernails.

"He's going to be more than dusky if those boys don't get here soon," I said, clenching my teeth, trying to keep from spewing obscenities.

"Is there more Epi in there? There can't be just one syringe," Jeannie said, and I heard the desperate hope in her voice that mirrored the one in my heart. I rummaged through the supplies scattered on the floor and found another box with another Epi syringe. With a quick flick of my wrist, I injected this one into his right thigh. The one-two punch of IV and then intramuscular medication should do it. At least I hoped it would. One for fast acting, one for slower acting. None of which would matter if we didn't get him an airway.

The distant howl of a siren caught my attention, and I jumped to my feet. "I'm going to go flag them down."

"There's got to be more we can do," Jeannie said, her eyes begging me for more answers, more medications, more something that I just didn't have. We weren't in an ICU and didn't have access to the tools we normally did.

"If this hasn't done it, it won't matter what else we do," I said. I didn't have to say it. She knew. The lack of oxygen to his brain could have been enough to end him already. The only thing that was going to save his life now was getting oxygen to his brain. Fast.

I raced out the door, arms waving, and I shouted, even though I didn't know if they could see me or not. Sully jumped out of his car, and I yelled at him. "Sully! Hurry. We need a bus now," I said, referring to an ambulance. He rushed to me, lips pressed together, jaw tight, hand on his weapon and took my arm, led me out of the parking lot so we didn't get run down by the other emergency vehicles right behind him. When an emergency call came for officer down, we generally ended up with more people than we needed on a scene. But in that moment, I'd take every helpful hand we could get.

"How is he?" Sully's long stride chewed up the distance between the parking lot and the apartment, and I struggled to keep up with him.

"He's dying. If we don't get him to the hospital he's

going to die." I swallowed, thinking of the respiratory stridor I'd heard as his windpipe swelled shut. "It may already be too late," I said. Holding onto his arm, we rushed to the apartment and burst through the open door.

The first thing I heard, or didn't hear, was the respiratory distress sound, the high-pitched crowing noise that had come from Charlie's throat. That only meant one of two things. Charlie had stopped breathing, or the epi was starting to work.

I dropped to my knees beside Jeannie who had her head bent over Charlie's face, her hair covering both of them. If his breathing had stopped she should have been doing CPR. Even though we didn't have an airway, compressions were the key to survival in the field.

Not trusting my eyes, I placed my hand on Charlie's chest. It rose. I felt the thrumming of his heart beneath my hand, and I turned back to Sully. "He's still with us. Get that bus here now, or call a chopper," I said.

Sully spoke into the shoulder mic, then rushed from the room. "They're here," he called as he hailed them with a sharp whistle.

In seconds so many things happened, I didn't know how I kept track. Jeannie was the one who usually the record keeper. In that moment, neither of us could think of anything else, except saving Charlie's life.

The paramedics raced in with their equipment.

"Oxygen, now," I said, as commander in charge of the scene. "Establish an airway. He's had two amps of epi and the stridor has improved. You'll have to intubate now. His airway's still not safe." I gave the short synopsis. "Give me the stuff, and I'll get a line in him." I wasn't going to surrender my patient and our friend to these men. In a similar situation they wouldn't stand by without helping us. We weren't going to stand by without helping them. It was a team effort for all of us to save Charlie. More cops arrive and entered the apartment, standing around watching the procedure. With so many people present, the atmosphere should have been loud, but no one spoke, except to give direction or ask for supplies.

An oxygen mask going full blast went over his face. I got an IV established in seconds, and the paramedic handed me a syringe of another medication, Benadryl, that I also pushed through the IV. That was an antihistamine that was slower to work than the epi, but was also a life-saving measure. Epi and Benadryl worked well together. One fast acting, short life. One slower acting, longer life. With those meds, a hope and a prayer, he'd make it.

A measure of calm entered the room once Charlie's airway was established with a tube down his throat and into his lungs. The EMT was the expert at that procedure and didn't falter. Good man. Then the tubing was connected, pumping one-hundred percent oxygen into him to re-establish the depleted resource to his cells and hopefully save his brain. Charlie had lost consciousness somewhere along the way. That was good. Hopefully, he wouldn't remember much from this event. If he lived through it.

Then the big, strong guys got him onto a gurney, strapped him in for a rocket-fast ride to the hospital. Usually, there was a measure of mirth hanging over a transport, the paramedics talking to a patient to keep them distracted and reduce anxiety. But not at that moment. Not with that scene having taken place. Charlie hadn't gone down in the line of duty, but he'd still gone down, was a police officer, and his life was hanging in the balance. We'd done what we could. The rest was up to him and the team around him.

I looked up, and I know my face reflected surprise. Cops were everywhere. Men and women. All somber-faced, looking to Jeannie and I for an explanation.

I felt like I was faced with a patient's family, the way we often were in the hospital. It was up to the nurses to explain a patient's condition to loved ones, and this situation was no different.

"Everyone? Step closer," I said. There were cops hanging around the outer door and in the grass. I wanted to speak to everyone at once and make sure everyone heard the same information from the source and didn't speculate if they didn't hear it right.

"What can you tell us?"

"What happened?"

"Is he going to make it?"

Questions bombarded me, but it was okay. They were afraid for him. Though some of their expressions bore the look of anger, at its roots was fear. Males who were used to taking care of things usually got angry when faced with a frightening situation they had no control over. Didn't matter if they were cops who thought they'd seen it all. It was different when it was one of their own.

"I can't give you all of the details, because I don't know them. But what I can tell you is that it appears Charlie had a severe allergic reaction to something, and it shut down his airway," I said, wondering if I was breaking HIPPA for real, but at that moment, I had to tell them something.

Grumbles and gasps from the group, letting me know they hadn't thought about that. Most people thought black male equaled high blood pressure and strokes, no matter what the age. While there was a valid relationship between those things, none of them had affected this situation.

"What did he take?" Shipper asked. I hadn't even seen him arrive. He stood there arms crossed over his chest, looking as irritable as usual.

"I don't know. We believe that it was anaphylaxis, or the overwhelming reaction a body has to something it doesn't like," I said. I was too fatigued to go into the scientific explanation of how it all worked, so that would have to do. "We'll have to wait for more information from the hospital. That's all we have for now."

The mass of men and women exited the small apartment, and I could breathe again.

Sully approached and held out his arms to both of us. We were a freaking mess. At least on the inside. We might still look like professionals, but inside, we were shaking in our sandals.

"What the hell happened? Why did he stay behind?" Disbelief colored Sully's voice. I was sure he showed more emotion to us now that his co-workers had all left, and it was just the four of us. Wayne hung by the door again.

"I don't know. We don't know," Jeannie said with her face pressed against Sully's neck.

"I'd just asked him what he did that landed him in the ER tonight, and he started behaving really weird. Confused. Sweating." I moved back from Sully and pushed my hair away from my face. I took a deep breath, needing to get some oxygen to my brain cells, too. "There was just something really off with him."

"Come on. Sit down and tell me everything. Maybe we can figure this out," Sully said and released us. Jeannie trudged to the fridge and got water bottles for all of us.

"Start at the beginning," Sully said and opened his

bottle. "I thought he was right behind us, going out the door, then he was gone," Sully said and looked at Wayne, who shrugged his answer. Apparently, he'd thought the same thing.

"He stayed behind, he said to give us a few tips in personal safety that were really important," I said, then repeated what we thought had happened. Sometimes it took a few repeats for the brain to really get it in a difficult situation.

Jeannie nodded, her lower lip trembling a bit as she took a sip of water. "It's a good thing he did, because if he hadn't, he'd be dead."

A confused frown covered Sully's face. "What's he allergic to?"

"I don't know. I'm sure it was something he received at the ER. We can't get his records, because we're not related. Not sure you can even get them. But he said he injured himself, his leg, and had to go for tetanus and antibiotic shots at the ER." I paused. "The doctor who is going to take care of him at Oak Island ER will be able to call for the records from Southport. That's where he said he went," I said.

"They could have put him on an oral antibiotic, too," Jeannie said. After a first shot, doctors normally prescribed seven to ten days of an oral antibiotic to ensure any signs of infection would be kicked out of the system.

"But he wouldn't have had time to fill a prescription before getting to us, would he?" Jeannie brought up a very good point. Since he'd been in such a hurry to get to us, he wouldn't have stopped to get a prescription.

"I'm thinking it was the injection. It was Penicillin or Rocephin. Those are the usual ones. As soon as he got it, he headed out the door. It was about fifteen, twenty minutes til he got here." I'd been mulling this in my mind from the time I suspected something was wrong with Charlie. It was those critical thinking skills that enabled Jeannie and I to be on it as soon as we were.

"Fifteen minutes is what is usually recommended to wait after getting an injection like that to see if there is going to be any trouble, any reactions, but he didn't have that time," Jeannie said. "He skipped that step because of us." She dropped her gaze onto her lap and shook her head.

"He was probably jacked up full of adrenaline when he came to help us, then when it wore off, the anaphylaxis symptoms became more apparent," I said. That made sense to me.

"So, it wasn't just a little reaction," Sully said. That was a statement, not a question, as he processed the information.

"No. You saw him. His eyes were swollen shut, his tongue was swollen badly and blocking off his airway," I said. I used layman's terms. Though Sully was a professional, he wasn't knowledgeable about all of the medical terminology.

Sully blew out a sigh and flopped back against the couch cushions. "Man. I'm never taking antibiotics again," he said.

"You probably will. But an allergic reaction can come from anything. Any substance, at any time. Even things you've taken before, you can suddenly develop a reaction to," Jeannie said.

"Wow. I had no clue," Sully said and shook his head, drank from his water bottle again.

"Most people don't unless they have a situation like this. I'm sure Charlie didn't have a clue, either," I said.

Pretty sure he wouldn't have knowingly allowed them to administer a medication he was allergic to.

"Oh!" Jeannie sat bolt upright. "Someone needs to notify his next of kin."

"I hadn't thought of that," I asked and turned to Sully. "Can you call the station and find that info? They've got to know asap."

Sully looked at his watch and stood. "I can do better than that. I'll call his brother, right now. He works second shift out of Southport, so he's just gone to bed. If I can't get him on the phone, we'll send one of the guys over to get him out of bed," he said and nodded to the people lingering outside the door. Sully took a deep breath, then huffed out a long sigh as he looked at the mess on the floor. The empty plastic and papers the gauze had been in, the empty boxes of supplies, the used needles I'd shoved into the couch for safe-keeping. I had no needle box to put them in, and didn't want to leave the needles exposed, so I just stabbed them into a couch cushion for the time being. I'd make a needle-proof container later.

"What a mess," Sully said.

"It looks like we had a code in our living room," Jeannie said and huffed out a breath. She was exhausted. So was I.

"We did." I stood, intending to get a trash bag from the kitchen to put it all in, but suddenly lacked the energy or the ambition, and I plopped own on the arm of a nearby chair. It could wait.

"It's past three, almost four am. Why don't you two get some sleep? We'll send someone by later to take your statements," Sully said and placed us in another comforting group hug. I felt a slight tremor from him. Looked like he needed the comforting touch from us as much as we needed it from him. We were all used to taking care of people we didn't know, not having life-threatening emergencies with our co-workers or friends. The luxury of having the emotional distance between caregivers and patients was essential, and had never been made clear than it had been tonight.

"Thanks, Sully. I don't know what we'd have done without you." Jeannie looked at the other officer. "Or you, too Wayne," she said and held out one hand to him. He took it, offering his own comfort in a more distant manner.

"Please keep us in the loop of what's happening to him," I said. "Either way." I choked back the emotion threatening my throat.

Sully only nodded, and I knew he was thinking whether he was going to call us later with good news or bad news. "Will do." He paused a second. "We're going to leave an officer on watch outside your door for the rest of the night. Just in case."

He didn't have to explain what that meant. In case the person who'd entered our apartment returned while we were asleep and the police were distracted.

"Thanks. We appreciate it," I said.

They left, and I locked the door, then engaged the deadbolt. I moved one of the overstuffed chairs from the living room grouping to right in front of the door. Then I placed two dining chairs on top of it.

"What are you doing?" Jeannie asked. Even at four in the morning this didn't make sense. Even for me.

"Making sure we're safe the rest of the night," I said. I didn't care if it made sense. I wanted it there.

"We've got a cop outside our door. That should make you feel better," Jeannie said and stifled a yawn.

"This makes me feel more-better," I said. I took one delicate lamp from its place in the living room and balanced it precariously on top of the pile in front of the door. "If anyone tries to come through the door that lamp is going to crash to the floor, and we're going to hear it. I'm tired enough to sleep like the dead now." A yawn caught me by surprise. Usually, after codes and high-adrenaline activity, I was charged up for hours. Tonight, the crash came sooner than expected, and the adrenaline had worn off. I was worn out.

Without further words, Jeannie and I hugged each other, needing the support and assurance that we'd done the right thing, and together, hopefully saved the life of a man we'd quickly come to call friend. She went to her room and closed the door. I went to my room, turned on my three fans, and fell face-first onto the bed.

❧ 13 ❧

E IS FOR EVIL STEPMOTHER - INTERNET

H e pulled at his hair. Bit back a whimper. Watched as paramedics loaded Mother onto the stretcher, an oxygen mask on her pale face. Her hands gone limp, her jaw slack. But it was her eyes. Open. Unblinking. She watched him. Stared at him. Blaming, with her milk-white eyes.

He'd always hated her eyes. Angry. Criticizing. Hostile. Filled with love only for his father. Never for him. Ever. And now look at them. Scolding.

He'd gotten home from work late again. Very late. He was never that late, but his work had taken extra time tonight. He hadn't finished the job. It ate at him to leave his work unfinished, but it couldn't be helped. He knew he had to hurry and get home quickly, leaving things un-done. For now.

Mother couldn't be left alone for long any more. She'd become restless at night. He didn't know why. All of her needs had been met. She'd been fed. Dressed for bed. A dry diaper. Just like a baby. She should have slept through the night, but she did it just to annoy him, to make his life harder.

At least that's what she'd told him when the situation had been reversed. When *he'd* been the child. When *he'd* needed something at night, she refused him, refused to comfort him, refused to acknowledge him. She'd gone back to her blissful sleep while he'd cowered alone in the dark.

Tonight, when he'd returned from his duty, she'd been on the floor at the end of the bed. Blood covered her face, looking like something from a horror movie. A large bruise bulged out of her temple on one side. It was that damned dresser of Father's. Ornate, with sharp corners. Heavy. Solid teak. He'd brought it with him from some foreign country after the war. Had refused to move it out of the way. It sat there like a trophy from his war days. He'd received no other awards, no other commendations, just that damned dresser he'd had to buy for himself. That was his medal, his prize, his ego.

Now, it was the object of Mother's destruction. She'd fallen and hit her head on a corner of it. Knocked herself unconscious, bled profusely, lying on the floor alone, calling out for him while she bled.

He clutched a bloody towel in his hands. She'd lain there bleeding while he'd been at work. She'd needed him, and he hadn't been there. But he *had* to work. He *had* to take care of things. For Father. For her. Didn't she know how much, how hard, he worked for her?

Trembling inside, he raised a hand to his mouth, pressed his thumb between his teeth and gnawed at the nail. The old habit came back to him when he was stressed. Now, with Father gone and Mother in distress, he couldn't stop it. Couldn't hold back from taking nips out of the nail. He chewed them, then spat them out.

"Sir, I'll need your signature in order for us to take her into our care now," one of the crew members said, and he snapped out of his reverie.

"What?" The word barked out of him. His heart hammered at what he'd heard. The words echoing in his brain.

"I said, I'll need your signature for transport," the para-medic said. The arrogant male stood there, just waiting for him. Like he was better than the others. Maybe he was their leader, their supervisor. Maybe he just thought he was.

"But the rest. What was the whole thing you said?" he asked. He'd heard it, he just had to make sure of it.

"That's all I said. I'll need your signature for us to trans-port her to the hospital." The paramedic stood there looking at him with an expressionless face.

That wasn't what he'd heard. He'd heard what the funeral home had said when he'd signed the release to send Father to the mortuary. *Are you ready for us to take him into our care?* Wasn't that the latest catch-phrase to make people believe the body of their loved one was going to be *cared for,* when the funeral home people were really going to just shove them into a gas chamber and burn them to ashes?

Take her into our care. That's what the paramedic had said. He was certain of it.

"Sir? Are you okay? You're bleeding." The man nodded at the bloody towel clutched in his hands.

"What? It's not my blood. It's hers, you moron," he said, dismissing the rescue worker as stupid as the rest of them.

"I realize you're stressed right now, but I don't appreciate the insult." The man took a wide-legged stance in front of him, gave him a look of impatience when compassion should have been oozing from him. "Check your thumb, dick-weed. You're bleeding."

He looked down at his left thumb that he'd chewed down to the quick without realizing it. He'd felt no pain. "It's nothing," he said. He wrapped the hand with the already-bloody towel and grabbed the stylus from the paramedic, scribbled his signature on the electronic page.

"Will you be coming to the hospital now?" the man asked him.

"No. I have things to do today. I'll come later," he said. There was too much to do now.

"Good enough. I'll give your contact information to the doctor who will be seeing her, and they'll take it from there," the paramedic said, with obvious relief.

Nodding, he watched as they escorted Mother from the house and loaded her onto the ambulance. Didn't seem to be in much of a hurry now. They'd come racing in with sirens blaring and lights flashing. After securing the patient, nothing but the distant hum of the diesel engine heading sedately to the hospital. Why didn't they have the lights and sirens going for Mother? Because they didn't care. Weren't careful enough with Mother, or concerned enough about Mother to use them. She was old. She was a waste of their efforts. He knew they thought that. If one of the tourists had experienced a similar incident, lights and sirens would be going for them, no doubt.

In a fit of rage, he strode forward, ready to charge the ambulance, when the shock of a lightning bolt struck his left leg, and he cried out in pain.

But they were gone, and not looking back at him. They didn't hear him scream and clutch his leg. Collapsing onto the nearest chair, he tried to breathe, tried to push away the moisture that had appeared in his eyes, but minutes passed before he could even begin to see again.

The hallway clock struck the hour.

Before the sixth gong had faded into the early morning, he hobbled down the hallway to change his clothing and headed to work.

"WE HAVE TO DO SOMETHING ABOUT THIS," I SAID TO JEANNIE. We were still in our jammies in the kitchen, trying to wake from an exhausting night. The night officer outside our door had left at his change of shift, about six am, and we were once again on our own. We'd always been on our own, never fearing for our safety. Until last night.

"What do you think we should do?" She turned the bacon over in the skillet. Nothing in the world smelled as good as bacon frying. Unless it was toast. The two together? Nirvana.

"I don't know. I just know we can't sit around doing nothing while nurses are being attacked and police officers are dying from anaphylaxis," I said. I was action-oriented. I had to do something today, even if Jeannie couldn't.

"Charlie's not dead. We saved him, remember?" Was I that sleep-deprived that she had to remind me? Apparently.

"I know. We sure did," I said and nodded, trying not to forget that impressive point.

"But you don't sound very happy about it." Jeannie paused in her stirring to give me an assessing look.

The tea kettle whistled its high-pitched interruption. Jeannie didn't care to have her tea zapped in the microwave, so she brought an old-fashioned kettle she put on the stove. With a whistle. Said it reminded her of her grandmother's house and good memories every time it whistled.

I wished I'd had good tea-kettle-memories. Mine from childhood weren't the best. The ones I could remember anyway. Some things I just blocked out entirely. Perhaps I didn't want to have those particular memories back.

Tea-kettle-memories sounded really nice. Maybe some day I would have them.

"I know. I'm so glad beyond belief that Charlie's going to make it. I just wish he'd waited longer after getting those medications instead of coming for us," I said and shuddered to think about that happening.

"You're feeling guilty about something that isn't your responsibility. Not at all. No one knew he had an allergy. No one knew he'd have a reaction. No one knew any of that. Think about this. If he'd waited and then the delayed reaction had hit him while he was driving between Southport and here, he'd be dead. He'd have crashed his truck, and no one would have known why until his autopsy," she said.

I looked at her and gave a smile as she cracked a few eggs into the skillet to fry nice and crispy in the bacon grease. "That is totally a point I missed as I sit over here feeling sorry for myself. You're absolutely right," I said and tucked my feet up onto the chair, feeling much better already, and I hadn't yet filled my gullet with the best breakfast on the planet.

"Of course, I'm right." She stirred another skillet filled with shredded potatoes, sprinkled salt and pepper on them like fairy dust. Maybe it was fairy dust, and that's why they tasted like magic. "I'm not smart for nothing, you know?"

"Don't I know it. You're so right. If he'd been halfway between the two places he'd have started feeling bad in the middle of it and not known enough to seek medical help. Would never have pulled over an called 911, because he *is* 911," I said.

"Pfft. No way." She shook her head and shot me an amused look. "What man do you know who considers himself a man would pull off the road, call 911 and sit and wait for help?" she asked.

"Uh-"

"Exactly. None. That's how many." Wow. She was sassy today. Apparently sleep deprivation worked well for her. But I wasn't letting her drive.

"True. Very true. You know they'd die before admitting they needed help." It was the sad truth of the American male.

"And he almost did. But it wasn't his fault, either. It was no one's fault. Sometimes, there's no one to blame," she said. Another sad truth that many people didn't want to hear in the midst of a crisis. Sometimes accidents happened, and there was no one to blame.

"So, who does a guy that needs help call when *he is* the guy you call when you need help?" Thinking about that made my brain hurt.

Jeannie paused, pondering that one. "I don't think I have a real answer to that."

"Yeah. We need caffeine," I said. It would be done brewing soon, I hoped.

What we were doing was something cops would call debriefing. Nurses called it a case review. After every big patient episode at the hospital, or a code, the chart and incident were reviewed to see if there was any way the issue could have been prevented. If not, what was the outcome? What was the inciting incident? Did the patient survive? Answering all of those questions with a yes or no created a different pathway, or a ginormous flow sheet that was reviewed by multiple people in multiple meetings that I never attended, because of my allergy to them. But in any case, Jeannie and I were reviewing the case of Charlie's incident as we would any other patient situation where a life-threatening emergency had occurred. This one had just occurred in our living room.

"I think the outcome would have been the same, no matter where he was," Jeannie said. "He has an unknown allergy. Discovered only when he had a severe reaction. He, or his doctor, will have to go back through his records from the ER to see what they gave him, maybe send him to an allergist to be officially tested. All that fun stuff."

"Yes," I said, hesitated. I needed a bit of distraction, so I rose to get some plates and utensils out of the cupboard and drawer. Since she was cooking, I was on the dishes.

"I wish we had an update on him, you know? They won't give us any information over the phone, 'cause we're not related or anything," she said.

"Screw HIPPA," I said, hating the Health Insurance Portability Protection Act, at the moment. Though protected all of our health information, and I loved it for that, it severely restricted my ability to call the hospital to find out what was going on with Charlie. They weren't going to tell me jack, no matter what I said.

"Let's eat and go down there. You know the hospital will be filled with cops. Maybe we can find someone to give us an update," Jeannie said and turned off the burners, then gave everything one last stir.

"Awesome idea." I got down the coffee mugs, filled them with life-sustaining brew that I poured a healthy dollop of flavored creamer into. I was *Créme Brûlée*. She was classic *French Vanilla*. "Maybe we should take some of this to Charlie," I said after I had a sip of the stout brew and felt the life-force being pulled back into my body, like a vacuum had been turned on and sucked my soul back from the nebula.

"Good idea. If he's allowed to have it yet," she said and served up the chow, and we sat at the table. "We don't know if he's been extubated, if he's awake, or even allowed to have coffee."

"Yeah. You're right," I said. Jeannie didn't have to say, if he'd survived. I'd already thought of that one myself. Either way, were going to find out soon enough.

"But let's take a thermos of it in any case. Pays to be prepared," she said. Once a Girl Scout, always a Girl Scout. Or was that the Marines? I got those two mixed up sometimes.

"Absolutely," I said. I dove into breakfast and after some fantastic food landed in my gut, then swirled its way to my brain cells, I felt better. Even with only four hours of sleep, we could deal with the day. We still had *three days off* before we had to be back to work at the hospital, so we needed to fill them with joy, sunscreen, and beach sand. *Mwhahaha.* The up-side of working twelve-hour shifts. Four days off in a row.

NURSES: WE CAN'T FIX STUPID, BUT WE CAN
SEDATE IT-T-SHIRT

We showered and dressed much like we had yesterday. Since I'd been the one to create the furniture structure in front of the door, I moved it all back.

Then we scooted to the hospital in Jeannie's hot little car with the top down, our hair flying out like we were gonna take off for the stars. If I'd had a scarf on, I'd have felt like a Hollywood movie star, but I didn't, and I wasn't. Not my lot in life.

We arrived at the hospital and parked, put the top back up. Even though it was a short ride, taking the top down was essential for a great ride on an island at the height of summer. As long as we drove faster than mosquitoes could fly, we were good.

We had to circle the parking lot twice before finding a space. "Must have some sort of thing going on today," Jeannie said.

"Probably we're just not used to seeing it during the day. Patients come in for appointments, lab draws, as well as the regular visitors. Probably just normal," I said. At least that was my take on it.

As we approached the hospital, a local television van painted bright yellow with their channel number and logo sat right in front of the door. If the color of the van were not enough to identify it, then the satellite dish on top was a dead giveaway.

"Wow. Something must be going on," she said. "Look at that, and all the cop cars for Charlie."

"I think the big deal *is* Charlie," I said as we passed the news van and entered through the front door.

We approached the visitor's station in the lobby, and asked where he was. The nice lady wearing a Pepto-Bismol colored lab jacket was going to help us out. If you had an upset stomach, all you had to do was look at her, and you'd feel better.

"Are you relatives?" she asked, peering at us over some fancy red-rimmed specs. Clashed with the pink jacket, but we'd let that one slide.

"No. We're concerned friends, right?" Jeannie said and looked to me for confirmation.

I guessed that was what we were. Pretty sure that's what we were. Yes, darned sure that's what we were. "Yes. Concerned friends," I said.

"He's in the ICU on the second floor, but they have very strict visiting hours, you know." *Yes, we knew.* She pointed the way to the elevators we already knew about. We thanked her and walked down the hall. Once in the elevator, we put our badges on, and I held my breath. We'd learned over the years not to have badges on when entering a hospital because people then expected us to help them, that we knew things we didn't always know. Like where the nearest restroom was. Or how to get to the lab. Things like that. But if we were off-duty and in civilian clothes, most of the time, we couldn't help. Was that passive aggressive? Or aggressively passive?

We got off the elevator, and I exhaled, then gasped. The hallway was filled with cops. Literally. It was like every cop in the station from Southport and probably the entire beach area had invaded and overflowed the ICU waiting room in support of their brother-in-arms.

"Whoa. There's enough eye candy for everyone," I said. I looked at the group of people there, and there wasn't a stinker among them. Must have left the old farts running the precinct behind.

"Yeah, right?" Jeannie said as she looked around appreciatively.

"Who has the insulin, 'cause I'm gonna need some later," I said. Indeed. We gave apologetic smiles, said excuse me, and pardon me a number of times as we swam upstream against the men and women in uniform.

At the heavy double doors to the ICU, we saw Sully and felt like girls spotting a rock star. "There he is. Let's talk to him." *Swoon.*

We could have used our badges to go into the ICU and our positions as staff to get information, but we didn't. Our roles were simply as visitors today, and we didn't want to overstep our boundaries. Actually, I wanted to, but Jeannie wouldn't let me.

"Hey, Sully," I said and waved, trying to get his attention.

"Piper, Jeannie," he said with a grin and swam through the masses toward us. "Good to see you two." Without a word of warning we were enveloped in those long, muscled arms of his, squeezed hard against his chest for a second and then released. "Heads up everybody," he said.

He gave that sharp whistle again, and I knew every dog within five miles of the hospital just sat at attention, wondering who'd whistled at them.

"These are the two nurses I was telling y'all about. They're the ones who saved Charlie's life," Sully said.

The somber faces of the officers and the heavy atmosphere lifted. Applause echoed off the cinder block walls, and we were serenaded, patted on the back, and I was propositioned. Twice.

I blushed and grinned, and I'd never felt better. Yes, I now felt like a Hollywood movie star with my adoring fans surrounding me. I just needed a pleated white dress, a blond wig, and a gust of wind.

"Thanks, everyone. We appreciate that so much," Jeannie said when the noise died down. "We were just doing our jobs."

"No, we weren't," I looked at her in surprise that she would downplay our roles. "We totally kicked ass, and saved Charlie's life."

The applause wound up again, and I laughed. It felt so good. Though we could have just sat on our butts after calling 911 last night, we didn't. We saved a life in a nearly impossible situation and beat the odds for Charlie. We were so awesome.

The ICU door swung open. A nurse with three pens sticking out of her hair, glasses on top of her head and a white lab coat tied around her waist, emerged. "I don't know what's going on out here, but y'all need to keep it down. We have very sick patients in here," Audrey said, shushing the masses like a school marm.

"Audrey, I"m sorry. It was us. We came to see how Charlie did overnight, and it got a little out of hand," I said, accepting the consequences for our awesome behavior.

"You two?" she asked. For a second her brows disappeared beneath her hair, and her jaw dropped slightly. She took a step closer to us. I thought she was going to give us an ass-whooping right there, but she put both of her arms around us for a quick squeeze. "Get in here, right now. He's been asking for you all morning."

"Really?" Jeannie asked as we followed Audrey into the ICU.

Asking for us meant he'd been extubated, had the breathing tube down his throat removed, and could talk. That was a huge first step to recovery. Meant the swelling in his throat and tongue had subsided, and he was able to keep his oxygen level at a normal level. Wahoo. Go us.

"Yes. I wish I could sedate him just to shut him up. He won't stop talking about you and what you did last night for him. He remembers most of it," Audrey said in a conspiratorial tone. She led us to door number three and stopped. A serious look came over her face, like a mother hen about to scold her chicks when she didn't want to, but knew she had to. "You know the rules. Don't wear him out, don't let him talk too much. If you can," she said and rolled her eyes at that one. "Like you're gonna be able to stop him. Hit the button if anything looks off to you, and I'll come running."

"Is he allowed to eat anything yet?" I asked.

"No. Just clear liquids for now," she said and reached for a pen from its perch, and I knew she had to go quickly.

I held up the thermos of coffee. "How about this?"

She grinned, knowing how southerners were about their coffee. "That's fine."

If it hadn't have been fine I'd have left it outside his

room and not even taken the temptation of it in to him. That would have been too mean, even for me.

We pulled the curtain back a bit. "Hey, you decent in there?" I asked.

"I don't think I'm ever decent, but I got some clothes on," Charlie said. It sounded like him, and the little nurse in my heart sighed in relief.

Jeannie jerked back the curtain to reveal our bright and shiny faces. "It's us."

"The dynamic duo! Come to see me," he said and struggled to rise from the prone position he'd been in.

"Hold on there, cowboy," I said. We rushed to either side of the bed. "Use the controls that are built into the bed."

I was afraid he was going to pull out the lines in his arms trying to sit up to hug us.

"No way. I don't care. I need to thank you ladies for saving my life," he said and held out those strong arms of his and embraced us from both sides of the bed. His heart alarm was screaming, but I was pretty sure it was because it was reading artifact, the junk that interfered with when patients moved around. Apparently, the makers of cardiac alarms believed people lie still when attached to a cardiac monitor. They know nothing.

I pulled back with tears in my eyes, brought on by the emotion in his voice.

"We did good, didn't we?" I asked through the veil of mist somehow covering my eyes.

He choked out a laugh to cover his emotion. "You've done more than good, Piper. I owe you two my life," he said.

There was hardly a mark on him now. His eyes were almost back to normal, the swelling having subsided significantly. A little squeak remained in his voice from having the tube down his throat, but it just sounded like he'd hung out in a jazz bar all night drinking whiskey and smoking cigars. And the rash had vanished from the skin I could see. All fantastic evidence that he'd make a full recovery.

"Now I know there's nothing wrong with you. I walk in on you, and you're hugging on two girls hanging over your bed," a male voice said. I didn't know who that was with the booming voice that sounded like Charlie's, but I could guess. I pulled back, and so did Jeannie, and the cardiac monitor took a break.

"Ladies, let me introduce you to my little brother, Elmo," Charlie said, and this time used the bed controls to sit himself up higher.

We turned to meet Elmo, and right then I decided I needed to open Wikipedia and seriously refresh myself on definitions. 'Cause Charlie's definition of *little* and mine definitely weren't the same. A large man stood there, his shaved head just inches from the ceiling. He had shoulders that could carry a quarterback holding the ball half the length of a football field a not tire. If he wanted to. But I'm not sure he did. He wasn't built for speed, but endurance and strength. Wow. Just *wow*.

He had those same, hazel eyes as Charlie, and his voice nearly matched. They could totally double their listening audience if they went on the radio together. We needed to talk about their future.

I held out my hand, half afraid he was going to crush it without meaning to in his large hand, but he was like Charlie. He didn't need to overpower someone to prove his masculinity. Instead, he pulled me forward by my hand and enveloped me in his arms. I sighed. I could have stayed there forever. Except my nose was firmly shoved into his armpit. Eventually, I'd have to breathe. He held out his other arm for Jeannie and dragged her in a similar fashion to him.

"Wow. Were making up for hug deprivation all in one day, aren't we?" Jeannie asked and pulled away.

"Shut up," I said. "Let me enjoy this." I snuggled deeper and the rolling laugh in his chest was just icing on the cake.

After we'd hugged and got the cursory laughs out of the way, we got serious.

"So what's going on now?" I asked. "When are you gonna bust out of here?"

"Are you going to be in the ICU for much longer?" Jeannie asked as she looked at the monitor again, noting his vital signs, and I'm sure she was interpreting his heart rhythm as we stood there.

"All looks pretty good now. They might move me to the regular floor after lunch, then home tomorrow," Charlie said.

"Wow. That's amazing," I said and shook my head in disbelief, then dropped my head as the emotion of the situation crept over me again. A large, warm hand went around my shoulders.

"I know, sugar. I know," Elmo said. He didn't have to tell me he understood. I heard it in his deep baritone voice and felt it in the simple comforting gesture. "If you two hadn't been on the ball, we'd be going to a funeral tomorrow instead of taking his sorry ass home."

I wiped the moisture from my eyes with the back of my hand. I thought of using Elmo's shirt to blow my nose, but I didn't know him well enough yet. "Indeed."

"Yeah, I had no idea an allergic reaction could almost

kill a man like that. No idea at all," Charlie said and took Jeannie's hand. "I have to thank you ladies, so very, very much. Our mother would also like to thank you. She can't come down to the hospital 'cause she's frail right now." He looked at his brother. "We're her strength while she's fighting a bad cancer, so if we weren't both here, I think she'd just give up and die. So we owe you for her life, too."

The tears kept returning, so I stopped fighting them. We'd done an awesome thing and saved this family with our knowledge, our hands, our skills and our hearts. There was no way to deny it, and pushing it aside diminished their genuine gratitude, so we didn't.

"It was our pleasure, Charlie," Jeannie said. Her voice was tight, too. "Our honor to help you."

"I'm just glad you're alive. I wasn't sure what was going to happen since you went without oxygen for so long," I said. It had been a real possibility I hadn't wanted to think about before.

"Me, too," Elmo said with a laugh rolling from his chest, "but he's no weirder than usual."

That crack got a tension-relieving laugh from everyone and a pillow tossed at his head by Charlie, without any heat on it.

"Well, we should get out of here and let you rest," I said, then realized I still carried the thermos. "Oh, Audrey said you were allowed clear liquids, so we brought you some, just in case."

"Bourbon?" he asked hopefully.

"Seriously? That's the first thing you think of as a clear liquid? You're a terrible patient," I said and stepped to the over-bed table and poured fresh coffee for him. "*This* is a clear liquid, dude."

"I'll take it, sugar. I'll take it." He clapped his hands

together once, then rubbed his palms together in anticipation. "This is gonna be the best coffee I've ever tasted."

"Why's that? You don't even know what brand it is," I asked and watched as bliss covered his face.

He grinned at both of us. "I know, 'cause it's been made by angels."

🦇 15 🦇

NURSES: THE FIRST PEOPLE YOU SEE AFTER
SAYING: HOLD MY BEER AND WATCH THIS-T
SHIRT

I f I wasn't blubbering away before, I sure was then. Jeannie was right there with me wiping her face on Charlie's pillowcase.

"We should probably go, let you get your transfer going and rest up a bit," Jeannie placed a hand on his and squeezed. "Call us though. Keep us posted on when the discharge party is, and we'll be there."

"For sure, for sure." He patted Jeannie's hand. "Don't you worry about anything, angels. We're going to look out for you the way you looked out for me."

After we exchanged phone numbers with Elmo, we all left together. "I need some more coffee," he said and followed us out of Charlie's room, turning the heads of the female staff in the area and half the men. He didn't bat an eye at the attention, which meant he was really focused on us, or he had a squeeze already and wasn't interested in branching out. "That brew they call coffee in the cafeteria is gut rot. Even the stuff we have at the station is better than that swill. Can I buy you ladies some more coffee? Somewhere other than here?"

We looked at each other. Hang out with a handsome gentleman and drink coffee together? Why not? "Sure. We don't have any set plans, just have to work on a security thing for the other travelers," I said. We could do it any time soon. And we certainly could use an extra dose of coffee.

"Charlie was telling me a bit about travel nurses. I never heard of that before. Why don't we go next door, have us some coffee, and you can tell me all about it," Elmo said. As we left the ICU, the lobby and waiting room had thinned out of police officers and only a few remained. Once they'd heard the news Charlie was going to be okay and discharged to his own home instead of to a funeral home, they headed back to their work of protecting the public and catching bad guys.

In minutes we were ensconced at a large table at Fat Pete's. We didn't get a booth because Elmo's size simply wouldn't be comfortable in one. He'd have squeezed into one for us, but we weren't going to ask him to do that.

In seconds we had an order of coffee and some pastries in front of us.

"What are you doing here?" A male voice asked from behind me. In a nanosecond the hair on the back of my scrawny little neck stood straight out and the fine hair on my arms did, too. I didn't like people walking up behind me without my knowledge, no matter who they were. I couldn't twist around to see, but I knew that whiny little voice. It was the skinny manager at Fat Pete's.

With an arrogant jiggle of my head I ignored him, but spoke out loud and lifted the coffee cup to my mouth. "Just sitting here in a public place enjoying a cup of coffee with my new best friend. Perfectly legal last time I checked," I said. After the nanosecond of going on high alert was over,

I was back to my sassy self. No one talked to me that way and got away with it. They got it right back.

"You got something to say to this lady, I suggest you say it to her face," Elmo said, his deep voice growling in his chest. I think he was a grizzly bear in a former life. His voice certainly sounded like it.

The manager, Fat Pete Junior moved forward, hanging onto the counter for support. As a trained observer, I quickly deduced there was something wrong, that he didn't want to put weight on one leg. Or he had a raging case of hemorrhoids. That also made people walk funny, but I was going with a leg injury.

"Hey, Pete. What's shaking?" I asked, knowing I really didn't want to know what was shaking in his life.

"You're not welcome here. I suggest you leave now before I throw you out." Though he spoke to both Jeannie and I, his focus was on me. What did I do? Oh yeah. I was the sassy one.

"Seriously?" The more agitated he got, the calmer I got. The tactic worked with patients having psychiatric issues. Made them either calm down too, or go ballistic and scream obscenities until they ran out of words. Either way, it ended a stalemate quickly. "My money is as green as anyone else's." I turned to Jeannie. "Right? Our money is as green as the rest."

"I don't know. I don't carry much cash these days, but my debit card works just fine anywhere I go." She gave a crisp nod, her eyes keen and assessing, too.

"I don't care about any of that. Get out of here." A red flush crept up his neck and onto Pete's face.

Elmo had been taking in the situation and then stood. Slowly. Deliberately. Like a giant rising up out of the earth. But he was in a restaurant and there was no dirt. Either way, it was good. Impressive. If I hadn't known Elmo I'd have been running like a frightened rabbit across the room, going Helter-Skelter looking for cover.

"Are you seriously attempting to disrespect these two women?" he asked. The look on his face was closed, dark, dangerous. I was sure he'd used that face many times when interrogating criminals or frightening small children at Halloween. He didn't need a costume. He just needed that expression.

"What?" Pete asked with an annoyed look on his face. He turned to Elmo as if he'd just now seen him, hadn't realized there was anyone else at the table except for Jeannie and me. Talk about narrowly focused. "What the hell do you want?" He looked Elmo up and down once and apparently found him inferior. That took some *cojones* to look a police officer of *that* size with *that* face and dismiss him. "Stay out of it. It doesn't concern you."

Elmo backed away from the table and took an intimidating step closer to Pete. "I'm not going to stand here and let you speak that way to the ladies who just saved my brother's life. Consider them protected, *very well-protected*, by the police force of this community now. You take one step out of line, and your ass will be sitting in the back of a cop car so fast you'll wonder how it got there."

Pete took another look at Elmo, then at us and swallowed, nodded once with narrowed eyes. He didn't like it, but he wasn't willing to get into a physical altercation with a cop. Or get arrested. "I get it." He took a step back. "They've gotten to you, haven't they? Apparently, the whole police force is in on it, too." He threw down the notebook he had in his hands. "I should have known they'd get to the cops first. They've infiltrated the hospital, now the police force, and soon they'll be everywhere." He took another step back, his eyes widened as his delusion took him over. "Just stay away from me." He hobbled away from us and moved to the back room where Emily said his office was.

"I hope he's not as sick as he looks," Jeannie said. She had compassion for everyone, even the dude who'd just threatened us.

Elmo sat again and picked up his coffee, then shook his head. "Something wrong with that dude. Seriously wrong."

"Yeah. The first time we came in here he didn't like us as soon as we said we were travel nurses. Until then he was all fake smiles and sunshine. Guess he thought we were tourists."

"He's a business man. He's supposed to be all fake smiles and sunshine. At least until he gets your money out of your pocket into his." Elmo sipped his coffee, then set it down. "Not half bad, but I'm sure the coffee you brought Charlie is better than this."

"Because it was made by angels?" Jeannie asked.

"Yes, ma'am." He leaned forward. "Anyway, tell me what a travel nurse is." He leaned back in the chair and looked like a giant kid waiting to hear a story, but his eyes were alert. He had cop eyes, too. He was prepared for the return of the psycho-Fat Pete manager to come screaming from the back, but so far so good.

So we told him our story about how travel nurses were just like regular nurses, but with restless feet and gypsy souls. We had a desire to travel, to move, to be on adventures, and the best way was to take short term assignments all over the country.

"Isn't that hard, packing up your lives and moving

every three months?" He asked the same question most people asked us, so we had a good answer.

"For us, it's harder to stay put. Harder to deal with the every day drudgery of life," Jeannie said. "We know one day we'll have to settle down, or want to settle down, and buy homes, get married, have kids and all that stuff. But for now, when we're young and single, it's a great way to go."

"Huh." He nodded. "I never would have thought of it that way."

We chatted about life on the island and the general area. Elmo gave us some great tips on places to check out, other places to avoid, and recommended a few nice restaurants that didn't have an asshole managing them. That was a bonus.

Then his phone gave a text notification that he looked at right away. "That's my mama. I have to go ladies. She's done with her latest treatment, and ready to go home." He stood, pulled out his wallet and placed a few bills under the plate that would cover our entire tab. When we started to protest he held up one big hand that stopped us. "My treat. Next time, y'all can buy." He looked around. "And we'll go someplace else, too."

I held my palm out to his for a high-five. "You're on. Just let us know when."

"You got it," he said and the giant of a man headed for the door. I wondered if they'd had to order a cop car in extra-long for him.

"Let's work on the other thing we need to do," Jeannie said and pulled a notebook from her shoulder bag. She had a handbag like Hermione from Harry Potter. There was no end to it. Sometimes I wondered if she was going to pull a tent out of it. It would make camping a lot easier.

"Okay. So what do we know? Some idiot, besides Fat Pete here, has it in for nurses," I said, recapping the situation.

"We need to come up with a phone tree, or contact list, or something to distribute to all of the nurses immediately," Jeanie said.

"Good idea. We don't know if this guy just happened to catch travelers, or if he has it in for all of us." The thought that someone was targeting *just* travel nurses was disturbing. Targeting nurses was bad enough. We were the caregivers of the world, and how someone could hate our industry so much they'd kill its workers was freaky. But if our safety plan worked, we'd just take the victims out of the game. We'd be ready for him.

"I have a basic database setup in my computer," Jeannie said.

"Of course you do," I replied. Didn't everyone have a database set up in their computers they could just whip out should the need arise?

"Oh, stop. You know I do that crap when I can't sleep. Helps me relax."

Gave me migraines.

"Go on. I'm sorry." I had a bad habit of interrupting conversations with sprinkles of charm, wit and sarcasm. It was a birth defect. Or a gift. I couldn't decide which.

"I'll plug in all the information we have from the HR file, on all of the travel nurses that are here, and that are scheduled in the next few weeks. We can call it a Safe Travels group, or something like that. We could even put it on the internet for everyone to add their experiences to," Jeannie said, her eyes glittering as she warmed to her subject.

She scooped her hair up in a high bun and secured it

with a tie. The day was getting warmer, even in the air conditioned building. She was getting excited at the depth of how far this little database could go. She was sick.

"Let's start small, and go from there. If people start dinging an assignment like bad food on YELP, that could affect how many travelers go there. The patients would be the ones to suffer." We didn't want to have those kind of repercussions, just wanted to outsmart the bad guy and save lives.

"Oh, I hadn't thought of that." She slumped for a second, disappointment in her demeanor.

I pulled the notes closer. "How about an electronic newsletter, just a short thing, to keep people informed of safety issues here. Or a texting system for alerts. Like one for smokers on shift. They shouldn't prop the back door open for a quick break, no matter how convenient it is. It's a security breach, and I'm sure the nurse who was attacked did it all the time."

"That's true." We puzzled it out, wrote down the security areas and issues we knew about already. "We need to talk to that nurse. Maybe security at the hospital, too, since they'd respond first to an issue before the police."

"Good ideas," I said.

We worked for another thirty minutes before I felt the hebe-jeebies on my neck again. "You know, I think they're out of coffee. We should go somewhere else." I stood.

"What? We're nowhere near done with this," Jeannie said, but went with my lead. We gathered our things, shoved them back in her purse.

"I can feel skinny Fat Pete's eyes boring into my neck. I'd rather not have a knife plunged into it when he goes off his nut. There are too many sharp implements in a restaurant."

"Oh, right. Who needs a gun when you've got so many weapons to choose from?" Jeanie said and gave a nervous laugh, then slung her bag over her shoulder.

"No kidding. Multitudes of knives and other stuff I probably don't want to know about." Now that I'd said that out loud, all I could think of was the inventory of weapons he had at his disposal back there.

"Yeah, who wants to be killed by a potato masher? Or *whisked* to death. Let's get out of here," she said, and I laughed as we walked out of the place.

I couldn't help myself. As she opened the door, and held onto it to leave, I looked back, just to see if I'd been right, if my instincts hadn't led me astray, and my reaction had been just too much caffeine.

But there he was. The skinny Fat Pete manager, leaning against the doorway to the back, glaring at us, spewing silent hatred as we left the building. I had my way of doing things, so I just pasted a big fake smile on my face and waved at him, seeing if I could send him over the edge of his mental cesspool and take a dive into the deep end.

He didn't move. Didn't give any indication he'd seen my red flag waving in his face. He just stood there glaring.

After today, we were never going back there. No matter how convenient it was to the hospital. I'd brown bag it and make my own coffee before I'd set foot in there again.

We drove to the Flying Pig and settled in. The atmosphere there was way more comfortable, and pigs hung from the ceiling. How cute was that?

We strategized and put together a plan. We just needed to institute it. Did we need to get permission from the DON to distribute our little newsletter? From HR? From anyone? It wasn't like we were organizing a nurses union or anything, we were just contacting other travel nurses to try to protect them from someone who obviously had issues.

"We should put a warning about Fat Pete's in it," Jeannie said and contemplated the idea as she sipped her tea.

"Can't we just put a general warning of general unfriendly types or something like that? I don't want to get sued for slander or anything," I said. Someone like that guy would totally sue, too.

"Good point." She wrote something on the margin of our document. "How about we just put friendly places, rather than unfriendly. People will gravitate to the good places without pointing out the not-so-good places."

"Brilliant. I knew I was friends with you for a reason," I said.

"That way there's no slander involved, just recommendations." She didn't respond to the compliment, but blushed lightly. The curse of fair-haired women the world over.

"Make it so, Number One." Like I had the authority to give a command.

"I'm on it."

So we messed around with the document another hour and by then it was lunch time. We took ourselves home for a quick sandwich and iced tea. We couldn't eat every meal out, though the temptation was there.

"Can you believe we had that nice dinner at Sharky's *just* last evening? Less than twenty-four hours ago?" she asked and took a bite of her sandwich.

"Wow. We sure pack a lot into our days, don't we?" An incredible amount.

"Unbelievable. And people wonder why we're

exhausted when we go back to work after four days off."
We were both experienced travelers and knew when to
pace ourselves, but this was an unusual situation we'd
been plunged into. Not every day, run-of-the-mill exhaus-
tion from over-doing it.

"Normally, we're just sight-seeing and stuff, not finding
bodies, rescuing cops, or anything like that," she said.

After our modest lunch we decided to try to find the
nurse who'd been attacked on her smoke break. That
meant another trip to the hospital to find out.

"Or," I said as the idea came to me and I twitched my
brows. "We could use our newly-acquired police connections. Not like we're violating HIPPA or anything because
police reports are public information, right?" I was looking
for validation in my thinking, not just a pat on the head
and told it was good idea.

Jeannie nodded slowly, following the way my little
brain was going. "Nice. We could just call the station and
find out without having to go to the hospital again."

We were so smart.

After a quick phone call to the police substation in
Southport and speaking with a very nice desk officer, we
had the name we needed and an emailed copy of the
complaint. Score. Normally we wouldn't get that information so quickly or so easily, but when she *somehow* found
out during the course of the conversation we were the
ones that had saved Charlie, she accidentally copied and
emailed us the information. I loved those kinds of
accidents.

"I'll print it." Jeannie hit the print button on her email
and in a few seconds I heard it coming up on her printer in
black and white.

"Her name is Lilly Cotton," Jeannie said.

"Good southern name."

"Her address is listed and the phone number." She raised her brows. "Should we try her?"

"Why not?" We weren't going to get anywhere thinking about it. I picked up my phone. "What's her number?"

Jeannie recited it off to me, and I dialed it. It rang three times, then someone answered. "I told you people I don't want to be interviewed. Leave me alone." Near hysteria screeched in her voice.

"Lilly, this is Piper Quinn, one of the nurses at the hospital, I'm not a reporter." I had to talk fast and get the words into her brain before she hung up. The human mind could process 400 million bits of information a second. So I had approximately half a nanosecond to say all of that. Wow. Maybe I should try out for speed talking. I could do commercials.

"What? Who are you?" Now that sounded like a nurse.

"I'm not a reporter. I'm one of the travel nurses, Piper Quinn."

"What do you want to talk to me for?" Suspicion was heavy in her voice.

"My friend, Jeannie, and I are putting together a safety newsletter for the nurses at the hospital and wanted to put something about what had happened to you in it. That's all."

"Oh. I see." She paused. "That still sounds like an interview."

"I'm sorry. I don't want to rehash the trauma of it for you." Something like that incident could trigger PTSD, Post Traumatic Stress Disorder, symptoms for someone, especially with it so fresh. I didn't want to do that, but I definitely wanted the information.

"It's awful." A tremor choked her voice, and I wanted to comfort her, but I didn't quite know how.

"Have you been back to work?" Work usually kept the mind busy. Keeping busy would be half the battle.

"It only happened last night."

"Oh, right. Sorry. A lot has happened in the last twenty-four hours. Have you been out of your house since then?"

"No, I'm afraid. I'm so afraid to go anywhere," she said in an emotional whisper.

"Why not meet Jeannie and I for coffee for something?" I wasn't going to sleep for a week with the amount of coffee I'd ingested today, but I was young and my kidneys functioned at full capacity.

There was a pause, and there should have been. She had to think of her safety and consider the odds, but she also had to know as a nurse that the best medicine for her was to beat the odds, beat the bastard who'd tried to kill her and survive. To thrive.

"I know you're hesitating, and I would, too. If you don't want to drive, Jeannie and I can come pick you up." She wouldn't mind and neither would I.

"No, that's okay," she said and I totally understood that reaction too. She didn't know us and after her brush with death last night, she hesitated.

There was defeat in her voice, and I shook my head, communicating to Jeannie that I didn't think this was going to work.

"I could use an ice cream," she said in a small voice. "That would be nice."

"Awesome. Why don't you tell us where to meet you, and we'll be there?" I gave Jeannie a thumbs-up sign and motioned for the notebook and pen. I wrote down the name of the shop.

"I don't know the address, but it's across the street from the Flying Pig if you know where that is."

"Sure do." As of today, its location was permanently imprinted on my DNA.

"Okay. See you in an hour." The line went dead.

Well, we had an hour to kill. I pulled up a search engine on my phone and plugged the name of the ice cream shop in and got us an address.

"Let's go." We opened the apartment door to the blast of heat. It was like an arctic blast, only in reverse, from the equator. I didn't think we were in tropical climes, but it sure felt close.

"I wonder why the weather is so heavy feeling today," I said. Jeannie hit the button to put open the convertible top to the car again. Way easier than it used to be with older models.

"I don't know. I think it's just humidity in the air we're not used to it," she said.

"There's nothing more oppressive than Pennsylvania in the middle of summer. Hot. Humid. Heavy. But this feels different somehow." I didn't have any fond memories of the summers in Pennsylvania, just memories of pollen, ragweed and molds. And carting boxes of tissues around with me wherever I went.

"I don't know, maybe check your weather app," Jeannie said.

"Good plan," I said, then promptly forgot about it as she squealed the tires leaving the parking lot, trying to get in front of a slow-moving vehicle with out-of-state plates. "Geez, woman. What's gotten into you?"

"I suddenly have an urge for ice cream, too. And I didn't want to get behind that van. I can't see around larger vehicles in this car." She grinned. "It's fast, so I can make it around them."

We cruised down the main drag and drove past the shop. We were early, so we just kept going for a bit, enjoying the day as the sun shone down on us. Pretty soon, my hair began to stick to my face, and I turned the AC on. Yes, even though we had the top down, I wanted the AC blasting straight at me. I like options that way.

I looked ahead at the dark clouds looming on the horizon. I also noticed people nailing plywood to their windows, taking in their outdoor plants and furniture. "Ugh-oh." I pulled up the weather app. "I think it's more than just a humid day."

"Why?"

"Look at the buildings, businesses. People are out hammering wood to them. That's a bad sign," I said.

"Rats. I hadn't noticed." She found a place to turn around safely in a parking lot, then we headed back down the main road toward the ice cream shop. "You're right."

"The app says there's a tropical storm headed our way."

❧ 16 ❧

"A tropical storm? That's not as bad as a hurricane, right?" Jeannie asked. I heard the hesitation in her voice. She was trying to remember the difference with that maniac brain of hers. She had a brain like Wikipedia sometimes, but apparently not on this particular topic.

"While that is correct," I said as I looked at the giant white clouds that looked like a bag of cotton balls blown up and filled with rain, wind and electricity, "hurricane's are built out of tropical storms. It just takes the right ingredients at the right time to spin it all into a hurricane." Who needed a blender when there were tropical winds spinning in circles at seventy-four miles per hour or more. Hurricane? Double the speed. It was kind of like the difference between lime juice and a Kamikaze. Some of the same ingredients, but turned into a explosive drink.

"Double rats. I don't really want to do a hurricane," she said.

"No, but it's not like we're going to have an option

soon." We'd killed enough time and pulled into the parking lot, buzzed the top back into place.

The shop was in the middle of a short strip mall filled with tourist shops that we had to check out another time. I had not yet begun to acquire my fill of shell necklaces and bracelets, t-shirts with Oak Island logo. Some were for friends, but honestly, most were for me. At least I was honest about my deception. I made a mental note that we had to come back here, soon.

We entered the frigid interior of the ice cream shop. It probably wasn't really that cold, but when you were hot and dripping with sweat outside, then the sudden change of temperature did feel like stepping into a walk-in fridge.

A few people already stood in line. One lone women sat in the back with a double scoop of something melting in a cup. She was lost in space, her gaze not focused on anything or anyone. She was average looking. Brown hair pulled back in ponytail off her neck. Beach clothes. Flip-flops, cropped shorts and a shirt with a beach scene on it. But it was her downcast eyes that gave her away. It wasn't that she just didn't want to make eye contact with anyone, she deliberately avoided making eye contact with anyone coming in. Although she should have been searching for us expectantly as we were for her, she wasn't. And that's what really made me think it was her.

I nudged Jeannie and tipped my head toward her table. "I think that's her. Lilly."

Instead of ordering, we adjusted our trajectory to her table. If she wasn't the woman we were looking for, that was okay and maybe we'd put a smile on someone's face. But if she was, I didn't want to leave her sitting by herself for too long. She didn't look very good. One of her legs twitched. It was a subconscious way to get rid of pent-up energy without pacing. A lot of people did it and didn't even know it.

"Hello. Are you Lilly?" I asked gently. I didn't want to startle her, but she hardly seemed to be aware of her surroundings, let alone having heard us approach.

She stiffened and sat upright, then focused on us. She didn't say anything at first, but visually checked us out to see if we were any threat to her, then she relaxed, slumped more in her chair. "Yes. I'm Lilly," she said in a strained voice that sounded like she was getting laryngitis. It was actually the injury to her throat that caused the scratch in her voice. She was fortunate the creep hadn't broken the hyoid bone in her throat. That could have ended her.

"I'm Piper, and this is my friend Jeannie."

"Is she a reporter?" Lilly asked and eyed me with suspicion, as if I'd betrayed her. As if she'd expected me to.

"No. She's a travel nurse, too. Okay if we sit with you?" I put my hand on the back of one of the chairs, indicating I was ready to sit. Most polite people wouldn't say no. And I deliberately didn't make any fast moves, so she wasn't startled. Things like that could trigger reactions of fear and anxiety, and she didn't need any more of that.

"Sure." She didn't make a lot of eye contact with us, indicating she really didn't want to be there, but I knew it would help. In some small way, it would help her. We took seats on either side of her.

"Are we late?" Jeannie asked and consulted her watch. Being late would freak Jeannie out. Me? Not so much. I've learned to go with the flow over the years. A few minutes waiting wasn't going to kill anyone, and wasn't worth the anxiety attack.

"No. I'm early. I caught an Uber over. I didn't want to drive, but I didn't want to stay alone at my house any longer. The kids are off at camp this week, and I was looking forward to some peace and quiet for a few days." She huffed out a tearful laugh. "Now that I have it, I don't want it." She shrugged and then looked at us as her eyes filled. "I don't know what to do." She was trying. She was hurting and looking for help. Maybe we could give her some.

She looked at us through watery blue eyes. When she tilted her head up to blink the tears away, she inadvertently revealed her neck. Angry purple bruises clearly demonstrated where the attempt on her life had been made. Unconsciously, she lifted one hand to cover the area. She probably wasn't aware she did that. Like when women placed a hand over their cleavage to cover it, after they realized they'd exposed too much. Unfortunately, while trying to cover it up, people just brought more attention to the area, the way Lilly did now. My heart went out to her.

"We'll help you," Jeannie said and placed her hand lightly over Lilly's. It was such a simple gesture, to touch a hand, that people forgot how easy it was. People gave hand shakes, or hugs, or bro-shakes that were entirely too complicated for me. The simple touching of one hand to another hand went a long way for comfort. And it was fat-free. No calories. No lengthy contracts, either.

"We certainly will." I adjusted the seat closer to the table, closer to her, so I didn't have to talk very loud and kept our conversation as private as possible. "Are you settled for a little bit? Do you need water or anything?"

"No," she said and placed her spoon back in the cup and tipped her chin down, covering the bruises and swollen skin on her neck. "I thought this would help, but really it's not." She patted her neck gently. "Hurts to swallow."

I examined her dish. "Rocky Road and Mocha Almond Fudge. Excellent combination."

At that she gave a quick smile. "You know your ice cream, don't you?"

"Never met a scoop I didn't like." Except one that had coconut flakes in it. Never again. Cue shiver of revulsion.

"So, let us tell you what we want to do, and then you can tell us if you'd like to help out," Jeannie said and pulled a notebook from her bag. "We've got a list of nurses who work at the hospital, travelers at this point, but I think all nurses should be made aware of the safety risks going on right now."

"Believe me," Lilly said with a wide-eyed look on her face, "everyone knows now. After what happened to me, going to the ER for treatment, then having to leave my shift in the middle? Everyone knows."

"Hospitals are among the very finest gossip centers, aren't they?" I asked.

"Yes. I'm sure everyone knows that I was attacked, and the smokers are going to think twice about opening that back door again. We've done it for years and had no problems." She shook her head. "I think it's time for me to quit though."

"Good for you," Jeannie said. "It's the number one thing you can do for your health."

"In more than one way," Lilly said, meaning that smoking was what had almost led to her murder.

"So, are you in with us?" I asked. "We decided to call the newsletter *Safe Travels*."

"But I'm not a travel nurse," she said. "That makes it a little different, doesn't it?"

I had to think about that. "That definitely deviates from the two murders we know of. They were travel nurses."

"It's not making sense," Jeannie said. "Once a serial killer has his mind set on a certain type, he rarely deviates. He can't help it. Whether it's like Ted Bundy who went for girls with long, straight, brown hair. Or John Wayne Gacy who targeted young homosexual males."

I gaped at her. "How do you know all that stuff?"

"I read. A lot. And watch the Investigation Discovery channel," she said, as if it were normal, everyday occurrence.

"Apparently. We need to get you out more, girl," I said.

"But she's right," Lilly said. "I don't think he was after me at first."

That was an interesting clue. "Why not?" I asked.

"The other nurse that was out smoking when I got there was a traveler. She was there first." Lilly huffed out a breath and her lower lip trembled. "I think I became the target when she came inside, and I went outside. We swapped positions."

"Wow," Jeanie said and flopped back against her chair. "I'd never have thought of that."

"Do you know the other nurse?" I asked, excitement thrumming through my system.

"No. I don't. But she was pretty distinctive. She was a tiny thing with short pink spiky hair. Looked like a pixie."

"Oh, I know her. I met her when we were spying in HR," I blurted out.

"When we were *assisting the HR manager,* you mean?" Jeannie said with widened eyes, correcting my slip-up.

"Yes. Exactly. When I was holding down the fort in HR, she came in looking for directions to the DON's office. Since I knew where that was, I showed her." I snapped my fingers. "And we exchanged numbers. I remember telling her to call if she needed help with anything, since she was pretty new to travel nursing."

I whipped the 'droid out of my pocket and opened the phone app. There were a bazillion people who weren't 'droid users, and loved iPhone systems. However, I couldn't deal with them. My brain simply refused to make the adaptation to learning how the iPhone systems operated. My theory was that people found the first operating system they've ever used to be the easiest one. Whichever one it was. Me? I was a 'droid user. Jeannie dealt with the other evil entity. Either way, we had both systems covered.

"Here it is. Mitzi," I said and pulled up her number. "We should call her."

"Let's wait. She worked last night, so she's probably sleeping," Jeannie said.

"Right." I looked at my watch. It was still early afternoon and night nurses needed as much sleep as possible before trudging through the next shift. Being up all hours of the night was an unnatural state for most people. But hospital systems operated around the clock, and therefore, so did nurses.

"So go through what happened, if you can." Maybe by now, she was ready to tell us her story. Telling the story of a tragic event helped to get it out of the brain, kept it from running on an endless feedback loop, preventing the person from letting go of it. Once it was out, it could be dealt with more easily.

I waited, and so did Jeannie. We'd asked for the story. It was up to Lilly to tell it.

"You have the police report, right?" Lilly asked, apparently changing her mind about telling us what had happened.

"We have the report, that's correct, but we want your impressions of him. The details that may have surfaced since then," Jeannie said.

"What did he smell like? Was he hard, soft? What body type was he? Did he have bad breath? Did he say something? Anything like that." I was hoping something stuck out to her.

"I'd just stepped outside to light up, took a few drags, then pulled out my phone to catch up on emails for a minute. Next thing I knew my face was plastered against the building, and my throat was in pain. It took me a second to realize there was a rope around my neck." She huffed out a breath as the memory of it overwhelmed her. "It's funny, you know. When you're in the middle of a situation like that, you don't realize everything going on until it's too late. Like it took a few seconds for my brain to get the gist of what was happening to my body." She turned her face to me and stroked a finger over the abrasions on her face. Probably from being scraped against the brick building. They were superficial and would heal in a few days. The rest would take more time. The internal injuries would take even longer.

"Take a breath. It's okay. We're here for you," Jeannie said, her voice soft and comforting.

"He was behind me. At first I thought he was going to rape me. That's probably what every woman in that situation thinks first, right? But when his body was against mine, I didn't feel anything like that, you know?" She grimaced.

"Meaning his male parts weren't involved?" I asked, wanting the clarification.

"Yes. I know that sounds weird, but it was an impression I had. Just for a second." She shrugged. "Like you said, it was an impression that didn't hit me until now."

"Fantastic job, Lilly," I said. "You might remember some more things now."

"Now we know he wasn't there to rape," Jeannie said. "He's probably impotent and taking out his rage on women. Nurses, he blames for some reason. Maybe he went to an impotency clinic and couldn't get the help he needed there." We were brainstorming. Getting into the meat of what made this man tick. What made his mind work in the demented way it was. It wasn't dementia, like a normal disease process. This was madness, psychological illness.

"But then, shouldn't he be angry at the doctor, not the nurse?" Lilly asked. It was a reasonable question and supposition, but when dealing with the criminally insane, nothing was reasonable or logical, except to their demented sense of why they were doing what they were doing.

"Maybe the doctor was female, and he's finding it easier to attack female nurses, rather than female doctors," Jeannie added.

I nodded. "That's a great realization," I said to Lilly.

Lilly looked at me. "Like you said, it didn't hit me until now." She leaned forward in her seat, more engaged. Great. She was going to be okay.

"Then what happened?" Jeannie asked. We were getting excited and in our enthusiasm, were thinking tangentially, when it wasn't necessarily the case. But we had more information than we had not long ago.

Lilly took a bite of her melting ice cream without enthusiasm, swallowed and took a breath. "Then something in me snapped. I have kids, you know?" She raised those eyes brimming with tears, but also with fierce determination shining through the storm. "If I was going to die in that moment, I was going to go out fighting, show my kids I was a fighter." She wiped a tear away with one hand.

I nodded. Jeannie and I were transfixed. The soul, the spirit of a person, was often the determining factor between life or death in any situation. We'd seen it often enough with our patients. Ones who should have died, but didn't, simply because their spirit was too determined to live. We remained silent, not prodding her. The bell over the door signaled people coming or going from the shop, but I was too engrossed in Lilly's story to really care.

"That's a sign of great personal strength," Jeannie said. "It's what helped you survive and will help you get through your recovery from it."

"Anyway, I felt a calm come over me. It totally could have been from oxygen deprivation, and I was about to pass out, but I felt peace. Somehow, I managed to reach into my pocket and grab a pen. With the last bit of strength I had, I drove it into him. Somehow, I did it," she said, shaking her head as if hardly daring to believe her own strength, her own ability to save her life, rather than depend on someone else to save her. "I stabbed him. I've never hurt anyone before in my entire life. I'm a nurse, for heaven's sake. I help people." Tears overflowed, and I pulled a few napkins from the dispenser on the table, silently pushed them her way. She took a few and wiped her face, then dragged in a few breaths and coughed that very distinctive bark most smokers had, whether they admitted it or not. It was a good think she'd quit smoking at this point in her life.

"That calm was your spirit coming to the surface," I

said. "You didn't need anyone to rescue you. You rescued yourself. That's an amazing thing."

She coughed out a laugh and a little glimmer of amusement shimmered with the tears in her eyes. "I guess it is. I'm the youngest of five kids, and so everyone was always taking care of me when we were growing up. I guess I don't need that any more."

"No, you don't. You do need to have some counseling for a while. That'll go a long way to your recovery and helping you understand your reactions, and in turn help your children understand. How old are they, anyway?" Jeannie asked, trying to distract her from the emotions, but at the same time keep her talking. It was a nurse trick. One we all fell for when we were in distress.

"I've been thinking about it. My husband's a fire fighter and he brought it up, too." She shook her head, agreeing now with the suggestion. "Our kids are six and seven." A sweet smile lifted the corners of her mouth. "We were high school sweethearts, Jimmy and me. Got married young, I got pregnant right away and went to nursing school when they were babies."

"Wow. You are a determined woman," I said. "That's going to get you through this, too. You're going to be okay. Your kids are too young to understand the whole thing, they'll just know when you're happy or sad, and you can explain that to them. They'll get that."

"They're great kids. They know when to let me sleep, but if there's blood or fire, it okay to wake me." The recollection of that make her smile. Then she snorted. "I actually have a spread sheet on the door to our bedroom, so they have to stop and think before they knock on that door.

"Aw. Another spread-sheet-devotee," I said and shivered on the inside. My left eye twitched, too, but I didn't think Jeannie saw it.

"What a great idea," Jeannie said and slid me an I-told-you-I'm-not-the-only-one-who-loves-spread-sheets look.

"Whatever," I said and waved it away before I broke out in hives. "The thing is, you did what was necessary to save your life then, and you're going to do what's necessary to continue living now. It's the best revenge against people who try to hurt us. Live well. Thrive, and be successful."

"You've given us some great information," Jeanie said. "Thank you for that."

"I'm sorry we pushed you to come out, but I think it was good for you, wasn't it?" I asked.

"Yes, it was. I feel better already, so thanks for the kick in the pants." She dove into her ice cream slush pile with more enthusiasm than when we'd first arrived.

"I think I'm going to get a scoop, too." Jeannie and I rose one at a time, not wanting to leave Lilly alone at the table. We got our choices, Butter Pecan for Jeannie. Chocolate Chip Mint for me. My favorite any day of the week and twice on Sunday's.

Lilly yawned and tried to hide it behind one hand. "Boy, I'm wiped out. I think the adrenaline of the last day has kept me going."

"And now it's worn off?" Jeannie asked with a nod. "We know all about that." In the past few days, I think we'd gone through twice our daily allotted amount of adrenaline squeezed from the small organs on top of our kidneys. They needed a break too.

"Yes. I feel like a rag doll now." She finished the last scoop of her ice cream and pushed it away. "I think that's all I need. If I go to bed right after ice cream I'll have bad dreams."

"Not that you need anymore right now," I said and finished up mine, too. "You said you took an Uber here. Want us to drop you off?" I made the offer, knowing Jeannie would be fine with it.

"No, that's okay. My husband is coming for me in a little bit. He had a meeting at the station, so the timing was good." Lilly leaned back against the chair and the lines in her face looked more relaxed than we'd first arrived. Not that I knew her well, but I knew faces. And I knew what strain on them looked like. She'd make it. She was going to be okay.

Jeannie and I decided to head out then, and threw our trash away in the bin by the door. Just as we were about to leave, I turned back to Lilly. "Just out of curiosity, where did you stab him?" I didn't have to elaborate.

"The left leg."

Jeannie and I turned to face each other with mirror expressions of shock on our faces.

❄ 17 ❄

TUT, TUT. LOOKS LIKE RAIN - CHRISTOPHER
ROBIN

We pushed out of the frigid ice cream shop into an afternoon that had darkened, the shadows deepened and the winds had kicked up. Higher than I'd expected, it whipped our clothing against us, tugging at our hair. We ran to Jeannie's car. "Hold on, Piglet," I yelled over the rising wind. We dove into her car, and I opened the weather app on my phone.

"I can't believe it," Jeannie said and tossed her bag in the back seat.

"There's really a big storm coming our way." I wiped rain from my face.

"That's not what I meant," she said, her breath coming in short gasps.

"Then what?" I asked.

"Charlie! He has a injury to his left leg."

"You don't suspect Charlie, for heaven's sake. He wouldn't do that." I was shocked she'd even considered it, but as I thought about the situation, I turned to face her. The wipers swished madly back and forth across the windshield as fast as my mind was racing. "Would he? Could he?" I started to have my doubts about the whole thing. "Seriously?"

"He was there when we found Kelly's crime scene. We called *him* to come to the scene of the lady in the marsh." She ticked off the counts against him. "We called *him* when out apartment door was open."

"We sat in his cop car and gave him our statements." Anger and outrage throbbed through me. I was nearly shaking with it. Or maybe that was the wind buffeting the car. Either way, I was moving involuntarily. "He was seriously pissed at us that we'd endangered ourselves. I mean, that was real, right?" At the moment, I didn't know what was real and what my naturally suspicious mind was creating.

"It could have been a put-on." She raised her hands to the wheel and clutched it, trying to make sense of it, as I was. "He was really angry when he closed the door at the apartment." She turned her head to face me. "Remember what he said? We *needed some lessons*. How are we supposed to take that kind of statement?"

I flopped back against the seat with the headrest made of genuine imitation leather as I remembered that night. "Then he collapsed. What would have happened if he hadn't collapsed?" My heart thrummed wildly. I felt like a deer that had just escaped a predator. Wary. Eyes wide. Looking for more danger. Waiting to hear a branch crack, signaling the threat had gotten closer. "How is that even possible? We trust Charlie."

"I don't know." She huffed out a breath. "We saved his life. What would have happened if he'd died? Would the murders stop?"

"We don't know. Can't possibly know," I said and

closed my eyes, pressed my fists to my forehead as I thought. "Did we just save the life of a serial killer so he could go on killing again?" I huffed out a breath. "Oh, my God. Tell me we didn't." I dropped my fists and faced Jeanie. Her eyes were wide, shock on her face and of course, she did the pursed lip thing while she considered all the angles of this situation.

I thought about Charlie when he'd been in the hospital lying on the bed, how he'd kept his leg extended, due to the injury. How happy he'd been to see us. Could that all have been a put-on? Could he have been faking it for the sake of everyone around him? Could we just be losing our minds and suspecting an upstanding police officer who'd just had a life-threatening event?

Lilly said she'd stabbed her attacker in the left leg. Charlie's injury was to his left leg. Lilly had no recollection of whether the attacker was black or white, or if she'd seen his skin at all. She'd been in panic and survival mode at the time. Those sort of details were veiled in the deepest part of her mind. But it triggered something in *my* mind.

Charlie had said he'd been cleaning out a shed and cut himself, sending him to the ER for a tetanus shot. Was that really it? Or was it a cover story he'd made up to hide a stab wound inflicted on him by a nurse he'd tried to kill?

How could we find out whether he'd visited a clinic for impotence? God, I was lame. There was one sure fire way of testing that theory, but I wasn't going to go down that rutted road. Neither would Jeannie. We'd made friends with those two fine brothers, Charlie and Elmo, and if my suspicious little mind was wrong, and sometimes it was, I'd alienate the whole family with my theory. I wouldn't risk it.

That would never be overcom-able. I knew that wasn't

a word. I'd just made it up, but it fit the situation right then. I wouldn't want to do anything to harm our friendship with this family. If we'd been talking about Shipper, that was different. I hadn't liked the man from the second we'd met him. If we alienated him, I'd be okay with that.

"No. I just can't make my mind accept that. It can't be Charlie. I don't want it to be Charlie. I refuse to let myself believe it's Charlie," I said, trying to convince myself it wasn't Charlie.

I shook my head, anger now surging upward. I was an excellent reader of human beings. So was Jeannie. My bullshit meter was finely tuned, and I'd gotten nothing from Charlie to say otherwise. He was true. I had to believe that, or I couldn't continue moving forward in this predicament. If people like Charlie were so good at masking their true selves, then I needed to reconsider a lot of things and send for a higher quality bullshit meter. Mine was obviously on the fritz.

"Well, the good thing is that serial killers rarely kill outside of their own ethnic group," Jeannie said in a small voice. "It happens, but not to often."

"That's it. I'm only dating men outside my own ethnic group from now on." Maybe some Latin men. Mixed race, too. That should cover all the bases and I'll never be the victim of a serial killer. Statistics don't lie.

"Piper, be serious." She clucked her tongue at me like an old mother hen.

"I'm sorry. I need some comic relief. I just can't put Charlie in the role of a killer. Sure, he'd kill in the line of duty, or if someone was committing a terrible crime-"

"Like serial killer stuff?" she asked, interrupting me.

"Yeah, like that." I pushed my lips out, thinking, the way she did, but it really didn't help. "But to kill for the thrill of it? Or revenge? Or any other reason? No way." I was certain we were barking up the wrong tree.

"I'm not sure the killer can help it. Or if it's thrilling. He's probably deranged in some way, and is thinking he's doing the world a favor, like the Green River Killer who targeted prostitutes. Or Ted Bundy, who went after women with long brown hair. Not that it made sense to us, but they felt they were ridding the world of something bad or evil."

"Discovery again?" I asked.

"*Investigation* Discovery. Great crime documentaries." She nodded, not even trying to hide it.

"So, I'm with you that the killer is deranged, but I can't see any of that in Charlie. Can you? Has he said anything or behaved in a way that when you look back would give you a high creep-factor?"

"No." Her answer was instant. That was a visceral reaction. That's what we were trained for. Lightning reflexes, except when it came to wet tile flooring. No one had fast enough reflexes to overcome that one. But right now, she was going with her gut and so was I.

"No. Just no," I said.

"I agree," she said. "I feel better knowing that." I took in a deep breath of very humid air and sighed. That felt better.

"Pisses me off that in this day and age we're questioning our friends and people who have dedicated themselves to working for the community instead of against it," I said.

"Me, too." She slapped the wheel once. "Darn it."

"What's the problem? Charlie's off the hook." That was great news.

"But we aren't any closer to knowing who the killer is,

or finding Kelly's body." She reminded me of the initial circumstance that had gotten us into this case. Kelly's murder and no body. "So far we haven't heard whether her body has been found."

"No. That's right. Charlie would have told us, right?" My racing thoughts screeched to a halt, leaving black scorch marks on the pavement of my mind. "But a hurricane would be the perfect cover to hide a body, wouldn't it?"

"Or to get rid of one you've got stored somewhere," she said with a downward pull of her mouth. "In this heat, I hope it's--"

"Don't say it." I held up my hand to keep her from completing that sentence. I shook my head. *Nix. Nada. Nope. Negatory. Never.* I didn't care how many ways or how many times I had to say it, she was not going to complete that thought out loud. Now that we'd seen Kelly's picture, she was real to me. I didn't want to think of her body turning to a pool of foul-smelling liquids. Sigh. I'd thought of her body turning to a pool of foul-smelling liquids. Gak.

"Sorry."

"I know. Hard not to go there." I took in a cleansing breath and suddenly realized we were fogging up the windows while sitting there idling in the car as the pre-hurricane storm unloaded on us. I wiped away the steam from my window and looked out. The parking lot was almost empty now. A hurricane had a way of chasing off the tourists. And apparently anyone else with half a brain. Except for us as we were still sitting there.

"So, now what do we do?" she asked and turned on the defroster, then changed tactics and wiped away the fog with her hand.

"We probably ought to check in with the hospital and

see if they're going to have us come in early or something."
I shook my head. I hoped not. I thoroughly enjoyed my
four-day stretches off, and I didn't want any hurricane
interfering. But denial would only get me so far. There
would be no beach activity going on with gale-force winds
coming, unless it was running for your life.

"I hate to say this, but I'm worried about my car." She
patted the dashboard, like it was a living creature. I was
just glad she hadn't named it Christine. "I just paid it off
two months ago. I don't want it to get wrecked from the
storm."

I thought a second. "There's no covered parking at the
hospital, but surely there's got to be a parking garage
somewhere around here."

Again, I consulted my phone as rain drops cascaded
over the car. "There's a place in Southport we could park
your car until the storm blows over."

"It'll probably be really expensive to leave it there for
several days," she said. It was outside her budget that she
strictly kept to.

"But a lot cheaper than having to pay for hurricane
damage, right?"

"Right-o." She nodded. Logic always got her.

"Let's go get my SUV. We'll take your car up to Southport and park it, then come back in mine."

"Great plan." She nodded. Of course she nodded. It was
my idea, and it was a good one.

My phone rang as she backed us out of the parking lot
and Elmo came up on the four-by-six inch high-def screen.
I jumped, like he'd caught me talking about him.

"Hey there, my friend. What's going on?" I put him on
speaker so Jeannie could listen. I tried to forget that
moments ago we'd almost convinced each other his

brother was a serial killer. Neither of would ever speak of it again.

"I wanted to see what you two ladies were doing. Charlie's getting out of the hospital today instead of tomorrow. And there's a storm coming, so we're having us a combination welcome-home-hurricane party to celebrate." I could hear the joy in Elmo's voice. If Charlie had turned out to be a serial killer, Elmo would have been devastated. I'd be willing to bet his mama would be, too.

"That's fantastic news," Jeannie said. "But isn't it pretty soon for him to go home? I thought they wanted him in for another day of observation." Having a life-threatening emergency was nothing to blow off, even in a hurricane. There could still be damage to his body from the emergency intubation and a need for further monitoring.

"He should, but they gave him the option." Didn't sound like Elmo was in agreement with that, but was going along with the decision. "They're trying to empty out the hospital to prepare as an evacuation center because of the storm."

"Good plan. First, we'll check in with our supervisor and get back to you. Not sure what their emergency plans are, or how we fit into them." Hospitals and emergency services all had disaster plans for events such as aggressive patients or visitors, internal fires, bomb threats, chemical spills, even airplane disasters that were part of our training at every hospital. But a hurricane was a whole new concept for us. It wasn't just RACE: rescue, alarm, contain and evacuate, as with a fire. This was another disaster altogether. It was going to be big, and it was going to be messy.

"We're going to go to Southport right now to put Jeannie's car in a parking garage, then come back. We'll let you know after that." A gust of wind nearly pushed us sideways into the next lane, but Jeannie handled it, and kept us in our own lane. Hydroplane anyone? She did slow down to a crawl, despite other cars racing past us willy-nilly in the rain. They could hydroplane into a pole, but we weren't going to.

"Oh no, you're not. Don't do that," Elmo said, his voice firm.

"Uh, why not? Is it a bad idea or something?" Jeannie asked. "I just paid off my car and don't want to take any chances it'll get damaged in the storm."

"You just bring it and yourselves over to my mama's place. She has a garage the size of an airplane hanger. It's a storm bunker. Nothing'll get damaged in there. Everything will fit. You, your cars, everything. Just bring what you need for a few days. We'll have the rest."

"Wow. Are you sure? We don't want to impose on her good graces," Jeannie said, but I agreed.

"Nonsense. She'll whoop my hide if I didn't bring y'all to a safe place for a storm like what's coming." Elmo chuckled. "Even sick as she is, she can still guilt me into doing just about anything."

"Okay. That sounds like a great plan, but just so you know, guilt is highly overrated." I knew this from many years of devoted practice and attempts to eliminate it from my life. That was my resolution every year.

"Ain't that the truth?" he said.

I ended the call, and we made the drive to our apartment. It wasn't home. The apartments we lived in would never be home, but it was the place we hung our stethoscopes. That was the way of life for a travel nurse. One day we'd set down roots. Until then, we just lived different places on a temporary basis and it was okay with me.

I called the ICU and talked to Audrey. She never seemed to take a day off. As a charge nurse, she was probably pulling double duty today if the hospital was trying to get the less acutely ill patients discharged and home before the storm.

"Audrey? It's Piper and Jeannie. We wanted to know what our roles are for the disaster. Do we come in as scheduled, or what?" I asked.

"Oh, thank you for calling. We've had such a mess here." I knew she was pulling one of those pens from her hair to write herself a note on her clipboard. "It looks like you'll be the relief crew. Storm is expected to hit when you're off, so we'll just keep it that way. You need to find a safe place to lay low, or head out of town for a few days. Then you'll come in on your regular shifts as the relief crew. The people who are on now are going to have to stay straight through, twenty-four-seven until the worst of the storm passes and will need you here to replace them as scheduled."

"What about the calm? Would that be a good time to trade shifts or something, while the eye of the storm passes over?" It was an idea that just came to me. Thank you, Wikipedia.

"No, that's actually a bad idea. Although it is a temporary lull in the storm, there will be debris all over the place and the roads will be impassable. Oh, and snakes. There's usually snakes everywhere." She said that so nonchalantly, it took a second to sink in. As if she'd said there was sand all over the beach or something. Like it was a regular daily occurrence, but not to me.

I sat up straight as did the hair on all parts of my body. "Snakes? Seriously?" Gulp. I was so not going out in the eye of the storm. Check that off my list of things *not* to do any time soon. Or *ever*.

"Yes, they get flooded out of their dens when the water rises. Last big storm that came through we had more snake bites than I'd seen in years, so I'd like to avoid that with you two."

"Me, too." Double gulp. Although I'd been raised in an area that grew massive-sized eastern diamondback, copperheads, and timber rattlers, I wasn't friends with them and didn't want to start any new relationships at this point in my life. I was busy. They were busy. It wasn't going to be a good fit.

"I don't know if either of you have experienced a hurricane or not, but I can't stress to you enough that you need to seek higher ground. Get away from town and off the island if you can. It's very serious business." She took a breath. "So, it's best you two hide out someplace safe for the storm, and then come in when scheduled unless you hear differently from me."

"Won't the phone systems be down?" I expected electricity wires to be down.

"No. Here, we have buried phone cables, so at least the land lines will be working. And the hospital has generators for power. We'll have to see about the cell networks."

"We're going to a friend's home. Once we're there, I'll let you know the land line number." And if by some outside chance, Charlie did happen to be a serial killer, they'd know where to come to find our bodies.

"Excellent plan. We'll get through this, and see you in a few days," she said.

"Okay, see you then." Background noise escalated behind Audrey.

"One more thing. If the hospital is destroyed, don't

come back. Call your agency and find another contact." She disconnected the line.

We looked at each other. "Do you think she was serious about the hospital thing?" I asked. That never would have occurred to me.

"She sounded pretty serious." Jeannie pushed her lips out as she drove, and we pulled into the parking lot moments later. We got out and raced to the apartment. I had my keys out first, and we burst through the door, soaked to the skin.

I shook off like a wet dog, and Jeannie brushed the water from her arms in a little more dignified manner. "Let's hit the shower. It may be the last one we get for a few days," she said.

"Oh, right." We took off to our own bathrooms, scrubbed, shaved, and shampooed everything necessary for a few days. We packed up the supplies we thought we'd need for the next few days, which was essentially everything we owned, and stuffed them into plastic trash bags to keep them from getting soaked by the time we got to our cars.

We called Elmo, and got the information for his mother's place, drove both vehicles over there and sat for a second in disbelief. She *did* have a cement block airplane hangar. A modest home, typical of the poor south, crop farmers, sat in the front of the property filled with trees and bushes that bloomed glorious colors. Behind the house were acres of fields in various states of growth. Towering over it all was the big building. Someone had certainly prepared.

Elmo appeared outside the giant doors and directed us to drive right in. There were tons of people and cars already there. And Charlie, grinning from ear to ear, not looking like he'd just had a near-death experience at all. No serial killer signs anywhere I could see in his demeanor, and my suspicion melted away. These guys were our friends. We weren't going to disrespect them again. Neither of them had overstepped our boundaries and totally deserved our respect and friendship.

Charlie limped closer as we got out of our vehicles.

"There's my angels. We wouldn't let nothing happen to you," he said and embraced us, looking like his old self again. I was so relieved he wasn't a serial killer. It totally would have changed our friendship. And I couldn't have in good conscience put him on my Christmas card list. "Let me introduce you to my mama. She's been wanting to meet you."

"Oh, man, I'm soaking wet," I said after a thorough hug. So much for the nice hot showers we'd just had. We were soaked again by the time we'd gotten to the parking lot.

Charlie brought us to his mother, who sat in an old bent-wood hickory rocking chair. I'm sure it was at least a century old, and had probably been made in the hills of western North Carolina. Many a woman had rocked their babies in chairs such as that. Though she might be gray in the hair, she was certainly keen-eyed.

"Mama? These are the two ladies who saved my life," Charlie said without preamble. "This is my mama, Lucinda King."

"Oh, bless you. Just bless you both." Lucinda held her old, gnarled hands out to ours as tears poured from her eyes. She'd been a hard-working woman her whole life. It showed in the history on her hands. No doubt about it. She'd washed clothes on a washboard in a bucket, hauled vegetables in from the field, preserved them for the long winters. She'd rocked her babies, and prayed over her Bible with them. People thought the road map of a life was written on the face. I thought it was the hands. Lucinda's life was written right there in the lines on her soft hands. "Come here, and let me hug you both." It didn't matter that we were of different races or were soaking wet. None of it mattered. We were the women who'd saved her son's life. Race didn't enter into it. It never had for any of us, and that was the part I found the most amazing in this new relationship we'd developed with the brothers King. They were just great guys. Both cops. Both amazing men. We, however, were just as amazing. Possibly more *amazinger*, since we'd saved Charlie's life.

We leaned over and hugged the tiny woman who had somehow given birth to two of the largest men I'd ever seen. She was frail. I could feel the bones in her shoulders, and her ribs. She'd obviously lost weight due to her illness, and was just skin and bones now.

"I thank the good Lord for putting you where you needed to be to save my Charlie's life." She sniffed away the tears. "I don't know what I'd do without him. Without either of my boys."

"I'm just glad you didn't have to find out," I said and looked at her sons, but spoke to her. "I'm sure you had your hands full while they were growing up, didn't you?"

"Oh, that's the truth of it, right there, now." She held both of her hands raised up in front of her. "I had the Good Book in one hand, and a switch in the other. Kept 'em both in line."

"You did a fine job, Miss Lucinda," Jeannie said. "We've become good friends with your sons quickly, and they've graciously invited us to be here through the storm. We hope that's okay with you." Always the politer, more conscientious one of us. But it mattered. Manners always mattered.

"I'd have been disappointed if they hadn't brought you here. Friends look out for each other in the good times and the bad." She shook her head, and for a moment she was reliving the bad, then she came back to the present with a big toothy grin. Still had all her choppers. That was a sign of a healthy life, too.

"Tell me you don't have to go to work in the middle of the storm, too, do you?" I asked Charlie. Elmo looked like he was geared up for Mad Max III.

"No. I have leave for a few days to recover from my recent brush with death. There's no way I can fulfill my duties as a street cop right now." He looked dejected. "They'll probably reassign me to a desk until I'm fit for duty again."

"Look on the bright side. It'll only be for a few days, and you get to hang out with us," Jeannie said, trying to cheer him up.

"But my boy Elmo has to go out in all that, and I worry," Lucinda said and placed one hand over her heart. "I so worry about him out there in danger."

"I'll be okay, Mama." Elmo put a comforting hand on her shoulder, then bent over and kissed the top of her head. "I'm just glad I don't have to be trapped in the same building as Charlie for three days."

"What? Oh, you," she said and patted his hand. "You're such a tease."

"People with a sense of humor live longer, Miss Lucinda. Did you know that?" I asked, trying to distract her from the very real possibility that Elmo could be injured or killed in the storm.

"No, I didn't. But I think that's right." The feverish pace

of her rocking slowed, so my sneaky tactic was working. Distraction was an art.

"I may never die," I said, and she laughed as I'd hoped.

"That's the way to think, baby girl." She placed both of her hands over her heart. "It's humor and love that will get you through the hard times and the good."

"You be safe out there," Jeannie said and raised her arms for a big Elmo hug, and I got in line behind her, like we were lining up for a ride at the fair. I was just glad he didn't charge, 'cause I didn't have any tickets.

❧ 18 ❧

WE ALL GO A LITTLE MAD SOMETIMES - PSYCHO

How dare they? How *dare* they? Rage filled him as he struggled to lift Mother from the back seat of the car and get her into the house before the storm hit. She was no help, just lying there in the back seat. Reaching in with one hand, he sat her upright. Even with the seat belt on, she'd fallen over, no longer able to keep herself upright. With one hand, he brought the wheel chair closer to the car, but the damned wind kept pushing it away. Finally, he got her into it, struggling against the wind, with her dead weight, and the stabbing pain in his leg. Pausing a moment, he clutched his leg above the injury. It wasn't going away like he'd thought. Father had always told him to tough out every injury he'd ever had and this was no different, or so he'd thought. Every movement hurt. Every day it throbbed with pain, no matter how many pain killers he took. He'd dug into his father's old stash of medications and took a few of them, but most were expired. Maybe that was why they hadn't worked. The pain in his leg kept him from focusing, resting or sleeping, clinging to him like a leach that ate at him, day and night. It was a constant, throbbing reminder of that woman's treachery, that nurse who'd stabbed him. Nurses were supposed to help others, not hurt and maim like she'd done.

A gust of wind swirled and whirled around the red brick house, tugging and plucking at the bushes and vines. The rose vine, climbing up the trellis, trembled at the power of the storm. He'd pruned and manicured the vegetation after Father had been unable to any longer. It was doubtful the roses would survive the storm. Mother would be upset to know her prized roses had been destroyed. She valued those damned roses more than anything. Even him.

Pushing Mother from the side door into the kitchen took nearly every ounce of energy he had, and he paused a second to catch his breath, brushed the sweat from his forehead. Though the temperature had dropped significantly, he sweated with his efforts. He pushed her inside the kitchen and applied the brakes on the wheelchair. "I'll be right back, Mother. I have to put the car in the garage."

She didn't say anything. She rarely did any more. After the ambulance had taken her to the hospital, she rarely made a sound. The doctor said she'd had a stroke. A big one that had resulted from her fall. She'd no longer be able to swallow or communicate again. But that hadn't been the case. She communicated quite directly with her eyes as she glared at him. She didn't need her voice to speak to him. He heard it in his mind. He knew exactly what she was saying. Her words echoed in his mind, telling him how incompetent he was, what a disappointment he'd been, how ungrateful he was to her.

"Mother?" Trying to rid his mind of the echo of the past, he shook his head, trying to remove the fuzziness behind his eyes, the stabbing pain at the base of his neck.

He called her name, waiting for her response. Hoping for a response. But there was nothing. Even now, when he'd saved her life, taken revenge for her, she had nothing to say to him.

Rain had plastered her thin hair to her pale scalp, making her look like she'd lost all of the hair and with it, her beauty. She was gaunt. Thin and ghostly-looking. Her sunken cheeks and prominent eye sockets gave evidence to her weight loss, despite the food he'd brought from work and fed to her every day. No matter how much he fed her, she still lost weight. With one glance back at her to ensure she wasn't going to fall from the chair, he pushed his drenched hair back from his face.

He limped to the car and parked it in the garage. The light switch to the garage door opener signaled something was in the way and it wouldn't go down. Cursing, he stalked to the entrance of the garage, looking for something that had interfered with the sensor. The garage was clean. Immaculate. Just the way Father had kept it. What could possibly be in the way?

His bag of tools. His backpack had fallen from the hook he'd hung it on and now blocked the eye sensor. He picked up the pack and placed it on the work station. That's where he should have kept it in the first place. Where he could find it easily enough for his work that was never finished.

The garage door then closed with a final, mechanical thump.

Trying to ignore the pain in his leg, he limped through the garage back to the house. There wasn't enough room to get Mother out of the car in the garage, that's why he'd had to get her out in the rain. Worried about leaving her alone for even a minute, he gritted his teeth and entered the kitchen.

She hadn't moved. Hardly blinked as she sat there staring into space. He had to get her changed, get her warmed up. "Would you like a cup of tea, Mother?" he asked and stroked her head. She was cold. Her skin very chilled. If she got pneumonia it would be *their* fault for sending her home in the rain. They should have kept her in the hospital until she was better. At least until after the storm passed.

Emergencies only. Disaster plan instituted. It was all a bunch of rot designed to eliminate the poor and the infirm from the community. He knew how the government worked. How they all worked. It was the same. Every man for himself.

He took off his rain poncho and hung it by the door, careful not to drip water on the floor, or Mother would be very upset. It didn't take much to upset her any more. If he were honest with himself, he'd have realized it hadn't ever taken much to upset Mother. He shuddered as the heat of a shameful memory blazed over him.

When he'd been eight years old, she'd taken a stick and beaten him with it until bruises covered his back, his arms and legs. He'd done nothing. Nothing, he thought, as he drifted back into the memory. He'd just been playing. Just been doing what eight-year-old boys did when they were bored.

But Mother hadn't liked it. Not at all. The situation had made *her* look bad. Had brought up questions about her mothering skills when the police were called and the firemen had to put out the blaze he'd started. He didn't remember anymore where he'd gotten the matches, or why he'd started the fire. That part of the memory was gone. Beaten out of him.

The matches had looked like fun. He'd been mesmerized by the flames as he fed dry pine needles and small sticks into the base of the fire, making it bigger and bigger. A gust of wind kicked up and took the flames from him. Took them down the alley behind the house and burned the open field behind the hospital.

He hadn't known that it had been the driest summer for decades in North Carolina history. He hadn't known the wind was coming. He'd just been playing, and she'd beaten him for it.

Silently, she'd stood beside him, one hand clenching his shoulder, one hand clenching a heavy stick, as the police and firemen drove away after a stern warning not to play with fire.

He'd learned his lesson as tears streamed from his eyes, sobs spurted from him. He'd told her he was sorry, but she hadn't believed him. And she'd taken out her rage on him.

She'd made him see it was *his* fault that the fire was so destructive. *His* fault people looked at her and clucked their tongues, gossiping about her and the wayward son she'd been forced to raise. He'd seen it, finally. It *had* been his fault, but he'd just been a kid.

Clutching the handles of the wheelchair, he seethed for the defenseless boy he'd been back then. It had taken weeks for all of the pain to go away, for the bruises to fade. He'd stayed in bed for three days, unable to move, unable to get out of bed to eat or get to the bathroom.

When Mother had opened the door to the stench he'd made, she'd made him clean it up himself.

He'd spent his life trying to make amends to her over it.

Now, he looked at her unblinking eyes, covered with the film of cataracts, and had trouble finding any sympathy for her. Now, she was just an old woman with no power over him.

She blinked and turned her milky gaze to him, and he pushed the wheelchair forward toward her room.

She had no power over him. She had no power, he reminded himself. But with those eyes, she could direct him to do anything she wanted.

Guilt surging up in him, he hurried. He placed the wheelchair beside the bed, then dashed as quickly as he could to the linen closet for dry towels. After changing her, tucking her into bed, and raising her up with pillows to ease her breathing, he stood back. "I'll get you some tea, Mother. You'll like that, won't you?" He retrieved the supplies from the car the hospital had sent home with them.

A feeding tube and pump, all the materials he'd need to keep her alive. At least for a while, they'd said. Somehow, he had to put it all together and remember what they'd said. He had to keep her alive. She had to live, or he'd die, too.

If she died, they'd all die. He'd make sure of it.

"Hello!" A female voice rose over the roar of the storm.

Startled, he reached into his pocket to grasp his blade. He'd expected no one. No one should be in their house. Had they come to take Mother away from him finally? He hurried to the hallway and looked into the kitchen. A woman stood in the open doorway of the kitchen. She was drenched from the rain. She was a tiny woman with pink hair, now plastered to her head. The blue scrubs hung heavy with water. "I'm sorry to come in like that, but with the storm, I decide to risk it." She shrugged and gave a shy smile. "I'm sorry."

"What are you doing here?" Seething. Trembling with the rage of it. How dare they intrude on him and Mother in their time of need. In their private space. She didn't look like a caseworker come to take Mother from him. She was alone. She wasn't going to take Mother by herself, and he released the blade.

"I'm one of the nurses from the hospital. I've come to check on you and your mother. I was worried when you were discharged so quickly that you wouldn't remember how to set up the tube feeding and stuff, so I came to see if you needed help." She hesitated, dropped her gaze to the floor for a second. "I hope that's okay I just came by."

A warm beat in his heart pushed past the coldness, and he stepped forward. "Yes, please. Come right in." He held out one hand to direct her inside. "Close and lock the door, if you don't mind," he said and smiled as she entered, then turned and locked the door behind her.

☙❧

"WE HAVE TO GET THE INFORMATION OUT TO THE NURSES now," I said, "before the cell phone towers are out of commission."

"Good point." Jeannie pulled her laptop from her bag and logged on. "I can send a group text to everyone, and they can decide if they want to be in the group after that. I'm including the nurse who's coming in a few days. I just hope it doesn't scare her off." Jeannie plugged away on the keyboard for a few minutes, then read back the text for my approval. "But at least they'll have the information."

"I like the part about being safe, coming up with a

buddy system to walk to the parking lot, and if people have to go smoke, do it in pairs, if possible," I said, approving of the plan. Short, sweet, to the point.

"I know. Seems like the security department should be doing this, don't you think?" she asked.

"They probably have their hands full preparing for the storm, getting the staff secured for the duration. That kind of stuff." Otherwise, they should have been all over this situation as well as the police.

"Probably right," she said and raised her brows at me. "Send?"

"Do it. No more time to spend on it." If we'd been able to, I'd have loved to have had an in-person meeting with everyone, sort of a Town Hall event. Since the storm caught us by surprise, there hadn't been enough time to plan anything like that.

My number was also on the list and in a few seconds, I had verification the text had gone out. In seconds, we had confirmation that the majority of the recipients responded positively, and were going to take this safety issue seriously.

"Awesome," I said as texts started blowing up my phone. "Look at that. Looks like it's a hit." I held my hand up, and Jeannie gave me a high-five.

"What kind of mischief are you two up to now?" Charlie asked, trying to see around Jeannie's computer, but she had one of those privacy screens on it. He couldn't see anything unless he was facing the screen square on.

"Not mischief," I said. I wondered what made him think that? We were innocents. Usually. Sort of. Mostly, anyway.

His expression didn't change. All he did was raise his

brows to question my intentions and integrity. I hadn't convinced him. "Uh-huh," was all he said. Cynic.

I narrowed my eyes at him. "You're a very suspicious man, Charlie King."

He chuffed out a quick laugh. "*Cop*. What else is new?"

That made me laugh. "For sure."

"Seriously, what are you doing?" he asked and leaned closer.

"We created a task force, I guess you could call it," Jeannie said and turned her laptop so Charlie could see the spread sheet.

"You did? All on your own without any authority?" he asked.

"It's a very small task force," I said. "With the storm coming, we had to act quickly, so decided we'd take the heat for winging it without authority." We were so good at stuff like that. Who needed authority when you could wing it the way we did?

"We just put together a texting group to warn nurses at the hospital to be safe, to have a buddy when going to the parking lot after work, stuff like that," I said. Those seemed to be the most important issues we could think of.

"And to quit smoking," Jeannie added with a nod. "Smoking will kill you."

"That's right," I said, then spoke to Charlie. "We talked to Lilly, the nurse who was attacked on a smoke break." That seemed like an important thing to tell him, since we were already divulging our entire plan to him. "She's decide to quit smoking after that experience."

"Are you two out of your minds?" His eyes widened. "You're doing the police work for us. That information should have gone out in a press release from the Southport station, warning people, not in a text from you two." He was irritated, I could clearly see that, but we had good reason for doing the things we did. Sometimes, not so much, but in this instance, we had good reason.

"The storm warnings and evacuations take precedence over everything else, you know that. There's no way the news station was going to trump the hurricane coverage for anything, not even this. And we couldn't wait until after the storm to send it out," I said. "I get it. You're worried about us, but we're not going to endanger ourselves by sending out a text to people to be more careful than they have been doing. Right?" I hoped he wouldn't stay mad at us for long.

"You're right. But I still don't like it," he said. "You're taking chances you shouldn't, and you have to stop. What if the killer is another nurse, and you've just given him all the information he needs to keep killing? Have you thought of that?" he asked.

"Uh, no." Jeannie and I looked at each other. "No, we hadn't," she said in a small voice, sounding much like Piglet. I guess that made me Eeyore. An ass, and didn't even know it.

"Wow," I said and slumped in my chair as something occurred to me. "The storm is the perfect cover for someone to hide a body," I said.

"Or get rid of one already hidden," Jeannie said. "Like Kelly."

Charlie looked at the two of us. "Are you sure you're nurses and not undercover detectives or something?"

"No, we're really not detectives," Jeannie said with a very pleased grin.

"It's covered in our contracts under, *other duties as assigned*," I said, trying to lighten the intense mood and decrease the feeling of guilt. If we'd inadvertently given information to a serial killer on how to do it better, I'd never forgive myself. "I like the sounds of helping solve the murders with you, Charlie. I'm not sure that's allowed, but we'd like to help however we can." Help people. It's what we did. How we were made. We were nurses and born problem-solvers. Being awesomely amazing was just whipped cream on top.

"I guess we'll have to see what happens after the storm. There's nothing we can do about anything until then," he said, and I could tell he was thinking hard.

"We just want to help. That's all," Jeanie said and placed a gentle hand on his arm..

"I don't know about that. There's a big difference between accidentally coming across a crime scene or evidence and purposefully seeking it out. There are protocols and processes that have to be followed or evidence could get thrown out in court," Charlie said. "I'm sure Elmo would discourage you, too. It's just too dangerous. There are too many unknowns."

"That's disappointing," Jeannie said and slumped in her seat. "I was hoping for some excitement on this assignment."

"Being a travel nurse and going through a hurricane isn't exciting enough for you?" Charlie asked, shock widening those expressive eyes of his. "You must be a thrill seeker, Jeannie. You may look like a closet accountant, with your sensible glasses and hair pulled into a ponytail, but you'd rather be jumping out of airplanes, wouldn't you?" He grinned, and I knew he was trying to imagine her diving from an airplane.

Jeannie shook her head. "No, way. I like my feet solidly on the ground, but I do like some adventure in my adventure."

"After a while, it's all about the scenery on an assignment. The nursing part is all the same. We can do it in our sleep," I said. Sometimes I thought I had. "But it's nice to shake it up, do something different." I shrugged. "That's why we take different kinds of assignments, not just ICU all the time. Gives us a break from the stress, and we always have something interesting to do."

"Like chase down murderers?" he asked, his voice flat, his eyes deadpan.

"Not by intention. If we find information that can help out, we'd like to do it." Jeannie looked at me. "Correct me if I'm wrong, but we believe it's our duty to do so."

"You got it," I said in total agreement. I considered myself a patriot on a small scale. I wasn't going to start a revolution or anything, but I had my standards and there were things I couldn't walk away from. Having grown up a big fan of one of America's first patriots, Ben Franklin, I couldn't walk away from this, either. Ben would have seriously disapproved.

"I think you need to stick to the safety alerts and let the dangerous stuff to the cops." A scowl pulled the corners of his mouth down, and he frowned. That was a mean face, but not nearly as scary as Elmo's scary face. Charlie would definitely need a mask on Halloween.

"Oh, look at you, all tough now," I said with a laugh. *"Watch out little lady, and let the men do the hard work."* I gave my best John Wayne impression, but it was never going to be even close. I didn't have enough testosterone.

"That's not what I'm saying," Charlie said and sat forward, suddenly more serious. "It's dangerous to go out there and put yourselves deliberately in danger to catch a criminal. You're not trained for it. You're not the right people to find him."

I looked at Jeannie as an idea crossed my mind before looking both ways. "But we're the right targets, aren't we?"

"Oh, no." He pointed a long finger at us. "Absolutely not. If you even think of trying to draw out a killer by being bait, I'll lock the two of you up until we catch him, and you'll have nothing to say about it." A vein pulsed in his forehead, and I could see another one ticking away in his neck. I hoped he didn't have high blood pressure. Just by being a black male he was at risk. I was beginning to think hanging around us was a health risk for him, too.

"Okay, calm down, Charlie. We're not going to do anything that stupid," Jeannie said.

"At least not without help," I said. To be that monumentally stupid, we'd need a lot more help.

"Yes, that's right." A nod from Jeannie let me know we were on the same wavelength. "Definitely. We can only do so much."

"What-are-you, out of your minds?" He nearly shot out of his chair. Though he was speaking to the both of us, he was looking at me, like I was the one responsible for all the bad ideas here. Maybe I was, but just didn't want to admit it yet. Denial has served me well for years, I wasn't about to kick the habit now.

The pulse in Charlie's neck drummed right along without any signs of slowing down. Rats. We really had to stop tormenting him.

"Seriously, we're just pulling your leg," I said and hoped I was telling the truth. "We envision years ahead of traveling and some day settling down with husbands and babies, so we're not going to do anything to jeopardize that future by putting our necks on the chopping blocks-"

"Deliberately," Jeannie added.

"-deliberately. But we're also determined to help out

where and when we can, to assist the cops in finding this jackass."

"Ja--Did you just say jackass?" Charlie asked.

"Yes. I did. Proudly. Why?" I knew way more bad words, but was trying to keep them restrained when in public or around nice old ladies like Miss Lucinda.

"Most nurses I've met swear like sailors, especially the ones I meet in the ER. Whew. They can filet the skin off your ears in seconds, but that's the first time I've heard you swear." He relaxed back into the chair, apparently having decided we weren't an immediate threat to ourselves, or to the general public.

"She does swear quite a bit when she's driving, though," Jeannie said giving away my secret.

"Damn. There. I swore again. Happy now?" I could swear right along with those ER nurses, but had been trying to at least pretend I had some manners.

The wind kicked up higher than it had been. The roof creaked and moaned, straining against the pressure of the gale-force winds. I looked overhead at the sturdy-looking wooden beams reinforced with steel girders that would crush me in half a second if they came tumbling down. They looked like they'd hold, but I didn't know anything about structure or the architecture needed to withstand a hurricane like we were suddenly in the middle of.

"Charlie? Is this place gonna hold?" I asked and reached for his hand. He took mine firmly in his large, warm one. "It's gonna hold, for sure." He looked up, scanned the roof and nodded. "We only had the roof blown off one time."

"Seriously?" Panic began to set in, and I clenched his hand.

Charlie laughed. "Just pulling *your* leg now. This is as sturdy as they come."

"So, the roof's not gonna come down and crush us to death, right?" I asked with a cringe. I still wasn't certain if Charlie was still kidding or not.

"It'll hold just fine," Lucinda said. She rocked back and forth a few times. "Charlie, I think I need some food, now. My stomach is telling me it's time to eat." With her cancer treatment, I was sure it was messing up her eating schedule.

"Good timing. I think Leroy has the grill just about ready."

Charlie stood, pushed himself up with his hands, taking some of the strain off of his leg as he got out of the low chair.

A loud metallic click plunged the whole building into darkness.

I screamed in my mind. I never screamed out loud unless absolutely necessary. I did jump. Since it was dark, and there were no witnesses.

"Uh, Charlie?" I asked. hoping I didn't sound like I was afraid of the dark. I wasn't. I was afraid of things *in* the dark.

A flashlight beam turned on and illuminated Charlie's face. "Stop that. You look like something out of the Blair Witch movie," I said.

After that, I couldn't take him seriously.

❧ 19 ❧

COME INTO MY PARLOR, SAID THE SPIDER TO
THE FLY - FABLE

There was so much to do. At work. At home. He had to get both of them boarded up before the brunt of the storm collided with the shoreline. Sometimes that slowed down a hurricane, but sometimes it made the storm linger to unleash its worst.

Now, a complication had been added to the mix. The nurse that had arrived on his doorstep. How could there ever have been a better gift given to him? He never would have thought it would happen that way.

"Please come in," he said. "My apologies. I remember you, but I've forgotten your name."

"Mitzi. That's okay. I'm sure you met so many nurses when your mother was in the hospital. It's easy to forget all the names." She set her backpack down just inside the door. "I'm going to take my shoes off so I don't track water through the house." She toed off her sparkly pink nurse shoes and left them beside the backpack. That was proper. Mother would appreciate the gesture. Mitzi was polite, respectful, and he relaxed a little.

"Let me get you a towel," he said and limped once

again to the linen closet. He hoped they'd have enough dry linens and towels to make it through the storm. If not, he'd have to set up a clothes line in the house when the power went off. Mother wouldn't like that, having a clothes line set up like the poor folk in town, but it couldn't be helped.

"I'll come with you," Mitzi said and followed him. "Where are your supplies?" she asked looking in the living room, but they weren't there. Mother never would have approved at having all of that stuff out where everyone could see it. What if someone dropped by, and they saw all that? She'd have been humiliated. Not that they had visitors any more. No one ever stopped by. Except for her. Mitzi.

"Everything is in her room. I just brought them in." He handed her a towel, and she accepted it with a nod of thanks, then dried her face and arms on it.

"I'm sorry, but I have to hurry. I have to go back to the hospital soon. Let's get it set up. I can show you how to adjust it so it will continue if the storm cuts the power off." She gave a nervous laugh and looked up at him with her bright blue eyes. "I'm sure it'll be off, what am I saying?" She placed the damp towel on the bedside table and approached Mother. "There she is," Mitzi said and spoke to Mother as if she understood. There was compassion in Mitzi's voice. Sympathy. And pity.

That angered him. He didn't need pity. Not from anyone. But he needed Mitzi. Definitely needed her.

"Yes, I'd appreciate it if you could get it set up and show me." He stood beside her, towering over the short little thing. He watched as she removed everything from the packaging with swift, efficient hands as if she'd done this dozens of times. That was good. She could keep Mother alive as long as necessary.

"The machine has to be plugged in to charge the battery, but when the power goes out, unplug it, and it'll run for several hours. After that, you take the tubing out of the machine to let it run by gravity." She put it all together, explaining as she went, but he wasn't as focused on it as he should have been. He was fascinated by her little body. How efficiently she moved. How much knowledge she possessed. Maybe he should just keep her with him to take care of Mother, so he could work. His mind raced with the possibilities.

"Thank you. I'm sure it will all be fine." He pushed his right hand into the pocket of his fatigues. He'd dug out his old clothing to wear during the storm. No use getting his good clothing wet when the old Army gear worked better for the situation he'd found himself in. The weapon he always kept there comforted him, and he closed his fingers around the firm length, used his thumb to test the tip. Sharp. Always sharp. Always at the ready.

"Darn it," Mitzi said. "I can't get this one open." She turned to him and held out a plastic package containing the bag the liquid went into. "Can you open it?"

He took the package from her with his left hand and pulled the dagger from his pocket with his right hand. Her eyes widened at the sight of the weapon. "Yes. I'll get it."

"You are prepared, aren't you?" She gave a nervous laugh and took the package back from him, glanced at the blade one more time. "Are you okay, though?" she asked. "I noticed you're limping. I didn't notice it the other day at the hospital."

"I'm fine. Sometimes the weather makes my bones hurt."

"I see. You're your own weather barometer, right?" She poured the contents of two cans of feeding solution into the bag and hung it from the pole the little machine was clipped to.

"You could say that." That was a good explanation for the limp that kept getting worse. People had started to notice it. He couldn't hide it any longer, so that was a plausible story for the issue. "I have an injury that flares up when the weather changes."

"I'm sorry to hear that. Chronic pain can take over you life, can't it?" Mitzi said.

He looked at Mother and nodded. "Yes, you could say that, too." *She* was his chronic pain that had taken over his life. There was truth in that.

Carefully, he returned the dagger to his pocket and the sheath hidden inside.

Maybe he didn't need it right now. He could use the jute if necessary. There was plenty of that to spare. If he needed it. He didn't know yet.

She adjusted a few things, then turned to him. "That's all there is to it."

"Really? It looked like a lot." He would forget it. He knew that. He hadn't paid enough attention, like Mother had always said.

"It can be overwhelming at first, but it's really not hard. Just has a lot of steps." She reached into her pocket and withdrew a square folded piece of paper and held it out to him. "I've written down the steps for you to make it as easy as I could."

For a second, he just looked at it and then at her. Then he took the paper from her tiny little hands. She would be so easy to kill. So easy to suppress. "Thank you for your help. I appreciate it." So easy to make disappear.

"I've got to get back to the hospital. I'm staying through the duration." She placed a warm hand on his arm in a comforting gesture and offered up the sweetest smile. One of his hands would fit around her neck. He probably didn't even need the jute. "After the storm, I'll come back and check on you again, if that's okay."

"Sure." She'd be back. That was good. Then she could stay longer. Much longer.

She turned her back and prepared to leave the room. He clenched his fists into his pockets. It would be so easy now. So very easy to take her now, but he couldn't. He still had too much work to do. "Oh, one more thing."

"Yes?"

"If she happens to pass away during the storm, just wait it out, or come to the hospital ER and let someone there know." Sadness filled her eyes. It wasn't pity, it was sadness. "I'm sorry she's not doing well. I know she means a lot to you."

"Thank you," he said as his throat tightened. She did understand. But she was wrong. Mother wasn't going to die. If she did, he would die, too.

Silently, he stood there are Mitzi walked down the hallway, through the kitchen, retrieved her shoes and backpack, and left through the same door she'd entered.

Turning to face Mother, he watched her breathe, then raised his eyes to hers. The silent stare she'd always given him. The unblinking gaze stared back at him now.

"Yes, I know, Mother. I should have killed her, but she was nice." As he spoke to her, a tremor shot through his leg, flaring out to his hip and down to his knee. He cringed with it. Clutched the door frame and clenched his teeth. "Yes, Mother. I'll get that cup of tea before the electricity goes off." He staggered to the kitchen and turned on the kettle. After that, he retrieved the camping stove and propane cylinders from the garage. They'd never camped. Not even when he'd been a kid. They'd promised, Mother and Father, but they'd never fulfilled that promise. There was always too much work to do. Something else always came first, before him. They kept the camp stove for emergencies. It was the same with every big storm.

Pull out the emergency gear. Put away the emergency gear. It was old and rusted in places, but it still worked. He just had to remember to buy new propane cylinders at times, but couldn't recall if he'd purchased any this year. The dust covering the ones he found was an obvious sign he'd failed. That he hadn't purchased new ones to prepare for hurricane season. How foolish of him. He was irresponsible, just as Mother had always told him. Always said with her eyes.

There was no way he'd find any now. Stores would already be bought out, and there wouldn't be a pack of matches within a hundred miles. They'd just have to get by with what they had. That's what Father would have said. He needed to think more like Father.

He hadn't built a fire since he was eight years old, so he didn't know if he even remembered how. Suddenly, his back ached. His shoulders pinged with pain, and he thought it might not be a good idea for him to build a fire.

HOURS PASSED AS THE STORM BATTERED ITS POWER OVER THE little island. The eye passed as expected, and I couldn't help myself. Jeannie, either. We begged Charlie to let us go out into the eye of the storm. Like kids wanting to go on a crazy ride one more time. We wanted to see what had happened outside. What it looked like. What damage had already been done, so we could brace ourselves for what was to come. As long as there weren't any snakes.

Charlie opened the heavy steel doors to a sky that was astonishingly blue. And bright. Not a drop of rain fell from above.

"What?" I took a few steps outside and took in breaths of fresh, humidity-saturated air. "It looks like a lovely day right now."

"It does, but it's the devil's handiwork, as Mama would say. Just the calm before the next part of the storm." Charlie shoved his shades on and looked like he did the day we met. Except for the missing uniform. He just looked he was out for a nice stroll on a beautiful day.

"Will you look at that?" Jeannie said, awe filling her voice. I didn't have to guess what she was looking at. We were surrounded by debris. Lucinda's home was far enough away from the beach that it wasn't affected by the rise of the tide, but everywhere we looked, something was out of place. Trash cans scattered all over the field. Palm leaves littered the yard. Trees looked as if they'd been stripped by a monstrous vacuum. Not a tree bigger than a sapling stood upright. Everything had been turned over and roots hung out of the ground. Someone's patio furniture had been upended, blown away and rested on top of Lucinda's roof.

"Charlie, look at the chairs up there." Jeannie shielded her eyes with one hand and pointed with the other.

"Oh, man. We should get that down before it scrapes her roof right off." He said a bad word. I felt better knowing he had a few up his sleeve, too.

"Yeah, and you got a new set of patio furniture. At least

a few deck chairs, right?" I said. "Look at the bright side. Free furniture."

Toys, clothing and boxes scatted all over the place like someone had just upended the town and shook it all out. Tools. A small car. Even the advertising van from a pest control company had been washed down the road and sat in a ditch like a dead cockroach.

"This is just crazy. If you didn't know we were in the middle of a hurricane, you wouldn't know what was going on. You'd just think it was a rainy day," I said, amazed at the landscape.

"Let me have the boys get that furniture off the roof. Hang tight and don't go anywhere," Charlie said, giving us a warning glare. He already knew us too well. What he didn't know was that we didn't always seek out situations. Sometimes they just fell into our laps. How were we responsible for that? He retreated back into the bunker, and we stood in the eerie calm, still in awe of the power of Mother Nature. Then I heard it. I turned my head to the side, trying to decide if I was hallucinating or not.

"There it is again. Did you hear that?" I asked Jeannie. I frowned, concentrating, listening intently for the noise to come again.

"What?" It came again as she spoke over it. I couldn't get a clear idea of where it was. I crouched down. Jeannie did too. "What are we listening for?" she asked in a whisper.

"Cat. Or kittens. I know I heard something." It was my soul that heard it. The soul of a saver.

"Oh, no. We have to find them," she said. We got down on our knees and listened some more. The unspoken understanding was that if they were out in the storm, they might not survive the next round.

That's when Charlie and two of his nephews, his sister's teen-aged kids, emerged from the building. *Of course* they emerged from the building at that very moment. And what did we look like crawling around on our hands and knees? Like we'd lost our minds. They all stared at us. Then Charlie directed them to quit gawking and get the furniture off the roof.

"Okay, crazy girls. What are you doing, now?" Charlie stood in the waning sun with his hands on his hips looking at us. Apparently, no longer surprised by anything we did. That was good. He'd become acclimated to our vibe. Nothing in the future should surprise him either. Not that I was planning to do anything stupid. Sometimes stupid just happened, and I was in the immediate area, so I got blamed. Go figure.

"Charlie, you have to help us. There's a cat out here," Jeannie implored him.

"Or kittens. I might have heard more than one," I added in case it wasn't just one. "Probably a mama cat with her babies." I tried to draw on his sympathies. Hearing there was a cat on the loose didn't always get the right reaction, but when referring to it as a *mama cat with babies?* Oh, that pulled on the heart strings of anyone who actually had a heart. I didn't know about anyone else who didn't have a heart. I tried to avoid hanging out with people like that.

"Oh, Lordy. You've gone and done it now," Charlie shook his head and groaned.

"What? What have we done?" Jeannie asked as I crawled away, closer to the corner of another outbuilding. Maybe they were in there. I could hear little mewls that I was now convinced were baby kittens. Kittens were babies, but *baby kittens* sounded just so much more pathetic.

"If my mama hears there's one of her cats out here with her babies in the storm, she'll be out here crawling around on the ground with the two of you looking for them." He cast a fearful look over his shoulder, as if he knew she'd be coming out the door any second.

A fat drop of rain hit me on the back, soaked through my shirt, and I looked up. Kinda hard when you were on your knees in the grass looking for lost kittens, but I managed. The sky was turning already. The bright white fluffy country clouds had met their angry goth cousins from the city. They were gonna throw down pretty quick. It was gonna get ugly again. Soon.

"Come on, people. Let's find them." Charlie bent at the waist, and did his best to try not to look as if he were looking for baby kittens.

"*Kitty, kitty, kitty*," I called in my best cat-caller voice. I knew how to call cats. It was the way I'd acquired my first cat, Puff, who'd wandered away from a neighboring farm. I was seven, I think. My sharp hearing had caught it's pitiful cries. I'd called and called as I'd walked through the hay field until I found that little orange and white tabby cat. I bundled him up in my arms and took him home with me, determined that he would be mine forever and ever. Or at least until my mother found out.

We wandered and called, as raindrops continued to fall. They weren't the drops of a nice summer storm, they were the big, fat ones that hurt when they landed in the middle of your forehead, like a bug on a windshield. Calling one more time, I got down on my belly and looked under the shed into a dugout hole, and saw eight sets of glowing eyes.

"I found them," I shouted and the others came running, even the nephews. They were more interested in seeing what the crazy girls were going to do next, than running from the storm. I just hoped they weren't taking pictures. Once on the internet, always on the internet.

I took a breath, knowing it might be my last for a while and wished for some swim goggles. I couldn't see into the dark hole very well. I only saw eyes. I could be reaching into a den of skunks, and I was about to get a face full of skunk piss in the next two seconds. Technically, it wasn't piss, but when it was in your face and mouth, it certainly was.

"Watch yourself. They could be feral," Charlie said standing to my right.

"Yeah. And I notice you're not down on your knees helping me, either." I stretched until I felt the fur of one little creature against my fingers. I grabbed it. And waited. Amazingly enough, a kitten and a baby skunk probably felt about the same in the dark. I dared to take a relieved breath. No skunk spray. Awesome. They'd let me back in the building again.

"What? I'm not the crazy one here," Charlie said. "Boys, get down there and help her."

Unlike their uncle Charlie, the two teenaged boys got down in the mud on either side of me and pressed their faces close to the hole, risking life and limb, and possible *eau de skunk*. "I think I can reach a few," one of them said and slithered forward.

"If they don't run," the other said.

"Let's hope not. If they go farther back we've got to leave them." I didn't look behind me, I just handed a kitten over my shoulder until someone took it, then I reached for another, and another. The boys each got two and passed them back. We kept at it until the rain was pounding hard again, and I was saturated. Again. Hurricane's were hell on dry clothes.

"There, I think that's it," I said and rose to my knees, saturated in mud.

"Where's the mother?" Jeannie asked. "They're still nursing."

"I'll get her. I see her." One of the boys crawled forward until only his legs were sticking out from under the shed. Then he started wriggling backward, but struggled against the slippery slope. He wasn't making any headway until Charlie grabbed him by the hips and pulled him out of the hole with a dirty calico mama cat in his arms. "I got her. I got her," he said, the thrill of victory in his voice. Instead of setting him on his feet, Charlie just scooped him and mama cat up and carried them into the building. The rest of us, hands full of kittens, followed right behind him. They slammed the door shut against the rising wind and barred it securely. We were plunged into darkness for the second time that day.

"Oh, my. They are so cute, but so wet," Jennie said. The pathetic little cries echoed in the dark and soon we were surrounded by others who wanted to see the kittens and hold them. Somehow, we made it back to Lucinda without tripping over anything, or losing any of the kittens.

"Oh, thank you, again. You girls are just the most wonderful people," Lucinda said as her grandson placed the mama cat in her arms. Mama Cat cried out as a towel was used on her head to dry her off. "Now you just hold still, Mama Cat," Lucinda said, talking to the cat as if it understood. "You'll have your babies soon enough."

Everyone had a towel, or something, to dry the kittens and Charlie placed a fluffy blanket on the chair beside Lucinda. He took the cat and placed her on the towel and one by one, we placed her babies on the chair with her. She mewled and purred and counted her babies to make sure they were all there.

"That's so beautiful," Jeannie said. "In the middle of all the destruction outside, we've ensured a family remains together." She sniffed. She was the more softhearted of us, but my heart was pounding away, too, with memories of Puff running through my mind.

It had been worth the effort to rescue them and get soaked again. For Lucinda, and Mama Cat, it had been worth it.

THE PERFECT STORM - SEBASTIAN JUNGER

He had to move it. The time was now. Mother was hooked to her feeding and slept. Lighting flashed and thunder howled outside, but the old brick home held steady. Father had built it to withstand the punishment of a hurricane. Not like new houses these days. They were the ones that splintered to pieces and washed away, not the older homes made to take a punishing from Mother Nature. The power of a hurricane was nothing to be dismissed, but he had to use it to his benefit now.

He removed his boots and slid each foot into an old bread bag. They would protect his feet from being saturated when he had to go out and do what he had to do. He put his feet back into the boots and tucked his pants in, then tied them up securely. His left leg pounded like a festering tooth ache. He hadn't taken his pants off to examine his leg recently. He'd been too busy boarding up the windows of the house, of work. The restaurant had entirely too many windows. He couldn't get to them all. If any of them blew out completely, he'd have to consider replacing them with something other than glass. They weren't cost effective during hurricane season.

Wiping away the sweat from his brow again, he ignored the trickle of it running down his back. It wasn't something he could deal with right now. He had to move. He had things to do. The storm was the perfect cover for him to do it in.

As long as Mother was resting, he could leave her for a few hours. She'd be fine.

He pulled two ponchos from the hall closet. One wasn't going to be enough today. He struggled to get the second one over the first and tucked the first one into his pants. Out of breath, he paused a moment. The brilliant lightning and reverberating crash of thunder erupting at the same time startled him. As if the hand of God had spoken at that moment, reassuring him, loudly and without question, that he was doing the right thing. He'd never heard from God as much as he had in the last few days. It was wonderful, and the validation he received in hidden messages were all he needed to continue his work. This was what he was meant to do.

Now, he knew he had to act. The message had become clear. Mitzi had been the last sign. He'd known it, but he'd been too overwhelmed at the time to see it. Now, he knew. Now, he'd find her, no matter what.

He hobbled out to the garage, grabbed his pack from Father's workbench and stowed it in the car, on the passenger seat beside him. No one would be out in the storm. No one *should* be out in the storm, so he had ample opportunity to drive unimpeded to where he needed to go, to get the last piece of his work done. He hit the garage door opener, but he'd forgotten the power had failed. Damn. He got out of the car and pulled the overhead rope to disengage the door from the electric opener. He struggled to get the heavy thing up high enough to shove it out of the way. It was an older model and heavier than the newer aluminum ones. Father had ensured no one was getting *into* the house through the garage, and no one ever had. Father had inadvertently ensured no one would get *out* of the house that way, either.

He propped the door up with a ladder, and backed out of the driveway. He paused a second, knowing the garage door was up and anyone could walk right into the house. But no one should be out in the storm. Mother would be safe.

He had to go. There was no more time to wait.

He hit the gas and turned on the wipers. The old heavy car would muscle through the streets, buffeted by the wind and the rain. Old Bessie, Father had named her. She was made for power and that's what he needed as he drove over downed branches and debris strewn about in the streets.

He used both lanes of the road and maneuvered the car to the restaurant. Parking against the back door, got out and squinted against the onslaught of rain stinging his face. He fished his keys from his pocket, nearly losing them as a gust surged up and nearly plucked them from his wet fingers. Trembling from the cold and the pain in his leg, he managed to unlock the back door.

A gust of wind snatched it from his hands and blew the whole thing open, banging wildly off the side of the building. Papers and small items were sucked in a whirlwind from the short hallway that led inside. He struggled against the door, tried to bring it shut, and slammed it from the inside, realizing the keys were still in the outer lock. He opened it again and discovered that when the door had banged against the building, it bent the key in the lock. He couldn't extract it. Standing in the blinding rain, he released the rest of his keys from the ring and shoved them into his pocket with his blade and pulled the door shut from the inside. He'd have to deal with the key later.

Inside, he leaned against the crates of non-perishable supplies stacked in the hall. It was a fire hazard. It was against the regulations. People could get hurt if they tripped over something. His employees should have known better than to stack things there. But they were all lazy. Father said so. Every one of them had to be told what to do, how to do it, and when. Father had been right. No one knew how to work any more.

He staggered past those items and moved to the large freezer. Fumbling for his keys again he shivered. He removed the industrial-sized padlock from one of the freezers. This was the high-quality food and meat locker that he had to protect. If he didn't keep it locked, the staff would steal from it. Though no one ever had, he knew they would if given the opportunity. That's just how people were. If you gave them a chance, they'd take from you.

He flipped the light switch. Power off there, too. He'd lose it all. All the frozen meat he so closely guarded would be lost due to the storm. Insurance didn't cover that, he didn't think. But his insurance agent was useless, too. Probably didn't want to do the paperwork to cover it. He'd have to see about that after the storm. He had his priorities scattered in his mind and couldn't get distracted right now.

A flashlight always hung on a hook beside the freezer, and he fumbled for it now. The beam was low, but good enough to do what he needed to do. First, he jammed the door open. It would be bad if he locked himself in the freezer. Mother would die if that happened. He would, too. No one would know he was there. No one would know to come rescue him.

Without any hesitation he moved to the back of the lengthy room. There it was. Still where he'd placed it two weeks ago. He'd even placed a date and time sticker on the wrapping in case someone had inadvertently gotten into the freezer. They'd think he'd just filled the space with a side of beef or something. Not what it really was. Not at all.

He pulled it off the shelf. It slipped out of his hands and fell hard against him, then clattered to the floor. Pain seared through his leg, and he cried out from the agony of it. He clutched his leg as tears filled his eyes. Blinded by the pain, he stood there, hanging onto the metal shelving. Panting, he tried to gain control of himself, gain control over the pain. He wiped the sweat from his face and took in a breath. He couldn't wait any longer, no matter how much pain he was in. He had to act now.

He propped the thing upright to get a better hold on it and tried to heft it over his shoulder, but it was too heavy, too awkward and frozen. He'd done it a thousand times with bags of flour and sugar, rice and beans, but this package was too rigid to complete the maneuver, and he dropped it again. It clattered like a piece of frozen fish on the tile floor.

Finally, he tied a piece of jute around one end and dragged it out like he was pulling a sled in the snow.

He dragged it out into the hallway now filled with water. The tidal surge must have hit. It raised the water level higher and higher, as long as the storm kept up, the water kept going up and up. It reached the restaurant and thus, the level of his house. Panic set in.

Mother was home alone. He had to hurry. If he had to evacuate her, there wouldn't be much time.

He dragged the plastic-wrapped package outside. The level of rain made it easier to drag and for that he was grateful. It floated along, bobbing like a toy boat on the water.

After opening the back door of the car, he eased the package up and slid it onto the back seat. He slammed the door shut, but it bounced off of the package and hung open. He hadn't realized the length of the package until now. It wouldn't fit. Fumbling and repositioning, he put one end on the passenger side floor, then propped the other side up and out the window on his side.

What an effort it cost him, though. He returned to close the freezer door. He slipped and slid his way down the hall and out the door. He slammed the door shut again and twisted the bent key in the lock. After several seconds of trying to extricate it, he gave up. No one would be out there trying to get in. He'd return with some tools and remove it later. After he'd seen to Mother.

Turning on the powerful engine, he gunned it several times as it coughed and choked. Water must have gotten into the engine, diluting the power. He didn't know how engines worked. He just knew this one had gotten through everything he'd put it through, and he needed it more than ever.

Backing up in the empty parking lot, he turned the big car around, careful not to back up and smash the tail lights in the dumpsters. He didn't want to have to replace them or explain while his tail lights were broken to a police officer. They pulled people over for the stupidest reasons any more, and he wasn't going to be stupid. Not now. He couldn't. He'd come too far.

He eased forward and, out of habit, looked both ways before pulling out of the parking lot on to the empty street. It looked like a war zone as he drove to the beach.

Trash, vegetation, all kind of debris was being flung around like a poltergeist had gone mad in town. Up ahead loose electrical wires blew madly in the wind. Sparks flew from the end of the wires as it scraped the wet street.

He turned in the street just before that one to avoid it. He'd probably be safe in the big old car, but he didn't want to take any chances on getting electrocuted. He had so many things to take care of. The street he took led to another and another and finally, he was at his destination. Or at least as close to it as he could get with the tidal surge having eroded the final three streets leading to the dock. The dock that used to be there. Now, it floated in the sea, battered by the waves, its destination determined by the madness of storm.

Parking wasn't easy, but he made it. The storm would erase any trace of tire tracks he left on the sand. He opened the back door and dragged the big piece out into the water, now two feet deep. The rain blinded him, and he pulled the hood on the poncho up around his head and face, tied it so only his eyes, nose and mouth were unprotected.

Fighting the raging wind he leaned into it, put the jute tie over his shoulder and dragged the package into the the boiling surf.

The storm buffeted and carried on, heedless of his struggle against it. He trudged into the surf up to his waist. The water having sloshed over the tops of his boots long ago, the bread bags had come in handy to keep his feet dry, but now they were useless.

Looking down, he made the mistake of looking at the package. At *her*. At the plastic wrap holding her face into place. Into the silent scream she could never make. He'd cut her throat. She hadn't talked. She hadn't breathed. She'd only died in front of him.

Her open eyes stared at him. Incriminating him. Silently raging at him. Silently crying at him. When he'd killed her, for just a second, she'd looked at him in shock, surprise on her face, silently asking why, then she'd gone down and struggled no more.

With a tremor in his hand, he placed his hand over her face. Over her pale face, distance blue eyes and pushed her out into the sea.

He timed it, timed the waves. One final wave crashed over him, and he shoved the package out into the roiling surf. In seconds it was gone, taken by the pitiless sea. He didn't wait to see where it went. The sea had a way of taking care of things.

He slogged his way back to the car, now up to the wheel wells in water. He didn't care. He opened the door to get in and buckets of water flooded in with him. He hadn't turned off the car and it still idled. He put it into gear and floored it.

Instead of moving forward, the tires spun against the wet sand, digging it in deeper. Deeper.

Struggling against the fear, against the anger, he pushed the engine harder and harder, determined to overcome the forces of nature with pure determination. He cursed. He raged. He hit the steering wheel with one hand, but it didn't move. His rage changed nothing. Mother Nature and the storm had all the power here, and he knew it.

The tide pulsed forward, giving the car a welcome

shove and he took advantage of it, guided the car until the tires gained traction again. Perhaps Mother Nature was on his side after all.

Blasting away from there, his heart thrummed in his chest. Sweat beaded on his face mixed with the raindrops. The exertion it cost him was monumental.

But now, he had to get home. Had to get back to Mother. He drove the car slowly, carefully, trying to find landmarks that led away from the beach. He passed the road to the marsh and recalled that he'd left one of them there. That hadn't worked out so well. This was much better. The storm. The wind. The waves. They'd take care of the disposal for him.

There had been no connections with either of the two to him. Confidence filled him now, as he turned onto his street.

Then he stopped quickly, fishtailing the car as the wet breaks grabbed and he hydroplaned sideways, viciously spinning the wheel, trying to save the car, but it hit a tree broadside and ground to a halt. He was dazed for a second, then he backed the car to reposition it.

Another tree lay across the road in front of him. He drove around it, right through the front yard of someone's home where it had once grown. It wouldn't matter that he'd dug up the grass, spinning his wheels in the earth for traction. The storm was going to cover everything up.

Erase any evidence he might have left behind.

With a sigh of relief, he looked ahead to the house through the mad whipping of the wipers. The ladder was still in place, despite the power of the storm surging around it. He pulled into the garage and turned off the engine. For a few minutes, he sat, catching his breath. He looked around for a dry cloth of any sort and found nothing.

Getting out of the vehicle took great effort. He had to pull his weakened left leg out with his hands. The pain nearly floored him. He lacked the strength to lift it out and place much weight on it. He used his right leg and his arms to lift the majority of his weight and braced himself on his right leg.

He had to get back to Mother. The ladder could stay there for now. If he needed to go out again, he could get out quickly and no one would dare enter the house. Or he'd kill them.

After making it into the house, he limped down the hall and clutched onto the bedroom doorway. Mother was there. Just as he'd left her.

The machine on the pole flashed. It was on battery. He'd have a few more hours before he had to do anything with it. He hoped he hadn't lost the paper Mitzi had given him.

Shivering, he undressed in the bathroom and threw his soaked clothing into the bathtub. A hot shower would have been so welcome, but without electricity, it wasn't going to happen.

He sat on the toilet lid, wrapped in a towel and removed the bread bags and soaked socks.

He was chilled to the bone.

I woke up in the dark. It seemed like I'd been in the dark for the better part of two days. Blinking, I struggled to orient myself and squinted at the digital number glowing on my watch. It didn't care if there was electricity or not. It just did its thing, no matter the weather.

I'd have to write an endorsement to the company after this event was over.

I'd gotten tired of sitting up a while ago. Now, squinting at the little screen on my watch, I could see it was four hours ago. I'd crawled into my car, into the back-seat, and created a nest for myself out of the things I'd shoved into trash bags. Everything was dry, so I pulled out a comforter and the pillows from my bed. I put the windows down in the car so I could breathe, but the air was still heavy with humidity and pressure from the storm.

That's what had awakened me. The air. The change in the air. Not that I was actually rested and refreshed from a few hours' sleep in the back seat.

It was kind of like working night shifts at the hospital. After four hours of sleep, I was awake, whether I wanted to be or not.

I stretched and tried to get out of the back seat while still maintaining my dignity, without falling onto the cement floor. It was close. But I made it. Once on my feet, I stretched again and took an inventory of aches and pains. Not too bad. I think I bent one of my kidneys. Or maybe it was my spleen. I hoped it would straighten out when I loosened up a bit.

"Hey, angel," Charlie called and flicked his flashlight back and forth to catch my attention. After being blinded by it several times in several seconds, he had my attention. Spots filled my vision as if I'd just looked at the sun too long.

"What's going on? Is the storm over?" I asked as I approached.

The little grouping of chairs was now empty. "Where's Lucinda?" I was worried about her not being able to rest during the storm.

Charlie lifted his chin and pointed to an area at the back of the bunker. "She's over there, sleeping on a bed like a queen."

"Lucky her," I said, then did a double take. "You brought a bed in for her?"

"Yes. We had the time, so we brought her bed from the house and a few essentials. Just set up her house inside here, so she'd be as comfortable as possible."

"That's awesome, Charlie. You and Elmo take such good care of her," I said, admiring the two more than ever.

"She took care of us for a lot of years, so now it's our turn to do it for her," he said, his voice husky with emotion.

That made total sense. Unfortunately, I'd seen too many people neglect their elder relatives because it wasn't convenient to take care of them. This situation with Lucinda, Charlie, and Elmo gave me hope in humanity again, even if it was only temporary.

❧ 21 ❧

AND ON THE EIGHTH DAY - BIBLE QUOTE

The storm stopped. Or at least ground to a slow halt. Enough that we could get out of the bunker, make our way to our apartment and see if it still stood. See if the hospital still stood. If we still had jobs, or if we needed to find a new contract outside the hurricane zone.

Our contract didn't include working through the aftermath of a hurricane. That wasn't included in the *other duties as assigned* clause, so we had an out if we needed it.

Jeannie and I pulled our vehicles out of the bunker and parked them to the side. Debris and fallen trees blocked the roads. We weren't going anywhere just yet, but at least we could get out and breathe fresh air. We found the patio chairs that had blown in and set them up beside our cars, like we were having a picnic. Just needed some iced tea and potato salad, and we'd be set.

Jeannie plugged away on her cell phone.

"What are you doing? Seeing if Mr Right called during the storm?"

"Yeah, right," she said with a snort. "No. I'm trying to

look at the text messages I got back from the initial text I sent out. I want to check them against the database and see who we missed." Her laptop sat open on the hood of her car. "I think I have most everyone, but that girl, Mitzi, didn't answer. I hope she's okay."

"She's the one I connected with at HR." I confirmed that. "She could be just out of cell phone reach or something simple like that." Could be, but with the crazy stuff going on with nurses, that explanation was going to have to be followed up on. I didn't just like assuming we couldn't reach her because of the storm. We had to know.

"Right. And then there's a traveler who is supposed to arrive today. Madeline Archer, but I haven't heard from her either," Jeannie said. That could be bad news or it could be nothing at all. I'd prefer to think it was nothing, but the other possibility was still a possibility. "That's some bad timing."

"Maybe the storm knocked out the cell service while that message was pinging around looking for a tower," I said.

"Maybe," she said and chewed her lip a second. "I have her address on the spreadsheet. Maybe we can go to her place and check it out, see if she's there, holed up."

I got why she was chewing her lip and why I had a sudden urge to chew on mine. The last time we'd gone to check on a missing nurse, we'd found a crime scene. Not sure either of us wanted to find another. "Let's put that on the list of things to do after we check our apartment and check in with the hospital."

"Got it. Delay that one as long as possible," she said and stopped chewing her lip.

"That wasn't what I said," I said and gave her a look.

"But that's what you meant." She knew me too well.

"Okay, so yes, that's what I meant." I shivered. "I just don't want to walk into another bad scene, you know?"

"Me, either. And I don't know whether it's better to know or not know if something happened to her. If we don't know, then we can at least plead ignorance for a while, right?"

"Yeah, until we, the self-appointed security team, really have to go to her place and find out for sure, because no one else will think of doing it." Maybe no one would. Except for us.

She slumped in her chair. "Right."

We watched for a bit as the friends and relatives of the King clan left the building in much the same way we had. Parked cars and trucks where they would fit, then everyone started the chore of clearing a path to the main road. We put on our shades, took some gloves that were offered, and bent our backs to the task right alongside everyone else.

In the background, the whine and buzz of a chainsaw working hard cut through the air. The longer we worked, the more chainsaws we heard. Smoke tainted the air, as people piled up debris and started to burn it. Or maybe it was a house fire. I didn't know, but at the moment I didn't care as I wiped sweat from my forehead and tried to ignore the biting insects that had descended on us. Come nightfall, it was going to be bad. Those little nasties had no boundaries at all.

"Ladies, we're all taking a break," Charlie said and waved us over to piece of shade provided by a sail-sheet they must have had in the bunker. Lucinda held court and handed out cool refreshments for us all.

"You look like you've got your own lemonade stand here, Miss Lucinda," I said and took the welcome drink from her. I'd always underestimated the simplicity of a glass of freshly made lemonade until then. It was heavenly amidst the destruction and chaos around us.

"Oh, I sure feel like it now. Just like when we was kids. Used to always find a way to have a lemonade stand in the heat of the summer," she said with a big smile that made the aftermath of the storm fade away, if only for a few seconds.

"It takes me down a memory lane I've never been down before." I sighed as a recollection of my own trotted down the dusty summer lane in my mind. "Back home, our version of this was setting up a table by the road and selling extra tomatoes, cucumbers, and squash my parent's couldn't use."

"That's it, too. The same thing. We all find a way to make a few pennies now and then." Lucinda nodded in agreement.

I looked around at the tree branches hanging from the power lines. "I think someone is going to make a few pennies putting this place back together again."

"For sure," Charlie said. "But the good thing is the power companies have been here since before the storm hit, getting a head start on keeping the lines open and going as much as possible."

"Really? That surprises me, but I guess I've never thought of it before now," Jeannie said, voicing my surprise as well.

"The companies in the surrounding states send crews in to help. I don't know where they hunker down through the storm, but they're here the second they can get out to start getting the power back on. That's the most important thing after one like this." He chugged a glass of lemonade then held his glass out for more.

"I can see why." This was going to be one big mess to get through and if the power companies could get a head start, that would make life so much easier for everyone.

"Even if everything is still a mess, as least you feel some comfort if you can turn a light on," Lucinda said as she refilled Charlie's glass. "Though, give me a candle and my Bible and I've got all the comfort I need right there."

"Have you tried to call the hospital to see if it's still standing?" I asked Jeannie as I saw her plugging away on the phone again.

"No. Just getting texts again. Finally got one from Mitzi. Her phone got wet and took a while to dry out." Jeannie said, clucked her tongue and gave a groan of frustration. "She apparently went rogue and helped a patient who was discharged before the storm, went to check on her and her son."

"Oh, isn't that the kindest thing? I know there are good people out there, risking themselves to help others," Lucinda said with a nod. "Just like my boys."

"Speaking of boys, how's Elmo? Have you heard from him?" I asked. I hoped he'd given an update.

"He's good. Needs some sleep, but he's okay." Charlie nodded and clenched his jaw. Though he tried to hide it, I could see right through him.

"You're chomping at the bit to get back to it, aren't you?" I asked him and clasped my hand on his forearm. He placed his other hand over mine and gave me a knowing look. "You read people very well, don't you?" he asked, no bitterness or machismo in his voice. Just an observation.

"Yes, I do. And friend, I can see you're eager to get back to it. Are you able to yet?" Physically, he was great.

"I feel fine." He released my hand and gave a champion

bicep flex that made me laugh. "Just feel that. Muscles at the ready," he said and danced on his feet like a boxer. He was back in action physically and showed no signs of any further allergic reaction.

"I meant, has the chief, or whoever, put you back in action? When do you go back to work?" The sooner the police force was at full capacity on the streets, the safer they'd be. Looters would think twice, I hoped. If I were his boss, I'd release him to the wild.

"In a few hours," he said and nodded. "I have the afternoon shift and probably the night shift too." He grinned. Knowing it was going to be exhausting, but ready to take it on anyway. It was an unfortunate oversight in the construction of the human body that we couldn't store up sleep the way a camel could store water.

After everyone was hydrated and had reapplied sunscreen, grabbed their hats and gloves, we went back at it, making piles of debris that could be burned, and piles that had to be carted off to the landfill at some point.

A few more hours into it, and we broke for lunch. We sat around in the shade of the sail again. The big oak beside Lucinda's house had held up, only missing a few branches, but all of the leaves that would have provided shade had been sucked off the tree. Now it stood as naked as a plucked chicken on Saturday night. Completely useless and ugly as sin.

As we chatted and planned how we were going to get home, a flickering light caught my attention, and I looked toward the front of Lucinda's little blue house.

"Hey, look at that," I said and nodded to the house. "The porch light is on."

Lucinda clasped her hands together. "Oh, praise the Lord. We got the power back." She continued her prayer under her breath. I was just as happy to thank the physical hands that had done the job.

"Wonderful," I said. "You can probably have a hot bath tonight and sleep in your own bed again." The boys had dismantled her bed and carted it from the bunker back to its place in her bedroom. That had been a sight to see. Two teenagers, all gangly limbs dragging a double bed with the brass frame from the bunker back to the house and up the stairs. Yes, laughter was the best medicine.

After that, they'd taken Mama Cat and her babies and put them in a nice big box, filled with fluffy warm blankets, in the living room so they could all be closer to Lucinda again.

"That will be wonderful," she said, but her eyes were sad. "But if you girls don't have electricity yet, you just come on back over here and bunk with me again til you do."

"That's so sweet of you," Jeannie said. "We'll take you up on that. After a few days, we probably won't smell very good."

That got a nice little laugh.

"I guess we'll have to face the music, and go see if the hospital is still standing," I said.

"We'll come back and help you get things back to normal when we can. If we still have jobs, we'll have to work the next three nights," Jeannie said.

"I'm sure the hospital is still standing," Charlie said and stood to hug us as we said our goodbyes. "Just come back when you can to visit. You don't have to work at all. Just bring your wacky rays of sunshine our way, and all will be good."

"Keep us up to date, about the hospital, and if they need any help down there," Lucinda said. That was a fine,

fine woman. As ill as she was, having just gone through a hurricane as well, offering her assistance to others in need.

"We sure will, Miss Lucinda." I bent and gave her a long hug. It had been a long time since I'd had a good hug from a mother figure, and I stretched it out as long as I could, savoring the strength in her heart and her arms that went around me. I almost teared up as we stood there in the afternoon sun holding onto each other in silence, knowing what we needed from each other.

"Bless you both," Lucinda said as we waved and got into our vehicles.

I took the lead as I had the SUV, and Jeannie drove behind me. I felt like a dog hanging out the window, waving as long as I could, watching them, without driving into a ditch. After we rounded the corner, the little blue house with the big-hearted woman in it was out of sight.

I drove slowly, in silence. I didn't even try to turn the radio on as without the majority of the power grid, there wasn't going to be any music playing. Maybe a public station for news alerts, but that was about it. I didn't really want to hear the state of anything yet. I just wanted to pull myself together and watch where I was driving.

The place really did look like a war zone.

Trees had been snapped off and lay in piles of giant toothpicks. Cars had been washed all over the place. I dodged a Mini-Coop on its side. Even a crane on a steel platform had been washed from its location and that took some power to do it.

Fires were burning all over the place, but it appeared the majority of them had been deliberately set by people burning debris. The thing that worried me the most was that with all the wet wood, people used accelerants like charcoal starters, or gasoline, which greatly increased the likelihood of having unexpected explosions and burn injuries. The hospital didn't have a burn unit, so I hoped people kept their fires contained. The hospital had just emptied out. I didn't think they wanted to fill it right back up again.

My phone vibrated with that obnoxious nuclear alert from the 1970's designed to get everyone's attention. It got my attention. The hairs on my arms stood out, and I pulled the phone closer to my ear to listen.

It was a weather alert, then a news statement that the Army National Guard had secured the island and surrounding areas, cautioning people in a mechanical voice against traveling unnecessarily at this time.

I remembered the warning about snakes, and I looked out the window onto the pavement, but didn't see any. *Yet.*

Though it took twice as long to get to our apartment, we made it. The parking lot was deserted, which gave it an other-worldly feel. Like a Twilight Zone episode was being filmed there. The sky changed as the sun moved, and had kind of a pea-green cast to it. The aftermath of the storm, maybe? I didn't know. It just looked weird. Creepy. And remarkably silent.

I got out of the car and moved a few branches that were in the parking spots closest to our apartment door, then got back in and parked the SUV and Jeannie parked next to me, then got in the SUV with me.

"So, what do you think?" she said as we sat there staring out the windshield. The whole apartment complex looked deserted and dark. There wasn't a light anywhere I could see. Not even the street lights. "Looks like we'll be in the dark for a while."

"We have some flashlights and candles. We can eat and

probably shower at the hospital, since they have generators." I remembered Audrey saying that.

"True. Wanna check it out here first or head to the hospital?" Jeannie asked.

"Let's go in and see if we can raise Audrey on the land line. If not, then we'll take a drive and see how far we can get."

"Good plan."

We unlocked the door and found the place just as we'd left it. It was weird, too. It felt devoid of life, devoid of our energy.

"Should we check the bedrooms?" Jeannie asked and hesitated in the hallway.

"And under the beds, too," I said, then I paused. "Uh, what should we do if we find anything?" The lemonade in my stomach curdled at the thought.

It wasn't like before when we called Charlie to come to the rescue. Charlie, Elmo, even Shipper, had bigger fish to fry than coming to hold our scared little hands again.

"I'd say, take a knife with you," Jeannie said and headed to the kitchen, grabbed a few steak knives and divided them between us.

"Right." When there was nothing else, there were always steak knives.

Of course, there wasn't anything under the bed, or in the closet, or behind the door. Except my overactive imagination and a few spider webs. I really had to stop watching horror movies at night. After *The Silence Of The Lambs*, I'd sworn never to do it again.

Her phone rang, and she pulled it from her pocket and put it on speaker. "It's Audrey," she said. "Hello?"

"Are you two okay?" she asked, concern in her voice.

"We're fine." Pfft. Who, us? We were always okay. Usually. Mostly. I mean, sometimes. Really often.

"I've been trying to contact you for a few hours. I guess it's hit and miss with the phones now."

"We took shelter on higher ground, like you said. Just got back and checked our apartment. It's okay, no damage, but no power here," Jeannie said, supplying her with the info.

"That's okay. You can take care of essentials here at the hospital and go there to sleep as long as it's secure," she said.

"Great. Good plan." Even though it would be weird. We'd done weird before. Not our first weird rodeo.

"But I'm wondering if I could give you the task of trying to find another travel nurse, Madeline Archer, who was supposed to have arrived, but didn't." Silently, Jeannie and I looked at each other wide-eyed. "I don't know if she can't get through because of the phones, if she didn't come, or she got here and isn't answering for other reasons," Audrey said.

We knew what those *other reasons* were that she didn't want to say out loud. We'd thought and fought them ourselves, and they remained hanging in the air between us.

"Yeah. We get you." How could we say no when we'd gone through the hurricane in relative luxury at the King home? "We were thinking about it, anyway. We set up a contact list via text with other travelers, and she was one we hadn't heard back from."

"Great," Audrey said, artificial enthusiasm reverberating through the line. I'm sure she'd had too few hours of sleep and entirely too much caffeine over the last few days. It was all about balance. "Let me know if you find her, and we'll go from there."

After a few crackles, the line went dead. Though the land lines were working, I wasn't sure they were playing nice with the cell phones.

"I guess we have our mission for today," Jeannie said and dropped the phone into her pocket. She replaced the steak knives in the kitchen and opened the refrigerator door, grabbed a few water bottles and handed me one. They were remarkably cool for having been sitting there for a few days with no electricity.

"Let's take my car," I said as we left and locked up. Although we'd left nothing of great importance in the apartment, no one else knew that and might be tempted to break in to find out.

We piled in, and I plugged in the address in the GPS. "It's a fifty-fifty shot at best," I said. Would there be enough signal to get the address to Madeline's place, or not? It took a few seconds of spinning around in circles, then it stuck and coughed up the map and a red balloon, indicating where it was.

"Score," Jeannie said with a big smile. She was so easily pleased. I needed to be more like her.

I backed out of the parking space and eased onto the road. It was down to a single lane now, chopped right out of the middle due to debris all over the place. I detoured around downed branches, or drove right over them if they weren't too large. I didn't have four-wheel-drive for nothing. I powered over cardboard boxes, random trash and the occasional child's toy. Though the GPS lady was telling me what to do, I had other plans.

"Man, she's bossy," I said and negotiated again around another blockade.

"Who?"

"The tiny little lady in the GPS that keeps telling me where to go." That's who.

"If she didn't tell you where to go, you wouldn't know where to go, right?" Jeannie asked.

"While true, I don't like her tone." Sounded prissy and superior. Bitch.

"Just do what the little lady says, and we'll get there just fine." She wrote in her notebook as we went.

"What are you doing?" She couldn't be that obsessed with her spreadsheets, could she?

"In case the GPS can't connect on our way back, I'm writing down the turns onto the streets so we can get home again."

"Wow, you're smart." I hadn't thought of that. It's a good thing we're friends, or she could be scary.

"Don't I know it," she said with a toss of her head.

Your destination--is ahead--on--the left, GPS lady interrupted.

"Okay, so here we are," I said and slowed the car to a crawl as we got closer to the destination. It wasn't an apartment building like we had, it was a private home.

"Maybe she rented a room or something," Jeannie said. "Like Kelly."

"It looks deserted," I said.

"Again. Gulp." She didn't have to elaborate. The last deserted house we went into had been a crime scene. Here we go again.

"Should we get out and take a look?" I asked and put the vehicle into park. I opened my door and left it open, left the engine running in case we had to run for our lives or something. There could be another crime scene, a dog on the loose, or snakes. There could still be snakes.

Together, we approached the front door and knocked. If the doorbell was connected to the electric, it wouldn't ring anyway. We waited. No answer.

"Maybe they evacuated before the storm," Jeannie said and slapped at a bug determined to land on her face.

"Hello? Can I help you?" A lone voice called to us. We backed up and looked for the person around the sides of the house, but didn't see anyone. .

"Hello? Where are you?" I asked.

"I'm up here," the voice said again from above.

"Here where?" Jeannie asked. "We can hear you, but can't see you."

"Straight up, sugar. Look straight up."

O-kay. We looked straight up.

"Oh. Hi, there," Jeanie said.

An elder woman was leaning out the upstairs bedroom window waving at us like Rapunzel in her castle waiting for her knight. Only this lady was no beauty from a fairy tale, and her luxurious locks had gone fifty shades of gray long ago. She didn't look like a travel nurse, so I immediately surmised with my exceptional powers of deduction that she must be the home owner. Snap. Was I on it, or what?

"How can I help you girls?" She asked that like it was just another sunny afternoon, and we were Avon ladies or something. Maybe Tupperware ladies. I wasn't sure if Avon still delivered.

"We're looking for a nurse. Madeline Archer. Does she live here?" Jeannie asked and shaded eyes with her hand as she continued looking up at the woman.

"Oh, she's not here, sugar. She called before the storm." Although the word was *before*, she pronounced it *be-foe*.

"She did? What did she say?" I asked, waiting for another southern colloquialism.

"Now, who are you two wantin' to know why she's not here?" The woman was smart to ask questions as we had no bags of makeup or sturdy plastic containers with matching lids on us. Not even a flier for the next party.

"We're also nurses at the hospital, but we got worried when we didn't hear from her, and this is the address we have listed," I said.

"Oh, sure enough," the woman said with a nod. "Mmm hmmm. She was gonna rent a room from me. See? I got this big ol' house with too many rooms and not enough people, so sometimes I take to rentin' one out for a while. 'Til I get tired of people, that is. Then I stay by myself agin awhile." She nodded.

I liked her logic. Sometimes I wanted people around, and sometimes I didn't. I could see how that situation could work for her. I might be looking at my future self hanging out the window of a big house.

"Can you tell us any more? Where was she when she called, did she say? And did she sound, you know, normal?" Whatever that was. But I wanted to know if she sounded under duress. Like if a serial killer had kidnapped her and had forced her to make the call. Simple stuff like that.

"Honey, I don't know, but she sounded jus' fine. Said she called from Greenville. Said she'd come that far and was turning 'round and headin' back to where she come from. Wasn't puttin' up with no hurricane."

"I can see that, too." Boy, could I see that.

"Okay. Thanks for the information and be safe." I waved to her, and she wave back.

"Are you okay up there?" Jeannie asked. "Are you by yourself? Do you have enough supplies?"

"I'm okay. I'm as tough as they come, sugar," she said. "I got fambly comin' by to check on me. So you take care of yourself, girls. You take care." She waved again and pulled back in the window, dismissing us.

"Well, I guess the GPS lady isn't the only one telling us what to do today," I said.

"We need to put her on the list of people to check on," Jeannie said as we returned to the SUV. She pulled out her notebook and scribbled something in it.

"We're going to be checking on half the people on the island at this rate." Seriously? How long was this list going to be?

"What else do we have to do in our spare time?" Jeannie said and got in, buckled up, then flopped back against the seat with a sigh. Something was brewing with her. "The beaches will be closed, stores are bought-out already, tourist attractions will be closed, and who knows how far we'll have to go to do laundry?" That in itself was a laundry list.

"I'll bet Miss Lucinda has a bucket and a washboard we could use," I said. At least I had an answer for that one. The rest? Not so much. She was right. We were living in a real-life post-apocalyptic world. Fortunately, there were no machines falling from the sky trying to take over the planet.

"Ha. Ha. Seriously? What *are* we going to do?" She looked to me for an answer I didn't have. That was unusual, but, we'd just survived a hurricane.

"I could think of a zillion things, but okay. Just this one time, we'll check on everyone on the island. Next time we go through a hurricane, they're on their own." That got a sideways smile out of her and a relief of the tension showing in her face. I had to draw a line in the sand somewhere. It happened to be on the beach on Oak Island.

"Okay. That's a deal," she said. "Let's get the heck out of here."

Somehow, we managed to get back through the area without getting stuck in quicksand or blowing out a tire on some unseen sharp object in the road.

"I'm going to try her again," Jeannie said and dialed Miranda's number again. It rang unanswered, then went to voicemail. Jeannie left a message to call us back. "We'll see if she does."

"That's about all we can do for now, right? That's assuming the information Senior Spice Girl in the window gave us was correct. She could be crazy as a loon and just gave us a bunch of bogus info, you know?" I wasn't sure if that was a rhetorical question, but I had a feeling Jeannie was going to answer it either way.

"Yeah. I still feel badly about Kelly. That we couldn't find her." Jeannie shook her head. "There's no telling where she could be."

I noticed she referred to Kelly in the present tense. I knew Kelly was likely dead. Very dead. So did Jeannie. But we couldn't help thinking of finding her body. Just couldn't help it. It's how we we're made. We had to see things through to the end. Nurses didn't walk away in the middle of a medical situation. We weren't going to walk away from this one, either.

"I know. She could have been left in the sand somewhere, buried in someone's basement, or any number of places. Even taken away from the area for disposal. Like the dump or something." I shuddered at that thought, thinking about seagulls and crabs picking her body clean.

"I hate it. I hate that we won't be able to offer any sort of closure for her family." She clenched her fists together on her lap.

"It's not really our job to do that, is it?" I asked quietly and leaned back against the headrest. I wasn't trying to be sarcastic or funny, just logical. At least for now. I had my moments.

"No, you're right. I guess since we discovered she'd been murdered, I want the satisfaction of being able to tell her family we found her killer, or her body. Or even both, you know?"

"Like Charlie said, are we nurses or detectives?" I asked.

"It's frustrating. Not having the end of the story." She stared out the windshield as she spoke, not focusing on anything, not even the two squirrels chasing around the street in front of us, who apparently didn't care that there had been a hurricane.

"Can you imagine what career detectives go through when they have unsolved cases?" I didn't even want to think about that.

"No. I don't want to."

"Me, either. But that's the end result we may have to look at with this situation," I said, voicing the realistic expectation we were faced with. We'd probably never know what happened to Kelly, and there was no way for us to find out. Just because we wanted to find all the answers, didn't mean we were going to get them by studying harder. We had to let go of the idea that we were going to.

"Okay. I'm done thinking about it for now," she said.

"Good call."

"For now, I guess we should rest up as much as we

can," she said, her voice dejected and sad. She had an analytical mind and didn't take not finding answers well.

"Look at the bright side," I said.

"What could possibly be the bright side to this situation?" A frown wrinkled her perfectly arched brows.

"We can walk away from it all right now." I was serious. "We can pack up the apartment and head out of town, right now." That was the simplest solution to everything. Just go. "There's nothing in our contracts that say we have to work through a disaster, natural or otherwise."

Her eyes popped wide. "Seriously? You'd abandon our assignment now, just because of a hurricane?" She huffed in a breath and continued to stare at me. "I can't believe you'd do that."

"I'm not saying I'd do that. What I'm saying is, we have the option. No one is forcing us to stay here. The hospital will understand. The agency will understand. Charlie and his family will certainly understand." I pulled the SUV to a stop and turned in my seat to face her. "We're not contracted to do this. We're contracted to work for the summer at a hospital and take care of ICU patients. That's all. We're not the Army National Guard, we don't have any chainsaws, and no electrician skills. We're nurses, that's what we do. The rest of this," I held my hand out and indicated the destruction all around us, "isn't up to us to fix."

"But--" she paused and took a look at the houses nearby. Some were missing roofs, some had the windows blown out, others had plywood coverings hanging off the window frames. All were in heavy states of disrepair. "But how can we leave?"

"We can do what we can do. That's it. We can take care of the patients we've been assigned to take care of, and leave the rest to the people who know how to do the other stuff, like the power company, the cops, FEMA." Although I didn't have much faith in FEMA, they were all we had.

For a few moments we sat in silence, contemplating our options. Birds fluttered into nearby trees. Crickets chirped from hidden places. And I didn't see any snakes slithering around where they shouldn't be.

"I don't want to leave," she said, her voice small, but I knew she was forthright in that decision.

"I don't want to, either," I said, just as committed. We each had to come to our own decision. "Just remember, if you change your mind, we have the option."

"What kind of nurses would we be if we abandoned our assignments now? Left our co-workers behind to deal with everything?" she asked, anger sparking in her eyes now. Instead of sadness, she was finding her motivation, her fire.

"I don't want to let Audrey down, you know? I know travelers haven't had a good reputation here, but this is a chance for us to help correct that," I said. In light of everything else, I'd almost forgotten about that part.

"Also not our job, as you say, but I want to do it, too. I don't think I can leave here without knowing the end of this story. If you want to leave, if you need to, I'll totally understand, but I can't. That's my decision." The anger faded from her eyes. More like resolution and determination flared in those baby browns of hers. "That's my decision." The repetition of it sounded stronger every time she said it.

Jeannie held up her hand and waited for mine. I clasped her hand like a bro' shake, only more girly and didn't hurt.

"Awesome. Let's go to work," I said and turned the vehicle back onto the road.

❧ 22 ❧

LIFE'S WHAT HAPPENS WHEN YOU MAKE
OTHER PLANS - ALLEN SAUNDERS

Nothing had gone the way he wanted it to. Nothing! Mother wasn't cooperating and had pulled out her feeding tube twice, leaving him with a disgusting mess to clean up.

He had to get back to the restaurant, to clean that place up too, but with Mother so ill, he wasn't certain he could do both. And there was no one to help him. Except that Mitzi girl. She might help, but he didn't know her phone number or how to find her outside of the hospital. The other ones he'd followed from work, but after the storm, everything was in chaos. Even his thoughts.

Skies overhead blossomed with white fluffy clouds, never guessing that just hours ago the rage of a hurricane had slammed through the area.

He dressed again. Carefully. He clutched his left thigh. Everything hurt it. Dressing. Undressing. Every step he took was an exercise in pain. But he had to get through it. Had to put everything back the way it was, or Mother wouldn't like it. Wouldn't be happy with it at all.

She preferred order and cleanliness. No, she required

it, demanded it, and he'd left so much undone. So much filth and debris around them. He should be ashamed of himself. Mother would be ashamed of him, too, if she'd known. Perhaps she hadn't seen the piles of clothing and stacks of unread newspapers piling up.

When she'd been in charge of the cleaning there wasn't a spot, or a hint of dust, anywhere. If he got to play with his toys, each and every one of them had to be put away when he was done.

Looking at the house now and the state of chaos it was in, his heart rate rose, his chest tightened, and he trembled inside. It couldn't be helped though. Mother would have to understand. She would have to. Though she wouldn't like it, she had to see. Somehow, he would make her see.

He had to earn the money to keep them going. Mother had to understand that. Somehow she had to understand that he had to keep Father's business alive. And it would keep them alive.

Gritting his teeth against the pain, he took four of the leftover pills that had been Father's. If two hadn't done the job, then maybe four would. He choked them down with some water he'd gotten from the bucket on the counter. The house had a well. All he'd had to do was use the hand pump. At least they had water, though they had nothing else.

He staggered out the door to the sidewalk and limped toward his other home, Fat Pete's. He had to open up, if he could. There would be hungry hospital staff waiting for him to open. Nothing had ever stopped Father from opening. Nothing.

As he rounded the corner, he couldn't believe it. The roof had been blown off of the building. All of the windows were gone. He'd run out of time to board them all up and now they were gone, glass strewn and scattered everywhere. His jaw hung loose, aghast at the destruction. He'd never imagined it would be so bad. He didn't have to unlock the door, just stepped through the empty arch where the door had once been.

Glass crunched beneath his feet, sounding like the end of his life as a giant stepped onto him. The giant had been the storm, and now, there was nothing left.

Rage filled him as he lumbered to the back room for the broom and mop. He'd clean it up. They'd see. He'd clean up the mess. Get the coffee going. And some toast. And bacon. Definitely bacon. That always attracted people. He was certain of it. As he thought of it, thought of the delight of having paying customers again, he felt better. The pain in his leg wasn't so bad. Maybe four tablets was a better dose than two. He pulled another bottle from his pocket. He'd given it to Father for anxiety, for agitation. Maybe that would help, too. He took two of those, and his mood lightened even more.

Buzzing around like a happy house keeper, he piled up glass, retrieved garbage cans and wiped down ten tables, put them in order. Salt. Pepper. Sugar. Napkins. That would be enough for starters.

He propped open the back door to let some fresh air in and hoped the musty smell of carpets, saturated with sea water and turning to mold in the heat, would be flushed out. He'd get to the carpets later. After there were customers again.

He stopped for a moment in the lot out back and leaned against his broom. Closing his eyes, he lifted his face to the sun and the light breeze. It was a glorious day. He'd see to it that Mother had a glorious day, too.

Returning to the inside, he tested the light switch and it

flicked on. Wonderful. The power had been restored, thanks to the close proximity to the hospital, just yards away. Now he could make that coffee and bacon. The food in the large freezers would be saved, now, too. Hurrying to the front window, he flicked on the *open* sign and set it to flashing. That would attract more people.

With the back door open and the scents wafting out, he was certain people would start showing up soon.

⚜

WE GOT TO WORK, AND I'D NEVER SEEN A GROUP OF NURSES more welcoming than those nurses we were relieving. They were all permanent staff members. I hadn't realized we'd been saved the task of staying in the hospital twenty-four-seven because we were travelers. That meant something to me. The people here, those people who had stayed, had the fortitude and stamina to tough-out anything. Jeannie and I were happy to be their relief.

"Sherm!" I cried, like I hadn't seen him in three days or something, and got bundled up into a great bear hug. "How are you doing, my man?"

"Aw, Curly. So glad to see you." He squeezed me tight enough to pop one of my lungs. Or at least my bladder. But both organs remained intact, just seriously strained their boundaries.

"Sweet. Glad to see you, but man, you've got bigger bags under your eyes than Clinton ever had. You need some serious sleep." I gave him a brotherly kiss on the cheek, and we set about the task of changing shifts, handing the patients over from one nurse to another.

Sherm stretched and yawned like the big bear he reminded me of. "Man, I'm going to sleep like a rock today," he said and gathered his backpack and slung it over one shoulder.

"I hope so. When are you due back? Not for a few days, I hope," I said. He needed more than one shift off after the marathon he'd just gone through.

"Not sure. I guess we'll see if I still have a house left," He said with a shrug, but I knew there was great concern behind his eyes. "Or a truck." He hadn't even been out of the hospital to see his house or if his truck had been washed away from the parking lot outside.

"I hadn't thought of that," I said. But if you need to get home, come back and you can take my SUV home."

A mischievous light filled his eyes. "I knew you was good people, Curly. Thanks for the offer. I hope I don't have to take you up on it, though." He gave a crisp nod and meandered out the door.

He didn't return.

The night was filled with the usual issues in an ICU, but the place was not filled with the usual boisterousness. The storm had taken some of the pizzazz out of people.

Sheila, the night's charge nurse, approached with a chagrined look on her face. Some people were closed. Some were open. She was readable from a mile away. I didn't have to wonder what she was going to say. She was either going to float me to another unit, or send me home. I didn't want to go home to a creepy apartment alone in the dark.

"Piper, I'm sorry," Sheila said.

"For what?" I asked, playing the innocent, hoping she was going to keep walking past me.

"I have to float two nurses down to the ER. Seems like we're pretty stable here, but it's a mad house down there."

She looked at her clipboard, then back to me. "Do you have any ER experience?"

"Oh, sure. Loads. So does Jeannie. If you have to float a second nurse, you might consider her. We work well together." There was no getting out of it. Travelers floated before permanent staff. If Jeannie was selected to go, she went whether she liked it or not.

I turned my patient over to another staff nurse and headed with Jeannie into the stairwell. ER was just one flight down, so I didn't need to get into the closet-of-death for that short trip.

We started in triage, getting people assessed and seen in order of the severity of their issue. Colds and hangnails took a backseat to chest pain and breathing issues. Fortunately, there were more minor injuries that could have been treated at home, but with the power out and the aftermath of the hurricane, I thought a lot of people came in just to be in a building with electricity, with air conditioning, and just for a little connection with humanity.

"How are you doing?" I asked Jeannie. She was buzzing by left and right all night and seemed to be thriving on the pace, but I knew at some point, she was going to have to take a break. Caffeine and adrenaline eventually ran out for everyone.

"Great. But this place is hopping tonight," she said and saluted me on the way past, dashing somewhere in the back. Seconds later, she returned. "I'm back. What can I do to help you? I've got everyone squared away in the back."

We finished that shift in the ER, spent the next night in the ER as well, then finally were able to stay in the ICU. As the ER filled up, they sent patients to be admitted and as a result of people over-doing cleanup in their yards or inexperienced people nearly whacking off their limbs with chainsaws, we were full in the ICU again.

"And that's why we don't use chainsaws," I said to Jeannie as she held the leg of one of my patients so I could wrap the bandage around and around the leg with a serious wound. The patient had been to surgery to repair the life-threatening injury, but blood still oozed from the beautiful line of staples in his leg. "That's another power tool I think you should have to have a license for, you know?"

"I see," she said and offered soothing words to my patient whose heart rate was heading higher. It was an indication of pain. Though I'd medicated him before the procedure, he looked like he needed a little more.

"Code strong, ER. Code Strong, ER. Code Strong, ER." The announcement came over the hospital paging system in triplicate.

"You want to go?" I asked. Her patients were less serious and one of us had to go.

"I'll go," she said and hurried to the back staircase that opened right into the ER.

She returned pretty quickly and out of breath, and I was sure she'd run up the back stairs. Just for the fun of it. There was something wrong with her.

"All settled?" I asked.

"All settled. Someone out of sorts because they weren't being taken care of quickly enough." She shrugged. It was the same story in every hospital we'd worked in, hurricane or no hurricane. There were impatient people everywhere. Sick impatient people were no fun at all.

So we returned to our duties, then Jeannie came racing back down the hall to me, holding her cell phone up in the air like she'd just won the Stanley Cup. I knew she hadn't because for one, she didn't play hockey, like I did. And two, it was nowhere big enough to be The Cup.

"What's going on? You win a new cell phone or something?" I asked, unable to fathom what her deal was.

"No. I heard from Madeline. While I was in the ER my phone rang, but I couldn't answer it. She said she was fine, but like Senior Spice Girl said, she wasn't contracted to do a hurricane, so she turned around and went back home. She's heading to California." She sighed dreamily. "San Diego."

"Party-pooper," I said. "She has no idea what fun she's missing out on here."

"Uh, maybe she does, and that's why she's going to Cali." Jeannie placed a hand over her heart. "That's a relief. At least we know she's not dead."

"Maybe not." Call me a pessimist, but that's why I've lived as long as I have. I question things. "Are you sure it was her?"

Dammit. I watched the smile slide right off of Jeannie's face. It started at her brows then just melted downward. I'd burst her bubble. Double dammit.

"There's no way to know, really," she said and looked down at her phone as if it would cough up the answer. "I just don't know. But it came from the phone number I have listed as hers." She looked back at me, big brown eyes worried again, then she snapped out of it. "No. I'm sure it was her. She had all the right information. Didn't sound like she'd been kidnapped and was being forced to leave the message. She didn't recognize the number, so didn't pick up when I called and was busy until now when she could call me back." Jeannie nodded. "I believe her. She did appreciate the call to check in on her, though."

"Good. That's good." We'd managed to check in with all of the travel nurses and everyone was safe and sound.

We dragged ourselves to our creepily quiet apartment to get some much needed sleep. The phone interrupted my plan to be unconscious for several hours. It rang in my ear just seconds after I'd lain my curly little head on my pillow. Or so it seemed. It was actually three hours after I'd lain down my curly little head. "Hello?" I tried to say, but my throat was so dry, it came out *help*.

"Piper? It's Charlie. Are you okay? Do you need help?"

"Hi," I whispered and cleared my throat. I turned over and sat up. My world spun like the hurricane that had just run over the island. "Uh, hi. No, just sleeping. What's up? Everybody okay?" My brain was still on the pillow.

"Yeah. Sure. Not why I called." Those words and the way he said them gave me pause. I wasn't sure I wanted to hear what he was going to say. I wasn't sure I didn't want to hear what he had to say. Either way, I knew he had something important to tell me, and I gripped the phone tight as my brain caught fire and I shot to a sitting position. "Tell me."

"We found her."

"What?" I shrieked. He didn't have to tell me who. I knew who. Every cell in my body knew who.

"What's wrong?" A disheveled Jeannie raced into my room and clung to the doorway for support.

"They found Kelly. They found her!" I shrieked again and motioned for her to come quickly into the room.

"Stop screeching in my ear, woman," Charlie said. "I know you're excited, but I don't have a hearing plan at work if you break my eardrums with that racket."

"Got it. I'm calm now," I said. I wasn't, but that was okay. I was excited beyond belief, and any fatigue lingering in my system got an immediate eviction notice. Jeannie rushed over and sat on the bed. Or fell over onto the bed, I wasn't sure which. Neither of us should be upright and talking on the phone with only three hours of sleep. We couldn't be held responsible for what we said. Our neurons hadn't regenerated yet. I put him on speaker. "Jeannie's here, too. Tell us what happened."

"Are you sitting down?" he asked.

"Yes, are you?" Seemed reasonable to ask him.

"Yeah," he said and huffed out a breath. I knew it was gonna be bad. "She washed up yesterday. At least she was found yesterday. Late in the day. A crew of Army National Guardsmen who were cleaning up brush to unclog an outflow pipe discovered the body yesterday." Putting distance emotionally, he referred to Kelly as *the body*. Using her name only made her too real all over again.

"What's an outflow pipe?" I asked. Don't make me think at that time of the day. Even though I didn't really know what time that was.

"It's for when we have heavy rain. It channels excess water back to the ocean," he said.

"I see." Made sense. Probably thanks to the Romans. Or the little Dutch boy. I wasn't sure which.

"So she was found?" Jeannie asked. There was satisfaction in that. At least now we knew. Another part of the story had been written.

"How...was she?" I cringed as I asked that. I'd had the image of her being eaten at the dump by seagulls and little creatures that I wanted to get out of my mind, but I wasn't sure if Charlie was going to replace it with one that was worse.

"Actually, pretty remarkable. She looked like she'd just

gone to sleep. Except for the laceration on her neck." He said that like he believed it, but I knew better.

"By laceration, you mean one big, giant slice across her throat that she bled to death through?" That's what I would have expected to see.

"Something like that." He wasn't telling us the truth. Or not all of it. I appreciated it, but I was no baby and neither was Jeannie. "Tell us the real story now, Charlie. We know that's not it."

"It's true. Elmo caught the call and called me to come. I saw her for myself," Charlie said.

"No Shipper?" I asked.

"No Shipper," he said with some amusement in his voice. Maybe he could do stand-up comedy as well as a radio show. That would work for me, too.

"Then what?" Jeannie asked and poked me to stop interrupting. I was terrible at the movies, too.

"She was encased in a huge amount of plastic wrap. I think that's what preserved her." He cleared his throat. "I shouldn't even be telling you any of this. I'm breaking all sorts of rules by telling you, but I couldn't not tell you."

"You're right. As soon as we saw you again we'd know you knew, you know?" It was confusing, but he knew what I meant.

He laughed. "You're so very right. You read me like a book and that's pretty hard to do, curly girl."

"But it's a good book, Charlie. A very good book. Since you've already broken the rules, how about you break some more and tell us the whole story?" We hadn't gotten to the end of this one yet. Of that I was certain.

"Oh, you are gonna get me in so much trouble," he said and I knew he was shaking his head, but he was going to spill it all to us.

"Only if someone finds out, and they won't find out from us," Jeannie said.

"And if they do, we'll bail you out of jail," I said. "What are friends for, right?"

"I'm not sure you two can be trusted with secrets," he said.

"What?" I gave my best shocked gasp. "Jeannie was a Girl Scout for years. And I was a Brownie for at least a week. Who do you think you can trust more than us? The NSA? I think not."

"Okay. But you are sworn to secrecy. Absolutely sworn to secrecy," he said.

"Got it." I watched Jeannie a second, then laughed. "Jeannie just crossed her heart, said her Girl Scout pledge, and is holding up three fingers. And I'm holding *one* finger up in the air and saying bad words. That's sort of a pledge, right?" I asked.

Charlie guffawed like he'd swallowed his tongue. "Girl, you are so not right."

"Thank you. Now, spill it."

DON'T CONFUSE YOUR GOOGLE SEARCH WITH
MY NURSING DEGREE-T SHIRT

"**L**et's go for coffee," I said and suppressed a yawn. "Surely we can find something some-where. Maybe even some food." I was still groggy after being awakened by the phone, and the short amount of sleep. So was Jeannie. Dog tired, as some would say. *Nurse tired* was what I called it.

"Since the hospital had power restored yesterday, maybe there's a restaurant close to it that's open," she said.

We'd heard from the morning staff coming in that more and more street lights and signs were lit up this morning. They were so excited to see it. It meant life was slowly evolving back into the island and maybe the aftermath wouldn't last as long as forecast by the weather guy. What did they know, anyway?

"Sure. Let's put our laundry in the car, and we can take off from there," Jeannie said. "That way we don't have to come back here and pick it up before going to Wilmington."

"Good idea." So we packed up our dirty scrubs and

other clothes, added the laundry soap and dryer sheets, threw in a few hangers, and we were on our way.

The closer we got the the hospital, we could definitely see more signs of life, just like the day shift people had said. Chainsaws still cut through the air and it was probably a noise we were going to hear for some time. It was hard to sleep through, though.

"Would you look at that?" I asked and leaned closer to the windshield, as if that would make a different in what I saw on the other side of it.

Jeannie looked up from her phone. "Oh, wow."

Fat Pete's looked like it had been nearly ripped in half by the storm. The roof was simply gone. Most of the windows were gone, too. Draperies fluttered in the light breeze. Bizarre.

"That's just so weird. My brain is having trouble making sense of it." What your brain *expects* and what it *gets* takes a few seconds to reconcile. Like when you ask for a Coke and get a Pepsi. It takes a few seconds for the mind to understand the deception that has just taken place, and you are *not* drinking the Real Thing. Like at that very moment. My brain wasn't easily replacing the image I'd had of Fat Pete's just three days ago.

"There are cars outside. Like it's open for business or something." Jeannie leaned forward too. I didn't think it was going to help her see things differently, either. Maybe she could wipe the dashboard while she was up there.

"The *open* sign is flashing *on*, so they've obviously got power," she said.

"And *coffee*. Squee!" I bounced my feet against the floorboard in a happy dance. "There is *coffee* in our near future. The only thing I want anyone to ask me today is, *one lump or two?*"

"That is a good question. Should we check it out?" She gave me an indication that she was game.

I looked at her and indicated I was game right back. "Wilmington is an hour away. I don't want to wait that long for coffee, do you?" I asked.

"Uh, no. No, I don't," she said and rubbed her hands together. "Let's go check it out."

We entered through what used to be the front door of the establishment. A hand written sign on a piece of cardboard that looked like a homeless person had written it, hung on the doorway. *Pardon our mess. Come on in.* Like they were having a construction party or something.

"I smell the nectar of life," I said and the little coffee fiend in me jumped up and down looking for the sugar bowl.

"And bacon," Jeannie said and clapped her little hands together. Yes, we were exhausted. Yes, we were weird. But it worked for us.

We stepped over the threshold and walked into what had once been Fat Pete's. Now, I didn't know what it was. *Flat* Pete's possibly.

The tile floor was amazingly free of debris as we walked through the entry. Half the seating area had been closed, a *please wait to be seated* sign indicated we shouldn't sit there. As if the missing roof and condition of the booths weren't enough of an indication. But the sign was a nice touch.

On the right side of the place, an area had been cleaned and the tables looked like normal. And people sat at them. Eating. Like usual. Like any cafe or restaurant or diner. With plates full of food and cups full of steaming coffee.

But with no roof. What the heck? We could work with that.

Perhaps it was the Oak Island version of *al fresco*.

We looked for an empty table, and noticed people we knew already seated.

"This is so weird, isn't it?" I asked them. Being sleep deprived, they might not be able to tell the difference.

"For sure, but we're desperate. I'd pay him double just to have a stack of pancakes and some coffee," David, one of the nurses said. "But he's not charging extra. Isn't that amazing?"

"Wow. Certainly is," Jeannie said with a suspicious tone to her voice. "I expected everything to be scalped pricing for a while."

"Not at Fat Pete's. He's charging the usual prices." David held up his cup and drank. "Coffee tastes a little weird, but I'm good with it." He shrugged, dismissing his observation. "It's probably just me."

"Great," I said to Jeannie. "Let's eat and get out of here."

We sat at a table, Emily took our order, and brought coffee back first. Bless her. She knew the needs of the caffeine deprived.

At the first sip, we knew there was something wrong with the coffee. It wasn't like we'd brushed our teeth, then drank orange juice, kind of off-taste. This was way worse.

After a few minutes of sitting there, the dark heavy scent of mold wafted upward to me. I looked down. We were sitting on restaurant grade carpeting. It looked okay. But I'm sure it had been saturated with the flood. Now, it was beginning to mold. Ew.

And we were sitting on top of it. Breathing it in. Double *ew*.

"Get up," I said and pulled Jeannie to her feet like we'd sat on a hill of fire ants. "We have to get out of here. Don't breathe," I said and pinched my nose shut as I dragged her out behind me.

"What?" she asked, but hustled out with me. "What's wrong?"

I waited until we were outside and took in some cleansing breaths. "We were breathing black mold in there." Mold of any sort was bad. Black mold was the baddest.

"What? From where? How?" she asked.

"The carpeting. I could smell it." Having grown up with an amazing lot of allergies, my nose was finely tuned. Mold was a huge trigger. "My throat started to close up right away." Or at least I thought it had. Probably my over-active imagination. Or not.

"Seriously? You could smell it, too? I thought it was just me." She fake-barfed into her hand. "Oh, that's so gross."

"No, it's not just you. This place shouldn't be open." We started for the car. "The coffee tasted weird, too, right? Kind of metallic, right?" I gasped and placed my arm on hers. "Will you look at that?"

"Oh, my God," she said and fake-barfed into her other hand. I almost did, too.

We stared.

Fat Pete's son, skinny Pete, pumped water from an outside well into a five gallon plastic bucket.

"That's where the water's coming from. I'd bet my Aunt Fannie on that one." If I had one. The well was prob-ably contaminated with who knew what. Heavy metals? Arsenic? Sea water? "If we get *Giardia* from this, I'm not going to be happy." Giardia was the second cousin to Montezuma of Mexico and had a revenge all its own.

Two people approached from the parking lot. We didn't know them. They looked like locals, though. "Excuse me, but we just came out of there, and there are some issues," I said.

"Yeah, they don't have a stinking roof, or hadn't you noticed?" the older male said in that fake kind of voice that though he was highly amusing. He wasn't.

"Uh, it appears they have some contamination issues," Jeannie said. I almost always took her advice. I wasn't sure about these two, though.

"Seriously?" the wife asked. "I was looking forward to something not heated up out of a can." Disappointment showed clearly on her face, and she gave a wistful sigh as she looked at the restaurant.

"That's a good thing to hope for. Just not here. We don't know if there are other restaurants nearby, but we're leaving this one and wouldn't recommend you go in there," I said.

"Good point. Tom, we're out of here." She tugged her husband's arm, and they went to their car.

Dave and his fiends came out. Dave patted his stomach. "That was good." He burped once. "I just need some sleep."

"Dude, you need to go back to the hospital. We saw Pete pumping water from a well outside for the water. That's probably why the coffee tasted so off. It's contaminated," I said.

"Oh, I'm gonna hurl," Dave said and dry heaved. "Seriously? You think so?" For some guys, it didn't take much to trigger their gag reflex.

"Pretty sure, dude," I said. "Look over there." I nodded to where the action was going down.

Pete trudged with a bucked of water, moving it toward the restaurant.

"Oh, man. That's so wrong," Dave said.

"Someone needs to call the health department," Jennie said.

"I'll be they're up to their eyeballs in it already," I said.

"Too bad," Jeannie said and asked her phone politely to call the local health department. They were gonna get an ear full from her.

Dave, however, was more straightforward and approached Pete. We followed along behind him and his pals in case someone needed to break up a fight. It wasn't going to be us, but at least we could pick up the pieces afterward.

"Yo, Pete." Dave said and motioned for the man to stop. "What are you doing?"

"Bringing water in, what does it look like I'm doing?" he asked and returned to his task.

"If you're bringing it in for food prep, you can't do that," Dave said and his throat worked again. He was gonna barf up that whole lot of breakfast he'd horked down. He just didn't want to do it in front of witnesses. And I didn't want to be one.

"Why not?" He looked insulted. "It's fresh water, pumped just a few minutes ago. Can't get fresher than that."

"But it's not treated, it is?" Jeannie asked.

"Of course not. It's pure well water. We've used it for years." He said it with a hint of pride.

"Dude. You can't just skip water processing and fill up buckets and carry them in there for public consumption." We'd all taken microbiology. We knew what kind of little beasties were doing the backstroke in that bucket.

The man offered a relieved sigh. "Oh, no. You mistake me. It's not for public consumption. We just use it in the restaurant." Duh. Same thing.

"Then what are you doing in there?" Dave asked and placed a hand on his gut that I could now hear roiling from where I stood several feet away. He was gonna blow any second. I took another step away. Slowly. Quietly.

Pete took a step closer to Dave, picked up his hospital badge, read it, then released it with a laugh. His eyes were glassy and wild. His face was flushed. There was something seriously wrong with this guy. Aside from the obvious lack of water purity education.

"Since I don't see a badge from the health department, it's none of your business, now, is it?" The man turned his back on Dave and the rest of us, and picked up the bucket and carried it into the restaurant.

"Dave, you really ought to go in to the ER. Something's not right with this," Jeannie said and watched as Pete made it all the way into the restaurant without spilling his bucket.

"You're right. I'm going in." He looked at his friends, who were also looking green around the gills. "You guys should come, too."

The trio waddled off in the direction of the ER, all of them clutching their guts.

"Should we put them on the list to check on, too?" I asked.

Jeannie silently eased her notebook from her bag and scribbled something on it. "We're never going to get this all done." We'd only been there three weeks, and gotten deeply involved in way too many things. Our assignment was going to be over before we got through our list.

"Wanna follow him and see what he's up to?" I asked, uncertain if this was something I wanted to do. Given all of the things we'd gotten into since coming to Oak Island, I voted no. With Charlie's warnings ringing in my ear, I thought we should listen to it.

"I don't know," Jeannie said. "He gives me the creeps. I made a report online to the health department. Those guys are going to make their own report when they get to the hospital, so I think we're really off the hook on this one." She didn't want to get involved, either. Besides, I suspected she was running out of room in her notebook for things we needed to follow up on.

"Right. We don't have to pick up every gauntlet we see in the path." Sometimes, there were just too many gauntlets, even for us.

"Yeah. And it stinks in there." Jennie wrinkled her nose.

"Let's go to Wilmington. We'll find something on the way for food," I said, accepting we'd have to wait a little longer for caffeine.

As it so happened, we found a set of golden arches not far from Fat Pete's that didn't have the roof blown in, and their coffee wasn't contaminated. Score. So we loaded up with two coffees each, several breakfast sandwiches and a load of hash browns. Skipped the pancakes. They're too hard to eat when you're driving.

❦ 24 ❦

FOR THE FIRST TIME IN SIXTEEN YEARS, I
SHALL SLEEP WELL - SLEEPING BEAUTY

The restaurant was gone. He stared at it in the dark. An orange sign had been placed on the frame where the front door had been. *Closed* slashed across it in giant words, ending his hopes of opening early. It was those damned nurses again. He knew who they were. They knew it, too. He knew where they lived. They'd outwitted him once. It wouldn't happen again. This time, he'd end them before they ended him. He shoved his hand into the pocket with his blade, clutched it in his hand. He'd end them and their interfering in his life. They were always interfering in his life.

But this? It had gone too far. He would end them, just as they thought they'd ended him. He'd outsmart them, just as they thought they'd outsmarted him.

Shoving away from the sight of the building, he tried to pace, but the pain was too much to bear. Reaching into his other pocket, he took the last four of Father's pain medications and then took two of the medications for anxiety. He didn't have anxiety, just nerves now and then. But whatever it was called, it was bad.

From the moment the health department had entered the restaurant with their hard hats and scowling faces, he'd felt the nerves gnawing in his gut. When they'd handed him that paper telling him Fat Pete's was being shut down, he'd known his life was over. It was the fault of those nurses who'd complained about the coffee. They'd complained about everything. All of them.

They weren't right. They were the kind who looked down on others. The kind who thought they were better than anyone else. He'd show them. He'd fix them, then he'd fix the restaurant. That made him feel a little better as the wings of relief the pills provided came from the heavens.

Mother would be so proud of him.

But now, he had to move, he had to go. He had to get things back in order. The house could wait. Everything else could wait except the restaurant. He'd get to work on it in the morning, getting it back to its former glory. The way it had looked when Father had run it. Spic and span, glass and chrome sparkled. Some days Father went in early to make sure everything had a shine to it. Those were the good days. When Father was happy, Mother was happy, and so had he been.

The smile faded from his face as he looked in the hall mirror and a man he didn't recognize looked back at him. Reddened eyes that looked like something from a zombie show stared at him. Hair slicked back revealed the gaunt cheekbones and sagging lips. Pushing himself closer to the image, he frowned, and huffed his breath against the glass, then wiped his sleeve on the mirror. Could it be playing tricks on him? he wondered.

The ghost of Father stared at him from the looking glass. No matter how he moved, Father mirrored his movements. Moving closer, he stared at his image again. He looked like Father had just before his death.

The image frightened him. *No.* It couldn't be true. He wasn't dying. He was in the prime of his life. Father had died and *he* was now taking care of Mother. He *had* to take care of Mother, no matter what. He'd promised Father. He could never break his word to Father.

Pushing away from the mirror, he moved down the hallway and flicked on a light. Cobwebs covered the wall sconce. In the night the bright light from the bulb revealed it all. Revealed everything. Revealed his incompetence.

Mother lay in her bed, just as he'd left her. She was a good Mother, now. She always did what he said. Always obeyed him. Not like when Father had been alive. Then, she'd told him what to do, and he'd obeyed. Now, things had changed. Now, he was the one in charge.

Watching her sleep always relaxed him. As he looked into Mother's eyes, he realized something else had changed. Something had faded. Her mouth fell slack. Saliva dripped from her mouth onto the pillow.

The sheet was tucked up against her chin, and he pushed it back to reveal her pretty flannel nightgown with the pink and red roses on it. It was her favorite. He watched her chest.

The hair on the back of his neck rose, and his heart seemed to freeze, then take off. A tremor built in his chest, then expanded through his body.

"Mother?"

He placed his hands on her shoulders and shook her. She was probably in a deep sleep, and he hadn't realized it. She would wake up angry with him and give him that terrible look she'd used on him since childhood. As he gripped her shoulders, he felt her stiffness in his hands.

"No, no, no, no, no." Tears overflowed his eyes. "Mother? Mother!" He shook her forcefully now. He had to wake her up. She *had* to wake up.

He scooped her up into his arms, and she lay stiffly. Rushing with her to the car, he placed her in the back seat. He had to get her to help. It would be faster than calling an ambulance. He was yards from the door to the ER, and the ambulance had to come from much farther away.

Turning the key, he cranked the engine and pushed on the gas. It coughed, and sputtered, and finally squealed to life. The sea water he'd driven through hadn't been good for the car, but he needed it so much right now. "Please," he said through clenched teeth. "Start!"

He rocketed out the driveway and into the street, not looking, not caring whether anyone was in the way. He had to get Mother to the hospital. Immediately. Someone had to save her.

He floored it and squealed the tires around the turns. Tears filled his eyes as the lights to the hospital came into view. He wanted to drive right up in front of the doors, but an ambulance was parked there. There were cars everywhere. He didn't care. Nothing mattered except Mother.

He dashed to the ER doors and rushed to the desk, spoke through the little vent in the window. "I need help! Now. Mother is in the car. I don't think she's breathing." Two of the nurses rushed to the side door and came to his aid.

"Show us where she is," one of them said.

"I'll grab a wheel chair," the other said.

"You'll need a stretcher," he said, certain Mother needed more than a wheel chair.

"I'll go with you," the first one said. She had kind eyes. "Show me where she is."

He took her by the arm, but froze, just outside the door to the building. "You have to help her," he said and stuck a thumbnail into his mouth as nerves shot through him. "You have to."

"Which car is yours?" the nurse asked. "Sir? Where is she? Are you sure she isn't breathing?" the nurse asked him and gave him a little shake on the arm, snapping him to attention.

"Yes. I'm sure." His voice had fallen to a whisper, as pain fell in on him from all sides. What was he going to do? He couldn't live without Mother. He knew that. She'd told him too many times to count.

"The others will be here in a minute, but you have to show me where she is, sir," she said.

"She's here," he said and led her to the running car. He opened the door to the back seat. "She's right there," he said. Maybe he'd been mistaken, and Mother hadn't stopped breathing. Maybe she was just quiet. Too tired to speak.

The nurse turned her back on him and leaned in to the back seat to check on Mother. She'd fallen over again. He'd forgotten to buckle her in, and when he'd taken a turn too sharply, she'd fallen over. He'd apologize to her later for his lapse in judgment.

He watched as the nurse placed her fingers on Mother's neck and pressed, then pulled back. She sat halfway in the car and had one foot on the pavement. It was her eyes that told the story before she spoke.

"I'm sorry, but I think you're mother is gone," the nurse said in a soft voice.

"What?" he asked, his worst fears were being realized. "No, she's not. Check her again. Check again! You have to save her. That's your job, isn't it?" he asked, near hysteria,

MOLLY EVANS

his jaw tight and fists clenched at his sides. A muscle throbbed in his temple.

"Sometimes there's nothing we can do for people. I'm so sorry."

"You're going to fix her," he said and punched her in the side of the head. She went limp and fell to the floor. He shoved her legs inside, closed the door and got in. Somehow, she would fix Mother. He hit the gas and took off.

He couldn't go home. He couldn't go anywhere with her. There was only one place to go. It was his safe place. No one would go there. The restaurant was closed. Shut down by the health department. No one would think of looking for them there. He drove there and eased the car around the back of the building.

Glancing in the rearview mirror, he saw no movement in the back seat. She was still out. That was good. She needed to be out until he got there. Until he got everything into place and then she *would* fix Mother, if she knew what was good for her.

In minutes, he carried the nurse into the restaurant, used the zip ties he always carried for binding trash and other things. He placed one of her ankles against a heavy steel shelving unit and placed her head on top of a bag of rice for comfort. When she awakened, she'd realize he'd made her as comfortable as he possibly could have, given the circumstances. Then she'd thank him for looking out for her.

He watched her breathing, just as he'd watched Mother's. The nurse breathed. Her chest moved up and down as it should. The pulse in her neck thrummed wildly. He hoped he hadn't hurt her too badly. He brushed her long brown hair away from her face. The right side of her face was red now and turning purple. "I'm sorry. I didn't mean to hit you so hard. I was just so worried about Mother."

He chewed the same thumbnail again and the pain of it broke into his focus. Blood tainted his mouth, and he swallowed it, then stroked her face again. "I'll be back. I have to arrange some things, but don't worry. I'll be back. I won't be long, I promise."

He rose from the painful position on the floor. His leg wasn't going to hold up much longer. He had to get some help for it soon. But not yet. Just not yet. He stood looking down at the unconscious form of the nurse. She was a beauty with all that long brown hair falling over her shoulders. He always liked long brown hair. Reminded him of summer days and the innocence of youth. Maybe he'd just keep her. If she couldn't fix Mother, maybe he'd keep her instead of killing her like the others. Maybe she could fix his leg, too.

❦

WE'D JUST RETURNED FROM WILMINGTON AND DROVE BACK to Oak Island. We were driving around, looking for the path of least destruction the hurricane had made, but also the inroads the people and Army National Guard had made into clearing the roads.

Heavy machinery had been brought in and bulldozed large trees aside. Sadly, the majority of the old oaks lining main street had been upended and now lay in piles for disposal later.

"I'm going to miss those trees," I said. We hadn't been there very long, but I'd developed a fondness for the trees right away. They reminded me of home.

"Me, too." Jeannie said. The sun was going down. I

wanted to get home before full dark as most of the street lights were still out, and I just felt safer. The National Guard had also issued a curfew for the majority of people to be off the streets by sundown, in any case. Looting in certain areas had begun and the fewer people on the streets at night, the better.

Jeannie's texts pinged like fifteen times all at once. "What the hell is that?" She pulled her phone out and looked. "Oh, my God!" She jumped in the seat like she'd been hit with a cattle prod.

"What's wrong? Do I need to pull over?" Had I forgotten to put my cattle prod away after the last cattle drive I'd been on?

"Keep driving. To the hospital. Fast," Jeannie said, trying to covey the sense of urgency she felt by gripping one hand on the dashboard and the other the seat beside her. I just hoped she didn't tear up the leather with her grip.

"What's wrong?" I asked, but did as she said. Something was seriously wrong.

She ignored me, but dialed her phone. "Charlie, it's Jeannie."

"Hey--"

She cut him off. "Don't talk. Just listen. One of the nurses from the hospital has been kidnapped. Like right now. She's tied to a shelf of some sort. The lights are out, she can't see any landmarks, and has no idea where she is."

"I just got the call. I'm heading to the hospital. Where are you?" Charlie asked, in his super sexy cop voice.

"On the way, too."

"See you there. We'll find her. I don't know how, but we're going to find her," he said, determination in his voice, then the line went dead.

Jeannie's legs twitched. She was agitated. I drove as fast as I could, but we were almost home when the texts came through. We were going to have to backtrack. "Tell me what she said. Who is it?"

"It's Maggie. She can't get a cell line out, but she can text. She said some guy ran into the ER and said his mother was in the car, and she wasn't breathing, so she ran out to help." Jeannie read the texts to me.

"She ignored the buddy system, didn't she?" I asked, but I wasn't judging. I was seriously unhappy, but there was nothing that could be done now. First we had to find her. I'd yell at her later.

"Yeah. The second nurse went for a gurney, and they didn't think." Jeannie held the phone in her lap. She was less agitated now, but still as determined as I was to find her.

"Caught them off guard, didn't he?" I asked. "Bastard."

"He did." Her foot twitched again.

"It'll be okay. What else did she say?" I asked.

"Just stuff about what it looked like inside. A lot of shelves with canned food. Like someone had stocked up for the storm quite a lot, and wasn't going to have to leave there for a while." Jeannie knew what that meant, and so did I. We might not find her for a while if the kidnapper had a load of provisions in his hidey-hole.

"What else?" If I weren't driving, my leg would have been twitching, too.

"He sounds crazy. He knocked her out, but then was chewing his thumb like a kid. Then he apologized for hitting her so hard." Jeannie gave a synopsis of the remaining texts.

"Whack-job for sure. We have to find her." I didn't know how we were going to do that, I just knew we had to try. We couldn't save Kelly or the other nurse, but somehow we had to save Angela. "Was that all of the texts? Did you tell her we got them, and the police are looking for her now?" My mind was racing with all the possibilities that could happen. The outcomes.

"No."

"Tell her. Tell her everyone's going to be looking for her, and we're not giving up. We're going to find her," I said, urgency shooting through my chest and my fingers clutching the steering wheel ached.

Jeannie texted her the messages. "Okay. I sent her the message."

"Keep talking to her. Ask her what else she sees. Anything. Everything. Something has to help. Something has to identify where she is."

"Light keeps flashing in a window. Red and orange kind of colors," Jeannie said. "I've never seen anything like that around here, have you?"

"No. What else?"

"Just the big metal shelves, like a prepper would have, filled with canned food, bags of flour and rice. Industrial sized bags of stuff." Jeannie cast an anxious look at me. "He could be holed up for months with that kind of food stock."

"That's good. That's really good." Thoughts churning, I kept putting it together. What did they all have in common? We drove past Fat Pete's parking lot. It was empty now. "Looks like you're health department report did the trick."

"What?" she asked, distracted and focusing on her screen.

"Fat Pete's. There's a condemned sign out front. Looks like your report to the health department did the trick.

There's tape across the door and a closed sign on the door, too." I sighed. "At least we got one good deed done today." That would have been a great end to my day, just to know Fat Pete's was no more.

"Thank God for that. That coffee was awful." She shuddered.

"So was he, you know? He's another whack job. Maybe they come out of the woodwork after a big storm or something." Kinda like roaches.

"I think he was weird before the storm, don't you? Remember how when he thought we were staff nurses he was sweet as pie, then as soon as he realized we were travelers he thought we were the scum of the earth." She shook her head.

"That's right. I'd kind of forgotten about that," I said. "Or tried to forget. We had quite a lot of excitement since we got here. It's a lot to remember."

"Right."

I slowed the SUV as we accessed the employee lot behind the hospital near Fat Pete's. I looked over and saw a car behind the building that hadn't been there earlier in the day. Weird place to park beside a condemned building.

Then I saw it.

I sucked in a breath, that nearly took all of the air out of the car as I stared through the windshield.

"What? Are you okay?" Jeannie asked.

"That's it! It's right there." Incapable of further speech at the moment, I pointed to Fat Pete's.

"What? I don't see anything." She looked to where I was pointing.

Coherent thought wouldn't form in my mind. I didn't say anything, but continued to point. She would see it. She hadn't seen it because her nose had been in her phone.

Then she took in a gasping breath that sounded remarkably like mine. I was surprised there wasn't a vapor lock inside the car.

"The sign," we said together.

In the front window of Fat Pete's restaurant, the red and orange OPEN sign flashed on and off. I remembered it from earlier in the day. He'd been trying to attract people to the place and apparently had forgotten to turn it off. As the evening deepened, the light became more visible and shone clearly in the near dark.

"Call Charlie." I put the car in park and turned off the headlights. I didn't get too close to the restaurant as I didn't want to alert the maniac running the asylum that more inmates were on the way.

"Charlie?" Jeannie spoke in a squeaky voice, the pitch rose as she spoke. "I think we found her. The nurse. Maggie. We think she's at Fat Pete's. Get some people over here to help us out. We're going in," she said and ended the call.

"Did you just hang up on Charlie?" I asked, my brows doing an odd trick. "You hung up on a cop with a full head of steam and sirens screaming out his ears?"

"Uh, yeah. I didn't want him to tell us not to go in. This way he can't say we ignored his orders, right?" she asked.

"You're hanging around me too much. You're stating to think like me." I would have thought of that myself, eventually.

"Scary," she said. "Let's go."

We eased out of the car and made sure there was no one else around. It was in between shift changes, so we were the only ones in the parking lot. We were in casual clothes and shoes. With all of the debris around, flip flops weren't going to cut it. Either way, we were in stealth mode.

Her phone rang, and she quickly silenced it. I was certain it was Charlie or Elmo trying to tell us to stay put, but we couldn't. We just couldn't. We approached the large vehicle parked by the back door. I looked in and grimaced.

"There's a dead woman in there," I said.

Jeannie took a quick look. "Yep. There is." She ignored the dead woman. We couldn't do anything for her now. But we could help Maggie. We hunkered down a little and peered into the open doorway of the back door. It was dark. It was a hallway. But we could see general shapes of things inside. "There she is. I see her," Jeannie whispered. She apparently had better night vision than I did.

🐾 25 🐾

I'M A NURSE. WHAT'S YOUR SUPERPOWER?-T
SHIRT

We didn't know what the hell we were doing.
We just had a strong need to rescue Angela.
Jeannie and I were the kind of people
who ran into burning buildings instead of away from
them. Maybe we should be firefighters. At least we'd have
better equipment.

"What are we doing to do now?" Jeannie asked.

"Winging it here. How the hell should I know?" Like I
had a plan.

Jeannie hunkered down and scurried to the parking lot,
then returned before I could yell at her for abandoning me.

"What are you doing?" I asked.

She held up a small stone, approximately the size of
three peas. "I got this."

"And you're going to hit him over the head with that?
A pebble?" She must be really strong, 'cause I didn't think
I could knock him out with that. "I think you a bigger
rock."

"No, I'm not going to hit him over the head with it. I'm
going to try to get Maggie's attention," she said with a

306

cluck of her tongue. She was getting testy, but I couldn't blame her.

"Oh." I got it. A bit slow today, but I was getting there.

Jeannie took the little stone and tossed it into the hallway like she was in a bowling event. The pebble clattered on the tile flooring and tapped the bottom of Maggie's foot. That much we could see.

Maggie didn't appear to notice it. She didn't look up, didn't look around. Maybe she was unconscious.

"I think you need a bigger rock," I said again.

Jeannie found another stone, repeated the same process and this time Maggie noticed.

She looked at the little rock, then down the hall. When she sat bolt upright and opened her mouth ready to scream. I knew she'd seen us. Or at least our shadows.

We held out our hands, motioning for her to keep her calm, to keep her from yelling out and giving away our position. Like we were SWAT or something.

She pointed to the dining room, and I interpreted that to mean Dumb Ass was in that area.

"Stay here," I said placed my hand on Jeannie's shoulder, for what possibly could have been the last time. "I'm going around to distract him. Get her out of there."

"Piper!" She grabbed my arm and tried to dissuade me from going on my quest of insanity, but we couldn't wait for the cops. Who knew when they'd arrive, set up a perimeter, find a negotiator and all the stuff you saw on TV. That could take hours. Or longer. We didn't have that kind of time. Neither did Maggie. We needed to end this.

The man was a nut that was about to be cracked.

And we wanted to save Maggie the way we couldn't save Kelly.

I could see Pete in the dining room. He was standing

over a table covered with knives. Apparently, he'd decided to polish the silver at that moment.

Before Jeannie could talk me out of it, I raced around the building to the front. I knocked loudly on the door frame. "Hey! Anyone in here?"

The man hobbled closer, holding onto the tables for support. "We're closed, can't you read the sign?" Pete's voice sounded raspy. Unnaturally weird. Even for him.

"I wanted to see if I could score a cup of coffee," I said, knowing I'd never drink coffee without a heavy metal detector ever again. Was there was an app for that?

"Coffee? Are you kidding me?" He pointed to the front. "Can't you see the sign? They closed me down." He took a step closer and squinted me, as if he just recognized me. "You! Get out of here. Haven't you and your friends done enough to destroy me?" He placed a hand over his face and sobbed. "You've done enough," he said, then gathered himself a little.

He held a butcher knife in one hand. Maybe it was a large vegetable knife. Possibly a chef's knife, I couldn't tell. In any case, it was big, looked really sharp, and I was going to have to get him to put it down.

"Your name's Pete, right?" I softened my voice, trying to sound non-threatening. As he'd already decided I was the devil's spawn, I was going to have to work hard to convince him otherwise. "I'm Piper. I'm a nurse at the hospital, and I heard your mother is ill." Big, freaking lie, as she was dead as Frankenstein's monster lying in the back seat of the car outside.

"Mother?" He nodded and lifted his head. "Yes, Mother. She's all I have now." He clenched his fist around the knife, his fingers working for a comfortable position on the handle.

"I know she's been ill, but my friend and I have come to help her. To help you." The only way I was going to help him, was into a straight jacket, extra-tight.

"She's dead!" Pete screamed, eyes haunted and delusional.

"I just saw her in the car. She looked okay to me," I said, trying to dupe him without lying through my teeth. I hated lying through my teeth 'cause I could never remember who I'd lied to about what. I was certain Mark Twain would have agreed with me.

"No, she's not. You're lying. Just like all of you. You said you'd help me. None of you did, and now she's dead!"

"She just needs a little more help than you thought, that's all." I took a step closer and didn't know if I'd regret it or not. My throat was dry and my hands trembled, and I needed to pee, but it would have to wait.

Behind him Jeannie eased out from the doorway, just enough for me to see her. She pointed toward the back entrance. I guess she'd gotten Maggie loose and was wanting me to go that direction. Why? I didn't know, but I had to trust her guidance like never before.

"Why don't we go see your mother, and you can decide for yourself?" I asked and held my hand out, indicating the direction of the back entrance.

In a flash, faster than I expected him to move, he raised the knife and a light glinted off of it. In that moment, I had a strange feeling of time slowing down. A sense of my mortality. And a vague sense of being right.

It *was* a butcher knife, unfortunately, he was going to plunge it into my chest if I didn't move faster than him.

I think I was a jackrabbit in a former life, because I took off and raced around the tables, headed to the back and started down the hall, running for my life.

"To the right," Jeannie screamed, and I veered my course to the right side of the hall, but didn't slow down. There was a maniac behind me, and I burst through the open doorway into Jeannie's arms.

Inside, Pete screamed in rage. Then I heard the most amazing sound. He was skidding and slipping and sliding on the floor, covered in stones. In a classic Keystone Cops blunder, his feet went out from under him, he flew up into the air and landed on his back with a serious grunt and didn't move.

"We have to tie him up, but be careful. Don't get too close." Jeannie said. She kicked the knife away from his stunned hand.

"How can I tie him up if I can't get close to him?" I asked.

"I don't know, just be careful," she said.

"I hear sirens. Can't we wait for the cops?" Angela asked from the doorway. "I want to wait."

"No. This guy is dangerous. We have to restrain him or something," Jeannie said.

"I have an idea. Come on," I said. Pete was stunned stupid from the fall and hadn't roused yet. He was twitching, so he wasn't dead, but I wanted him contained. "Grab an arm." Jeannie and I took his arms and dragged him down the hall. It a was kind of like mock fire drill where we practiced carrying patients away from danger. Only this time we were dragging danger away from us.

"What are you doing with him?" Maggie asked, fear in her voice. I think she was definitely a rabbit in a former life. Maybe a baby deer. Possibly a squirrel.

"Maggie, open that door." I nodded to the big stainless steel door. Jeannie and I dragged him into the cool room, then raced out and slammed the door shut.

"Ha! We did it. We did it!" I cried and gave the girls each a high-five.

"Maggie, are you okay?" Jeannie asked.

Maggie turned shocked eyes toward us. Her breathing wasn't looking right, and her eyes rolled upward.

"She's going down," I said. Amazingly enough, we were able to keep her from hitting the floor very hard, but it's really difficult to keep someone from falling over, so Jeannie and I went down with her.

Seconds later Charlie, Elmo, Shipper and the gang stormed the building, guns drawn, and super-duper flashlights shining in our faces. The three of us were in a pile on the floor. We'd caught Maggie, but she dragged us down with her. I was okay with that. My legs were rubbery, and my hands still trembled from being chased by a lunatic with a knife.

"What are you doing?" Charlie asked. There was serious disbelief in his voice. He had no idea what we'd just gone through.

"Are you okay?" Elmo asked and looked around. "Where is he?"

"It's okay," I said and tried to sit up, but my hand was caught beneath Maggie's hips. "He's in there." I pointed to the large stainless steel door with my elbow.

"The freezer?" Charlie asked with raised brows. "Seriously?"

"Yeah. He's taking a chill in there," I said.

"What happened?" Charlie squatted down and held out a hand to Jeannie.

"He chased Piper through the restaurant and slipped on the stones Maggie and I put in the hallway." She extricated her leg from beneath Maggie's legs and allowed Charlie to help her to her feet. "He sort of fell down."

"Then we shoved him into the freezer," I said. "We didn't have anything to tie him up with, so we contained him the best we could."

"Awesome," Elmo said, a look of admiration on his face and laughter rolled up from his chest. "Just awesome, ladies."

"Should we get him out of there?" Jeannie asked. "He didn't look good."

"Let's get you three clear first." Charlie held out a hand to help me to my feet, and I held onto him for just a few seconds longer, needing his strength and warmth after such a crazy experience.

"Thanks," I said. "Oh. And there's a dead woman in the car."

"In your car?" Charlie asked.

"No, not in my car. Why would you think there'd be a dead woman in *my* car?" I asked and frowned at him.

"Sorry. Just covering all bases," Charlie said.

"The body is in *his* car. I think it's his mother. She died, and he freaked out," I said, giving him my opinion on the topic whether he wanted it or not.

"Okay. One stupid thing at time," Charlie said and helped us to get Maggie out of the hallway. An ambulance was just feet away with a stretcher, and Charlie put her on it. Her eyelids fluttered as a paramedic placed an oxygen mask over her face. She was rousing already.

"Elmo, let's go get him," Charlie said and pointed to Jeannie and I. "Stay here. We're going to bring him out."

"Got it." For a change, Jeannie and didn't argue with him. It was getting late in the day and the half-life of my coffee had just about worn off. My sarcasm level increased with the level of caffeine in my system. Mornings were the best. Now? Not so much.

We watched as the two big brothers moved down the hall, guns drawn, and yanked the freezer door open.

"Well, that's a first," Charlie said, relaxed and holstered his weapon.

I couldn't help myself. I had to hear it. I had to see for myself. I had to watch the end of this story being written.

Charlie stepped into the freezer and hauled Pete to his feet. "Come on Popsicle. Time to thaw out." Charlie spun him around and cuffed him.

"Ow. That hurts. What are you doing? Where's Mother?" He kept up a non-stop rambling of nonsense. As Charlie led Pete out, he limped badly on his left leg.

"That must be where Lilly stabbed him," I said, finding great satisfaction with a job well done. I wanted to buy her two more scoops of ice cream.

"He probably tried to treat it himself, and now he's got a raging case of sepsis," Jeannie said.

"Worse," I said with a wrinkle to my nose as a distinct odor I hadn't noticed when I was running for my life, but now it hung like a dark cloud around him. "Way worse."

"Oh, man." Jeannie knew what I meant. The infection had gone from a simple infection to massive gangrene. He was going to lose the leg if he didn't lose his life. Once you knew what it smelled like, you never forgot it.

"We've got to get him to the ER, now," I said and waved the second ambulance crew over. "Get a line in him. He has a probable septicemia from a puncture wound in the left thigh approximately ten days ago. He'll need antibiotics, a vascular scan and probably a vascular surgeon right away."

"Thanks ladies. How'd you get all that from looking at him," one of the paramedics asked.

"Just a hunch," I said. I wasn't going to go into the

whole thing. They'd do their own assessment and figure it out. "Just get him over there fast. He's septic, and isn't going to get any better standing here."

Charlie had another scowl on his face, or was it amazement. "You'd see him cared for before Maggie?"

"He's more seriously ill than Maggie. She just fainted. She'll be around in a minute. He's got a bad infection, has probably had a psychotic break, and smells really bad."

"He takes priority," Jeannie said and lifted one shoulder. "As upset as we are for what he's done to the nurses, he's ill in more than one way and needs to get seen by a doctor." There was her compassion again, even for one who's caused such pain and destruction.

"Thank you, ladies. You've made my day," Elmo said and pulled us into a big hug.

"We need to take Angela to the ER too, just to make sure she's okay and then we can debrief you," Jeannie said.

"Okay," I said. It had been a long day and didn't look like it was going to end any time soon. Maybe they had some coffee at the ER.

I guess we could sleep in our next life.

"Okay, now. What the hell is going on here?" Shipper stepped up and scowled. "I'm going to arrest these two for interfering in an investigation."

"Shut up." We all said it together. At least we were all on the same team. We just needed matching shirts.

Shipper jerked as if stunned. "Are you all insane?"

"Yes," I said and stepped closer to him, narrowing my eyes, invading his space. Although I'd met the man only a time or two, I didn't like him. "Either you walk on the wild side with us, Shipper, or you're out."

"Don't talk to me that way, lady. I'll have you know--"

"Can it." Elmo took another step closer, putting his

body between Shipper and me. I liked that in a man. Stepped up to protect the women and children when the time came. He was an alpha male. I didn't know what Shipper was. Maybe he'd been a snake in a former life. Looking at his narrow-set eyes, I was thinking so. "Leave this to us, Shipper. If you want to help, then help, but you're not going to stand there barking orders at us like you have any authority over us."

He looked up at Elmo. "I don't like the way they do things," Shipper said and took a step back, surrendering the fight for now.

"I don't care." Elmo turned his back on Shipper, a sure sign of dismissal. "Why don't you go secure the front and leave this to us?"

"Fine." Shipper wasn't ever going to play well with others, not even with his home team. Maybe he needed to learn an independent sport, like chess or something.

Charlie pulled each of us into a hug. "I really ought to arrest you two for disobeying orders"

"First of all, Angela just fainted. We caught her, and she'll be fine in a few," Jeannie said.

"Second of all, we don't take orders from you," I said and gave him my stare I usually reserved for naughty patients, but he gave me a cop stare right back. They canceled each other out.

"And third, you actually didn't give us any orders," Jeannie said, bringing up that happy point.

"What? I told you to wait," Charlie said, certain he'd said those words.

"Actually, you didn't. I hung up on you before you could tell us not to go in." Jeannie was right.

"But you knew that's what I was going to say," Charlie said with a frown.

"Yes, which is why I hung up, so you wouldn't be mad at us for disobeying an order you didn't give, and one we wouldn't have listened to anyway." She was so boss.

Elmo laughed in a way that eased my mind. They weren't going to be mad at us for long. "They got you there, big brother." Elmo placed a hand on his broad chest and laughed again. "Twisted as it may be, they got you there."

Charlie pinched the bridge of his nose and closed his eyes. "I know I'm gonna sound like Shipper, but, I don't like that at all."

"Let's get Angela to the ER and have her checked out, then you can arrest us if you want," I said. "It's been a while since I've been in cuffs."

The entire event took less than twenty minutes, but it felt like two days had been squished into that time span. I know Einstein had a theory about bending time, but I couldn't believe I was thinking like Shipper, either. I didn't like it at all.

W e finished our thirteen-week assignment on Oak Island and won over the hearts of the nurses, the administration, and the community at large. Somehow we managed to work through the massive list we'd accumulated at the beginning of our assignment and through the hurricane, checking on everyone and everything we'd put on it. Mama Cat raised her litter of kittens and was promptly spayed.

Charlie and Elmo kept us in the loop of closing down the case. Pete went to the nut house to be with others of his own kind. There, he would be contained forever, and not able to hurt anyone again. Even himself. Gangrene had set in to his leg and he'd walk with a permanent limp, but at least he could walk. More than he probably deserved, considering the destruction he'd wrought.

Our actions in persisting to find out why nurses had been pursued by a psychopathic killer had bought us attention from the local government. We were given the keys to the city for a day by the mayor, and a lifetime supply of frozen yogurt from a local shop. As long as we lived on Oak Island it would be a lifetime. Even I didn't think we could eat that much frozen yogurt in the time we had left on the island, but would give it a try.

We'd secured a new assignment in Arizona. We were going from the ocean to the desert. A three day drive lay ahead of us and there would be lots of places for me to take pictures.

Being a travel nurse was an exciting adventure, and I was taking pictures to document it all.

We turned our vehicles west and headed to into the sunset.

FROM THE AUTHOR

Dear Reader,

Thank you for picking up *Murder In The Marsh*. The first book in this series was inspired when I was a travel nurse on assignment in Winston-Salem, NC in 2017. I was gassing up my car at about midnight, in the middle of nowhere, and a thought occurred to me: I could totally disappear from that gas station and no one would know.

I was a single woman, renting a room from a lady in the area. I had no friends nearby and my employer would only know I was missing if I didn't return from seeing the patient I'd been sent out to visit. I was working home hospice at the time, and we saw patients 24/7. Fortunately, nothing happened, but the thought kept persisting and finally I made enough time to start writing this book and it just zipped out of my fingers.

Watch out for more books to come in the series as Piper and Jeannie take more travel assignments and solve more mysteries. To keep up with the news about the series, about my other writing, and all things about Molly Evans, sign up for my newsletter at: http://www.mollyevansro-mance.com

Email me at: Mollyevansromance@gmail.com

As a free gift, I'm giving you a novella written under my other pen name, Sierra Woods, for signing up.

For medical romances, click here:

https://tinyurl.com/yxw27v6q and go directly to my author page.

Love, Molly

Printed in Great Britain
by Amazon

71562893R00190